KAGNEW
STATION

CHRISTMAS
2005

Paul Betit

KAGNEW STATION

The Sequel To Phu Bai

Paul Betit

Just Write Books

Published by

Just Write Books
Topsham, ME 04086

SUMMERTIME BLUES
Words and Music by EDDIE COCHRAN and JERRY CAPEHART
© 1958 WARNER-TAMERLANE PUBLISHING CORP. (Renewed)
Lyrics reprinted with the Permission of Alfred Publishing Co., Inc.
All Rights Reserved

Library of Congress Catalog Card No.: 2005933366
Betit, Paul
Kagnew Station: a novel/Paul Betit
p. 256
1. Fiction-Mystery & Dectective-General. 2. Fiction-Suspense
3. Fiction-War & Military
1. Title.

ISBN 0-9766533-0-3

ISBN 978-0-9766533-0-3

Printed in the United States of America

Acknowledgements

Thanks to Deborah Kennedy for setting me on the right track. Thanks to Bruce Redwine for keeping me there. Thanks to my wife, Deborah Betit, for her timely suggestions and editing help. Each has made this story much better than it would have been.

Kagnew Patch on Cover

The red, white and blue antelope patch was worn by soldiers at the 4th United States Army Security Agency Field Station from 1955 until the listening post ceased operations in 1973.

The Kagnew Station patch artwork on the front cover was created with the use of an artfile provided by Charles Rysticken. His website www.idsardar.com sells specialty products with custom graphics specializing in military and veteran gear/products.

To my sons,
C. J. and Chris,
who continually
remind me
who I really am.

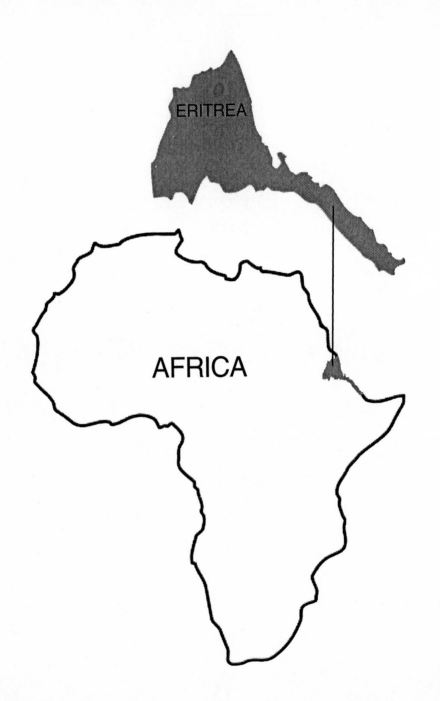

July 1968

AFTER DROPPING the piece of newsprint to the ground, the man pulled up his pants and carefully picked his way through the brambles back to his Land Rover.

A cloud, so thick he could feel the water crystals touch the skin on his face, had settled over the East African plateau, blocking the moonlight and making it difficult for him to find his way.

As the man slowly walked, he could hear the lines from Johnny Cochrane's "Summertime Blues" blaring over the loud speakers from Tract C: "*I'd like to help you son, but you're too young to vote.*"

He'd been waiting for more than an hour in the antenna field not far from the U.S. Army Security Agency site. He'd timed the meeting to coincide with the trick change. He hoped the two military policemen posted at the entrance to the top-secret facility would be too busy checking the security badges of the soldiers coming to work to notice his Rover.

He let out a stream of curses as he bumped into the vehicle. Keeping one hand on it, he inched his way along the driver's side and took hold of the steering wheel before pulling himself into the seat.

He was beginning to lose patience. For a moment, he even considered turning on his headlights so they could find him. Even in this pea soup, there was a chance the MPs would see the beams from the headlamps. They would come to investigate. The lights stayed off.

Over the din of the music blaring from Tract C, the man heard a metallic click come from the backseat. Gradually, the sound slowly registered. A few moments later, he turned just in time to see a blinding flash of light. That light and the loud report of the rifle held five inches from his head were the last things Sergeant David Wallace saw or heard.

"There ain't no cure for the summertime blues."

A MAN WHO SAID his name was Smyth met John Murphy at Asmara International Airport.

Claiming he was from the American consulate, Smyth interceded when the Ethiopian customs inspector asked to see the travel bag slung over Murphy's left shoulder. Then, he handed the inspector a $20 bill.

"Welcome to Asmara," Smyth said, brushing a wisp of blond hair from his forehead.

Murphy grunted, unsure of the stranger who had come to his aid. "Are all these guys crooks?" he asked.

"Only those with a little power." Smyth was tall and slender, immaculately dressed in a light brown tropical suit. Despite the poor lighting, he wore his dark glasses inside the customs area. "Normally, your diplomatic passport is enough to keep them out of your things. But sometimes it takes a little extra."

Murphy kept a tight hold on his flight bag. He watched as the inspector retreated into the other room to search his suitcase.

"Let me take care of your passport," Smyth offered.

Murphy pulled out the red-covered passport. He handed it to Smyth, who joined the customs man in the other room. Several minutes later, Smyth returned with the suitcase. He led Murphy through a set of swinging doors into the passenger terminal.

As they walked out into the bright East African sun, Murphy saw several young white men in civilian clothes and sporting short haircuts. They loaded duffel bags and suitcases into a small olive-drab bus parked in front of the terminal. "I thought U.S. military personnel were supposed to travel incognito," he commented. He followed Smyth to a black Rover sedan parked in a lot across the street. "Those guys stand out like a sore thumb."

Murphy had avoided the small group of young Americans during the 18-hour flight from New York to Athens, the 10-hour layover at the small hotel across from the seawall in Piraeus, and the overnight flight from Greece to Ethiopia.

"The Ethis do like us to maintain a low profile," Smyth answered. "But there's only so much we can do."

As a special agent with the Army's Criminal Investigation Division, it was part of Murphy's job to maintain a low profile, on duty or off, no matter what the country. While on assignment in the States, in Vietnam, Korea or the Philippines, he nearly always wore civilian clothes. He brought none of his military issue to Ethiopia.

"By the way, what's in the bag?" Smyth asked as he drove the car out of the parking lot.

Murphy placed the black leather bag on the floor in front of him. "Some personal belongings."

A compartment in the bottom of the bag housed a .25 caliber Browning automatic. In the past, Murphy's diplomatic passport had enabled him to carry the weapon undetected into a half-dozen countries. He'd never had to bribe his way through customs before.

Murphy had been told he wouldn't need a gun during his trip to Ethiopia. He'd left the .45 caliber pistol the Army issued him at Fort Dix. But Chief Warrant Officer Charles Van Dyck, his old partner, had advised him to always carry an extra weapon. "Keep it in your boot," the short, stubby warrant officer, called "V.D." by his friends, had told him. "You never know when you're going to need another piece."

Murphy took that advice to heart after he found himself, unarmed, trying to arrest a soldier who held an M14 in his hands at Camp Casey in South Korea. He finessed his way out of the dilemma by sticking his index finger against the spine of the highly-agitated buck private, who had accidentally killed one of his buddies while on guard duty along the demilitarized zone then tried to blame it on a marauding band of North Korean soldiers.

"Extremely imaginative," were the words used in the after-action report to describe Murphy's technique for disarming the suspect.

"Extremely lucky," V.D. countered, "Get yourself a gun."

At the start of his first tour in Vietnam, nearly three years before, Murphy bought the Browning from a dealer in the Cholon section of Saigon. It went everywhere he went.

After getting the car up to speed, Smyth turned on the radio. Buck Owens' "I Got A Tiger By The Tail" blared out. "Good cover music," he sarcastically chuckled, reaching to turn the volume down. "That's Kagnew Station."

Less than 48 hours before, Murphy had not heard of Kagnew Station, a U.S. military base located in the Ethiopian province of Eritrea. Three days before, David Wallace, a military policeman, had been found shot to death in an antenna field less than ten kilometers from the main post. Murphy had been sent from his unit at Fort Dix to lend his expertise to the CID investigators at the remote base. During his brief CID career, he'd earned a reputation for his relentless investigations of the suspicious deaths of American soldiers.

Van Dyck, his mentor, had employed a more laid-back approach in his inquiries. In his slow, methodical way, he covered all the bases until every lead had been followed, every shred of evidence thoroughly sifted and evaluated.

Murphy's style was more intuitive. He still followed proper police methodology. But he wasn't afraid to trust his gut. Oddly, the two men, with vastly different investigative techniques, had worked well together.

Murphy's temporary assignment to the remote African base had been a rush job. No travel orders were issued.

Ordinarily, nothing moved in the army without a thick stack of orders. "Pretty soon," V.D. had often complained, "we're going to have to submit a requisition form, in triplicate, to get authorization to take a piss."

This time, Rupert Johnson, the Special Agent in Charge at Fort Dix, simply told Murphy to pack his bags and grab his passport. He was given a limousine ride to Kennedy International Airport and a ticket for a midnight flight on Trans World Airlines to Athens. There he changed to Ethiopian Airlines; but no travel orders.

"Report to Major Hilton," said Johnson, the crusty old warrant officer who ran the investigation unit. "He'll tell you what to do."

Normally, CID investigators worked in pairs. But Murphy had been working alone since his return from Vietnam nearly six months before. The big military buildup in Southeast Asia had stripped the state-side CID units of many of their special agents, making it difficult to partner up.

That was fine with Murphy. Ever since Van Dyck was killed in Vietnam, he'd become accustomed to working alone. In truth, he was unsure whether he could work with anyone else again.

"The major wants me to show you around," explained Smyth, after they began the drive to Asmara.

A short time after leaving the airport, Smyth swerved to his left to avoid colliding with a couple of brown-skinned men on bicycles who had rolled into his lane from a side road. Both wore the same dull blue, cotton coveralls. Heavily engrossed in conversation, neither of the men paid any attention to the few vehicles on the road as they pedaled along.

Smyth rearranged his glasses on the bridge of his nose. "Nobody looks where they're going in this country. Those guys on bikes are always running into people."

Murphy didn't mind the small talk. He felt exhilarated about finally reaching his destination. It had been a long trip, at short notice, over parts of three days. Murphy had gotten eight solid hours of sleep over the Atlantic, but he knew jet lag would hit him sooner or later. For now, he thought it best to take things slow until his body and, more importantly, his mind, became acclimated. So he listened while Smyth went on complaining about the driving habits of his hosts.

As Smyth spoke, his cultured voice dripping with sarcasm, Murphy tried to place the accent. Philadelphia Main Line or Greenwich? Swarthmore or Wesleyan?

It took about ten minutes to drive into Asmara. Along the way, amber fields gradually gave way to small stucco houses colored in faint pinks, blues and yellows. Murphy noticed some of the houses were surrounded by tall stone walls, topped with shards of broken glass. As they neared the city, the view from the car became more urban; two and three-story beige apartment buildings, long faded by the sun lined both sides of the road.

When Smyth finally stopped talking, Murphy put in a word: "Been over here long?"

Smyth kept his gaze on the road. "I came here about two years ago. It's my first posting, and I've been running errands ever since."

"I hope I'm not putting you to any trouble."

"Oh no." Smyth looked at Murphy from behind his dark glasses. "Usually, the errands are quite interesting. It breaks up the monotony. Nothing much happens over here." After a slight pause, Smyth added: "That is, until this week."

"**KAGNEW STATION** is an American oasis in a desert of barbarism," Smyth said as they drove onto the base.

Before he took Murphy to Wallace's room, Smyth gave him a quick tour of Tract E. To the locals, and to the men stationed there, this compound was Kagnew Station.

The base was named for the rider-less horse credited with leading the charge against the doomed Italians at the Battle of Adua more than seventy-five years before, the only time a European force had lost a battle to a native army in Africa.

During the twenty years the American Army had operated its base in Asmara, the U.S. government had lavished more than $50 million on the facility, making sure its three thousand American soldiers, sailors and airmen, and their families, lived comfortably.

It was as if a large slice of Americana had been plunked right down in the middle of the African wilds.

"Uncle Sam likes to keep his ASA boys happy," Smyth said. "After all, they're in the top ten percent."

It was a belief, commonly-held by ASA personnel anyway, recruits had to score among the top ten percent on the Army's basic intelligence test before they were asked to join the highly-secretive organization. That hint of elitism was a great recruiting tool, a device often used to get recruits to sign up for the ASA's initial four-year enlistment, rather than the three years other Army volunteers served.

The square-mile, walled compound, hidden from the view of most Ethiopians, contained a fully-equipped 66-bed hospital, a gymnasium, swimming pool, a 20-lane bowling alley, basketball, tennis and hand-ball courts, softball fields and even a miniature golf course. There were also well-appointed clubs for the officers, NCOs and lower-ranking enlisted men, as well as a large, well-stocked PX, a commissary, a chapel, a gas station, a movie theater, a credit union, a library and a USO facility. Dependent children attended elementary and high school at Tract E, and soldiers and sailors stationed at Kagnew could take courses at a branch of the University of Maryland.

Inside a smaller compound nearly two kilometers across town at Tract B, site of the old Italian Radio Marina, where the ASA originally set up shop nearly twenty years before, a large housing complex had been built for the families of the post's senior NCOs. In addition, R & R facilities had been developed in Keren, a small town located in a valley less than one hundred kilometers northeast of Asmara, and at Massawa, a port on the Red Sea little more than 100 kilometers east of the provincial capital by road.

Murphy was impressed. "All the comforts of home."

Smyth drove down the road leading to the back gate before pulling into a small gravel parking lot, next to a small grove of trees where more than a dozen motorcycles were parked. Across the street was the gray-colored BEQ.

Murphy wasn't surprised to find the BEQ, where Wallace's quarters were located, empty.

Even the house boys assigned to weekend duty had made themselves scarce, leaving their shoe-shining equipment in the downstairs landing.

It was Saturday.

At Fort Dix, most of the sergeants who lived in his BEQ usually took off on weekends. This time of year, they headed to the Jersey shore, looking for action at Atlantic City, Seaside

Heights or Wildwood. From all of their bragging, they usually found it.

Since his return to active duty four months before, Murphy spent most of his weekends on post, except for an occasional drive back home to visit his mother on Cape Cod.

He'd come back from Vietnam, where there was no such thing as a weekend off, in terrible shape. His second tour in Southeast Asia had left him exhausted, underweight, and carrying small pieces of shrapnel from a mortar shell. Surgeons at the Naval field hospital in Phu Bai had removed what they could from his back during the Tet Offensive.

Murphy was told the small metal fragments would eventually work their way out, but he had to take care of the rest of his body. At Fort Dix, he devoted most of his free time to whipping himself back into shape.

Long jogs through the pine barrens at the far-flung south New Jersey post had improved his stamina; he was now able to lead morning physical training exercises at one of the basic training companies, and to serve as an instructor in the O'Neal Method of Self Defense.

Murphy's weight had come back, too. Nearly six feet tall, he now tipped the scales at a solid 185 pounds.

Despite the improvement in his physical health, Murphy still didn't feel right. He felt less than whole, as if something was missing. Even before he was wounded, Murphy had felt this way. Maybe, that's why he preferred to work alone, and to be alone.

Wallace had been assigned a room on the top floor of the two-story barracks, a miniature version of the three-storied B Company and Stratcom barracks up the street.

"The major thought you'd might like to check this out," Smyth said. "Maybe, you'd see something the others had missed."

Wallace's room was ready for inspection.

The houseboys had made up the bed, located near the door. Under his rack, boots and shoes, shined to a bright black sheen, were lined up in the correct order.

Wallace would have been responsible for the appearance of the rest of his military kit. From his experience in various Far East postings, Murphy knew the houseboys weren't allowed to open foot or wall lockers.

Inside the double-wide metal wall locker, Murphy found all of Wallace's uniforms hung in conformance with Army regulations.

A quick pat-down of the clothing revealed empty pockets. Murphy noticed the two lines of ribbons above the left breast pocket on the dead man's khaki uniform. Wallace had been awarded the bronze star. He also had worn ribbons indicating he'd served in Vietnam and Korea.

The display in Wallace's wooden footlocker, where the dead man's toiletries, skivvies and towels were kept, also conformed to regulations. Nothing out of place. Nothing extra.

"This guy was a good trooper," Murphy commented. "A lot of NCOs I know don't even bother with their displays. Nowadays, nobody ever checks them, anyway."

He leaned down to take a closer look at the two pairs of boots and two pairs of dress shoes lined up under the dead man's bed. "Here's a gig," He pulled a small white business card out of one of the boots. "That's worth two demerits at The Point."

Murphy handed the card, which advertised a place called Luigi's, to Smyth.

After removing his sunglasses to look at it, Smyth returned the card. "It's a little hole-in-the-wall bar downtown." Murphy put it back where he found it.

After lighting up his first cigarette since getting off the plane, Murphy walked across the small room to the window overlooking the broad field separating the post's enlisted men's barracks from the brick-faced family housing units. He recalled how Van Dyck would often tell him. "Sometimes, no evidence is the best evidence." Was this one of those occasions?

Even by U.S. Army standards, Wallace's living quarters were sterile. His wall locker had yielded two packs of Lucky Strikes, a back issue of *Field and Stream*, a couple pairs of jeans and a bright orange Tennessee Volunteers sweatshirt. Aside from that, there were no signs anyone had settled in. No letters from home. No Playboy centerfolds taped to the inside of the wall locker. Wallace hadn't made much of an attempt to personalize his living space.

Murphy gazed about the small room. "This guy didn't stay home much."

"Nobody spends much time on post." Smyth said.

Murphy wondered aloud: "I wonder where he spent his time."

A FEW MOMENTS after they left post, Murphy noticed a little black man squatting in a cultivated field about twenty meters off the paved road leading to Tract C.

The man's pants were pulled down around his ankles. In each hand, he held a large stone.

The scene puzzled Murphy. "What's he doing?"

Smyth slowed almost to a crawl. "He's making fertilizer. If we had come out here earlier, that field would have been filled with men, each shitting on his little plot of land. They come out here to void their bowels before they go to work. For most of them, it's the only way they can fertilize their field."

Murphy had heard the Chinese used "night soil," human waste, to fertilize their fields. However, that was usually composted before it was spread. Here, the process was more direct.

Murphy took another look. He saw the man knock the two stones together.

"What's with the stones?"

"A bit of flatulence, I suspect," Smyth said. "When he farts, he believes he releases some sort of evil spirit. So he smashes the rocks together to scare it away."

Murphy chuckled. "I know some old master sergeants who should carry rocks with them."

There was no traffic, and wheat fields extended for several hundred meters toward hills on both sides of the two-lane road.

"That fellow back there doesn't own his little plot of land," Smyth said. "It's like the middle ages here. Most of the farmland around Asmara is owned by very few people, and they lease out small sections of it. The landowners don't do anything to keep up the land. They just expect the poor fellows like our little friend back there to pay the rent."

On the way to Tract C, they drove past the Stratcom facility and Naval Communications facility, squat cinder-block buildings located across an intersection from each other behind chain-link fences about two hundred meters off the main road.

"Asmara is a perfect place for a radio relay station," Smyth explained. "We're nearly 8,000 feet up, and it's a straight shot from southern Europe to Asmara, from here to Vietnam and Thailand. It makes for direct and relatively secure radio communications."

A bullet-nosed Studebaker passed the Rover.

Murphy watched it pull away. "Now, there's a car you don't see too often."

Smyth followed the old car down the road. "There's a lot of cars over here you don't see much back in the states anymore. American soldiers have been shipping cars over here for nearly twenty years. A lot of them are still on the road."

The paved road ran for more than five kilometers out to Tract C, site of the highly-classified ASA operation. Only a large grove of trees on Murphy's side of the road broke up the wheat fields. Between the road and the trees lay a small pond.

After turning the black sedan into a parking lot, Smyth slowly pulled up to the entrance to Tract C, a large compound surrounded by two tall double-chain link fences. He climbed out of the car. "I just want to tell the guards we're going into the antenna field. Wouldn't want them to sic their dogs on us." Then he chuckled.

Smyth left his door ajar, and Murphy heard the old rock-and-roll song "Sea Cruise" blasting from a loudspeaker placed on a corner of the large windowless concrete building inside the compound. A Spec 5, who Murphy assumed was the driver of the Studebaker, stood inside the small guard shack, showing his security badge to an MP.

Close by, inside the narrow corridor between the two fences, another MP placed a large bowl on the ground. As the corporal warily backed away, two Doberman Pinchers ran around a corner and dashed down the corridor toward their brunch.

Murphy possessed a top-secret clearance. Sometimes, CID's special agents needed access to sensitive material. But he knew his clearance wouldn't get him past the MPs guarding the operation site at Tract C. ASA personnel held Top Secret Crypto clearances, a level higher than his.

Smyth returned to the car. "I told them we weren't planning to blow up any towers while we were out there."

Smyth rolled down his window before turning around in the parking lot. "One of my favorites is coming up." Soon, the air filled with Frank Ifield yodeling "Lonesome Cattle Call." "They play that same tape over and over again. If anybody is out here trying to listen to what's going on inside that building, the music will drive them crazy."

About one hundred meters beyond the entrance to the parking lot, the paved road changed to a dirt track. Smyth kept the car inside the wheel ruts, and the Rover sedan gently swayed from side to side as they drove along. A few moments after leaving the pavement, Smyth pulled over to make way for two motorcycles bearing down from the opposite direction. The two small dirt bikes roared past, throwing up a large cloud of dust in their wake, and headed for the paved road. "The guys from Kagnew come out here and ride," Smyth said. As dust filled the car, he coughed. Too late, he rolled up the window. Murphy turned away. Looking out his window, he saw several tall radio towers rising above the scrub grass and brush.

"For obvious reasons, not too many people come out here," Smyth said. He was locked in a battle with the steering wheel to keep the car rolling along the wide ruts in the dirt track. "One night, a couple of months ago, the MPs found one of the sergeants from Tract C out here in his car with a bar girl."

"The colonel get upset about that?"

"No," Smyth said. "But the guy's wife got quite miffed."

About five hundred meters beyond the end of the paved road, Smyth turned right. As the car lurched up a slight incline, more towers became visible. When the Rover reached the crest of the small hill, Murphy could see dozens of towers. Erected in intervals, they marched toward the horizon across a large, flat plain.

"Asmara is a good place to relay messages," Smyth said. "But it is an even better place to listen to them." The antennas, connected by cable to radio receivers inside the ASA facility at Tract C, ran for more than five kilometers down the valley floor and for nearly two kilometers across it. "From here, the people in that building can listen to radio communications for a radius of twenty-five hundred miles."

While in Vietnam, Murphy had spent time on an ASA base at Phu Bai, outside the former imperial city of Hue. He was aware of what the security agency did. Smiling, he repeated it's unofficial motto: "In God we trust. All others we monitor."

"Amen," Smyth said.

After bringing the Rover to a stop, he took off his sunglasses. "These are parabolic antennas. The wires which make up the antennas are strung between a series of towers. They're like magnets for radio signals." It took Smyth about five minutes to drive to the spot where Wallace's body was found, just off the dirt track about fifty meters from one of the antenna towers.

As soon as he got out of the car, Murphy lit up a cigarette. While he smoked, he leaned against the side of the car, slowly surveying the area. "What was Wallace doing out here anyway?"

"Nobody knows." Smyth had come around from the driver's side of the car. "He was off-duty. Nobody saw him drive out here." As he leaned against the car beside Murphy, Smyth pulled a white handkerchief out of his pocket and began to wipe the dust from his sunglasses. "There's a lot of traffic out on the road when eves shift ends around eleven." He paused to inspect his glasses. "That night, there also was a low cloud hanging over the area. It was thick as pea soup, and the guards reported they couldn't see beyond the parking lot from their post."

"I don't suppose anybody heard anything?"

"The watch commander must have had the cover music turned on full blast that night," Smyth replied. "Nobody reported hearing a thing."

Just then, Murphy heard the tinny whine of a motorcycle laboring in low gear up the dirt track. He looked toward Smyth. "That's a Suzuki. I'd know that sound anywhere."

Smyth finished wiping his glasses. "You ride?"

"I learned to ride on one of those in the Philippines."

After watching the rider on a 250cc Suzuki speed past, Murphy resumed talking. "I don't suppose anybody did a sweep of this area."

Smyth shrugged his shoulders. "A couple of antenna repairmen found Wallace slumped over his steering wheel." He put his glasses back on, then carefully folded his handkerchief before wedging it back into the inside pocket of his sports jacket. "They come here all the time to adjust guy wires and replace antenna wire. From what I understand, the repairmen hauled the body out of here in their three-quarter ton truck. Later, the MPs came out and drove Wallace's Land Rover back to Kagnew Station. I don't think anybody looked at anything out here."

Murphy flicked his cigarette away. "Time to go to work."

He walked to the front of the black sedan. While Smyth watched in silence, Murphy slowly surveyed the area, walking in an ever-widening arc around the spot where Wallace's body had been found, his eyes glued to the ground. The quiet ended about five minutes later when Murphy stopped about thirty meters away.

" 'Ello! 'Ello!" Murphy mimicked a Cockney accent. "What 'ave we 'ere?"

Smyth moved to his side. Removing his glasses, he looked down to the ground in front of Murphy's boot, where a long brown turd lay, dried and decayed. "That could have come from anybody."

"I don't think so," said Murphy. He leaned over and gingerly picked up a crumbled page from the Stars and Stripes military newspaper he found clinging to a thorn bush nearby. It had dried excrement on one side. "I don't think that guy we saw in the field down the road, or any of his buddies, read this." After noting the paper had been published the day before Wallace's death, Murphy dropped the piece of newsprint to the ground. "If we had a decent lab, we might get a blood type from that." Murphy knew bits of blood were often found in stools. "At the very least, we could find out what he ate for breakfast."

The CID maintained an excellent forensics lab in Frankfurt. But Murphy knew there wasn't enough time to ship his discovery to West Germany for testing. As V.D. would say: "We don't have time to dick around."

Van Dyck often counseled Murphy about jumping to

conclusions. At the same time, the older investigator marveled at how often the younger man's hunches proved correct. "There must be a direct connection between your gut and your brain," the old warrant officer joked.

As he walked back to the car, Murphy shared his most recent leap in logic with Smyth. "I think Wallace knew his killer."

"Really!" Smyth sounded skeptical. "And how did you reach that conclusion?"

"I don't think Wallace drove all the way out here to take a crap. Do you?"

Murphy didn't wait for an answer.

"No. Maybe he was waiting for somebody, or maybe he was with somebody. In any case, he felt comfortable enough to answer the call of nature. When he got back into his vehicle after he was done, somebody wasted him."

Smyth put his dark glasses back on. "What makes you think it was Wallace who took that dump?"

Murphy took a long drag from his cigarette.

"I don't know of too many killers who take a crap at the scene of a murder."

THEY MET MAJOR HILTON in the bar at the King George Hotel.

During his brief tour of the main post, Murphy had wondered why Smyth hadn't stopped at the Provost Marshall's office to introduce him to Kagnew Station's top cop, or why he hadn't paid a courtesy call to the local CID unit. Smyth had gone out of his way to avoid having Murphy meet any military personnel during their short stay on post. It was as if he wanted to keep his presence at Kagnew Station a secret.

Now, as they went off-post to meet the man who was supposed to give him his orders, it dawned on Murphy something was different about this case.

The King George was located on a quiet tree-shaded street off Emperor Johannes Avenue. The broad thoroughfare ran for nearly three kilometers across town from the Empress Menen statue, the tall centerpiece in a wide roundabout just down the hill from Kagnew Station, to Ghezzabanda, a neighborhood on Asmara's east side.

The two men found the major nursing a scotch and water at a table in the hotel's small lounge. A much younger man sat nearby. Otherwise, the bar was empty. Both men were dressed in civvies - Levis and short-sleeved shirts. Their faces looked sun-burnt.

"Back from the golf course, I see, major," Smyth opened.

Ethiopia's only 18-hole golf course, a rough layout at Kagnew Farms, was located a little more than a kilometer from the hotel in the open country west of the main post.

Hilton ignored Smyth's remark. He stood, reaching out to shake Murphy's hand while offering seats to the new arrivals. "So you're our hot-shot detective. Why, you're young enough to be my son."

Murphy felt anything but young. Despite his appearance, dark, wavy hair worn a little longer than Army regulations and a dark complexion that made him look much younger than his age, Murphy felt tired and worn. But his smile, a smug upturn of the lips which Murphy flashed at the slightest provocation, masked his true feelings. It also enhanced his youthful appearance. That smile, or "shit-eating grin," as Van Dyck called it, made Murphy a difficult person to read.

Hilton, a tall, thin man in his late thirties, was trying to do just that. All the major got was a smile and some small talk.

"Oh, I don't think I'm young enough to be your son, sir," Murphy said. "But thanks for the compliment."

Murphy's use of the word "sir" came from his innate politeness. Military protocol did not require CID investigators to defer to higher-ranking officers. Investigators, many of whom were non-commissioned officers like Murphy, were supposed to treat officers as equals. It made it easier for them to do their jobs if everyone forgot about rank.

The lounge took up an enclosed veranda that ran along a portion of the King George's front, separated from the sidewalk by a tall hedge. Screens made it difficult to see inside from the sidewalk, only a few meters away. However, the view over the hedge into the street was unimpeded. A pretty secure location, thought Murphy, a good place for a covert meeting.

Most residents of Asmara took an afternoon siesta, a tradition introduced by Italian colonists. During the brief meeting, no one walked past the hotel, and only a few cars passed by. A radio behind the small bar was tuned to the country music show, broadcast each Saturday afternoon on the United States Armed Forces Radio Network.

The major turned to the young, crew-cut man sitting next to them. "Logan, get these two fellas a beer."

After Logan jumped to his feet and busied himself behind the bar, Murphy thought to himself: a real eager beaver. Murphy tabbed Logan as a graduate of the Army's Reserved Officers Training Corps, a newly-minted second lieutenant extremely happy he hadn't been assigned to lead a rifle platoon in South Vietnam. There, Murphy knew, the young officer's peers were being gobbled and spat out at an alarming rate.

This guy feels fortunate to have been sent to this African backwater, Murphy thought, and he would do anything to stay here. So eager to please, Murphy knew there was no job too menial, no task too small for Logan to do in his efforts to ingratiate himself with his superiors.

"A kiss-ass with a personal agenda," Van Dyck would say. "A very useful person to have around."

A few moments later, Logan returned with two stubby brown bottles of Melotti beer. After setting the bottles down, he took a seat at an adjoining table.

Smyth took a long swig. "Ah. Panther piss."

After frowning at Smyth's comment, the major turned to Murphy. "Have a nice flight?" A little more small talk.

Murphy took a swig of the bitter-tasting beer. "It seems like I've been in the air forever. But I did catch a nap during the stopover in Athens and slept a little on the flight down here."

Smyth finished his beer in a few large gulps and put the empty bottle on the table. That was the signal for the official start of the meeting.

The major looked at Murphy. "You do know why you're here?"

V.D. would have answered the question by paraphrasing

the CID motto: "I do what needs to be done."

But Murphy often used a vague catch-phrase of his own. Placing his flight bag, which had been resting on his lap, on the floor, he said: "Usually, sir, I'm sent in to tie up loose ends. But I thought there were no loose ends in this case. I was told the MP was killed by Eritrean rebels."

Smyth turned toward the colonel. "Mr. Murphy, here, thinks Wallace may have known the people who killed him. He thinks—"

The major put up his hand. "No, we don't think so," he interrupted. "We think he ran into a group of rebels trying to leave the area. Sergeant Wallace happened to be in the wrong place at the wrong time."

"What do the Ethiopians think?" Murphy asked.

Smyth answered matter-of-factly. "The Ethiopian government doesn't officially recognize the existence of the Eritrean Liberation Front." He folded his glasses and slipped them into the inside pocket of his jacket "Of course, they don't officially recognize a lot of things here, like the famine and droughts that regularly visit this country. No, they are blaming the killings on the Shifta, bandits."

Murphy took a sip of his beer. "Sounds like a question of semantics."

Smyth chuckled. He went on to give Murphy a brief history lesson.

The liberation front began operating in earnest in 1962 when Emperor Haile Selassie's army marched in and took control of Eritrea, which had been federated with Ethiopia since 1952. It had become a British protectorate in 1941 after a British force helped the Ethiopians kick the Italians out of East Africa during World War II.

"When the Brits left, many Eritreans expected to gain their

independence," he said. "Instead, Eritrea became the 14th province of the Ethiopian Empire, such as it is."

Murphy took another sip of his beer. "That's interesting. But I still don't see any loose ends here."

Hilton interjected: "If it wasn't for this, there wouldn't be any loose ends." The major reached into his breast pocket and tossed a bullet to Murphy. "Know what that is?"

Murphy caught the bullet and looked at it. "Looks like a thirty-caliber round."

After clearing his throat, Smyth resumed his briefing. "Since the uprising began, ELF has depended primarily on the Ethiopian army for its weapons. Some of their men started with old muzzle loaders. The liberation front has gotten most of its weapons by stealing them or by taking them from dead soldiers. They've got quite a collection of small arms, including our hand-me-downs like the M1 carbine."

Murphy took another look at the bullet, noticing the little red dot at its tip, making it a tracer round. "What makes this bullet so special?"

The major leaned over the table. "We're pretty sure it's part of a shipment air-freighted to Kagnew Station six, seven years ago following a coup attempt. Someone was in a big hurry so they shipped 100,000 rounds of ammo used for night-firing exercises. Every round was tipped with phosphorous."

"We think there was a misfire the night Wallace was killed, and that shell was ejected from the chamber before he was shot. We found it on the floor of his vehicle. We would like to know how the liberation front came by that bullet."

Murphy took another look at the shell before setting it down on the table.

"You've got your own investigators. Why can't they look into that? They know the territory."

Smyth spoke up. "Yes, they do know the territory. But I'm afraid the territory knows them, too. Each one of our investigators has to be accompanied by an Ethiopian every time he steps off post on official business. It would be difficult for the local CID detachment to carry out a discreet investigation."

Smyth whipped a green-covered passport out of his jacket pocket and tossed it onto the table in front of Murphy. "But you, sir, are a tourist."

Murphy picked up the passport. He looked inside to see his picture staring back at him. He turned the page and found an Ethiopian visa stamped on the page following the Greek entrance and exit stamps.

"You pulled a switch," Murphy said. Impressed with Smyth's slight of hand, he wondered just what the slim man with the sandy blonde hair did at the American Consulate.

Smyth, who now held Murphy's official government passport in his hand, rewarded Murphy with a little grin. He pointed to the passport in Murphy's hand. "It came from Athens on the same plane as you. There was no problem getting it off the plane before you did. But I don't know how I would have made the switch if our little friend at the airport hadn't tried to be so thorough."

Smyth explained: "As a tourist, you really can go just about any place you want in this province, and the local authorities won't know who you are or what you're up to."

"Look, Murphy," Hilton continued. "We didn't ask to have you sent over here. But now that you're here, you might as well make yourself useful." The major, leaning forward in his chair, lowered his voice. "Your investigation must be handled discreetly. We don't want the Ethiopians to know we got a wild card here. We just want to make sure no American arms are finding their way to the rebels. The Ethiopian government wouldn't like it."

Smyth continued. "Some of the young Turks in the Ethiopian Army have spent time at Patrice Lamumba University in Moscow, and they would like nothing better than to see their Russian mentors replace us. They're looking for any excuse to get us kicked out. Soviet stock is on the rise in Africa, especially since the Russians agreed to help the Egyptians build the Aswan Dam after we refused to get involved in the project."

"I know this is a difficult assignment," Hilton said. "Look around. Maybe you'll find something. Maybe you won't. We just don't want any surprises."

The major stood up. "We want you to work through Smyth. In spite of the shooting, it's business as usual here."

Business as usual. Murphy smiled.

In Vietnam, where American soldiers were dying everyday, it was also business as usual.

However, American soldiers weren't supposed to die in Ethiopia.

THE DREAM SPILLED out of Murphy's sub-conscious, snapping him back into the real world.

It was the same nightmare.

He was a little boy running up the high dunes near the tip of Cape Cod while trying to escape from a giant wave about to break onto the beach. The harder Murphy tries to run up the huge bank of sand the more difficult it becomes for him to make any headway; the more he churns his little legs, the deeper his feet dig into the soft sand, holding him in place. When he looks back over his shoulder, the terrified little boy sees the storm surge above him.

Murphy woke up in a cold sweat, in a strange bed in a strange room. Through the louvers of the closed wooden shutters, he could hear the gargled strains of the muezzin, calling the Moslem faithful to afternoon prayers at the Kulafah Al-Rashidin mosque more than a kilometer away.

Murphy had fallen asleep after trying to take a shower in the bath down the hall he shared with the other guests on the second floor. The water had suddenly slowed to a trickle, and he'd barely been able to rinse the soap off his body.

The dream always provoked the same response. He was terrified. Normally, within moments of awaking, the feeling passed. This time was no different.

No one knew about the dream, nor its effect on him. The nightmare bothered Murphy. He saw the recurring dream as the lone chink in his armor. To others, he appeared fearless. But the dream told Murphy something else; deep inside, where no one else could see, resided a little boy. He worked hard to make sure no one saw that little boy.

An only child, Murphy had been raised by his mother on the Cape. His father never returned from the South Pacific after his National Guard unit was activated in the early days of World War II. Murphy had no memory of him. The only tangible evidence he had were the snapshots of a young couple with their new baby taken on the beach in Truro and the few letters his father had managed to write before he was reported missing in the jungles of New Guinea.

Growing up, Murphy felt different from the boys whose fathers had survived the war. They seem to share in a completeness he lacked. For a time, he even envied those boys whose fathers were abusive or indifferent.

Murphy's mother, who worked as a cook at a school in Dennis during the school year and as a chambermaid at a large hotel in Chatham during the summer months, gamely tried to fill the void. While he was growing up, she even played catch with him or accompanied him on his hikes along the Cape Cod shoreline.

But his mother worked long hours to make ends meet. Murphy was left alone a lot, and he'd learned to take care of himself at a very young age. This early self-reliance helped him become an extremely resourceful young man.

His three uncles, his father's brothers, provided Murphy with strong male role models. All three of them had become detectives in the Boston Police Department. Although none of their own sons decided to follow in their footsteps, Murphy found their profession intriguing. Growing up, he always enjoyed the family get-togethers at his grandmother's crowded tenement in South Boston, where his uncles sat around the kitchen table and talked shop.

From them, Murphy learned respect for the law, and the responsibility a policeman had in seeing it properly enforced.

That didn't mean Murphy went by the book completely. From other investigators he learned it could be beneficial to let some things slide, to look the other way. It depended upon the circumstances. "The CID walks a big beat," V.D. use to tell him, "and we can't arrest everybody."

The mission of the U.S. Army's Criminal Investigation Division was global in scope. It was charged with investigating all felony crimes involving U.S. Army personnel anywhere in the world. That mandate allowed the CID to get involved when soldiers were accused of committing crimes against each other or against civilians, both foreign and domestic, or when they were victims of crimes. When jurisdictions did overlap, the CID normally would work with the other police agencies with an interest in the case.

This time, however, Murphy had been left to operate on his own. Unusual, but not unprecedented. He'd been sent out into the cold before.

Other CID investigators would handle the meat of the case. But a seemingly minor detail, something that didn't fit, had been left for Murphy to sort out. He was sure no one else had been assigned to find out how a single .30-caliber bullet, supposedly issued to American soldiers, had wound up in the hands of a group of Eritrean rebels.

Still, Murphy couldn't help but feel like the poor relation at his rich cousin's wedding reception. He'd been relegated to a table at the back of the ballroom, far from the head table, the buffet, and the dance floor.

AS HE SAT in the bar at the St. George Hotel munching on a hard roll, Murphy heard a lion roar:

"I didn't think lions came this close to town, Waldo," Murphy said to the little brown man who stood next to his table pouring thick Ethiopian coffee into a cup from a ceramic pot.

"We have no lions here, Mister John," Waldo said. He had particular difficulty getting his tongue around the letter r, so the word "mister" came out as "mistarr" in his soft, heavily-accented voice. "The lion is at the emperor's palace." One of the walls of the large palace compound, built by the Italians for the colony's governor after the First World War, abutted the back of the hotel. "His majesty keeps his animals here in Asmara."

Smyth had introduced Murphy to Johanes Woldegibremerriam, concierge of the small hotel. "Waldo's a good man," Smyth said, explaining how the nickname had evolved from his rather long, difficult-to-pronounce last name. "During the war, he worked for the Brits." Smyth didn't elaborate.

Before he left, Smyth handed Murphy one of his business cards. Embossed with the state department seal, it introduced Smyth as a Foreign Service Officer. "You can call me. Anytime. Day or night."

After Waldo left, Murphy waded through the contents of a large manila envelope Logan had given him. The pile of documents on the table in front of him included copies of Smyth's after-action report, an autopsy report, an extract from Wallace's 201 file, a report from the provost marshal's office, a wad of Ethiopian money and two $10 chit books.

Murphy stuffed the wad of money, two hundred Ethiopian dollars in colorful fives, tens and twenties, into the pocket of his jeans. Generous, thought Murphy. In his other front pocket, he carried a money clip holding ten U.S. $20 bills.

Murphy slid the chit books into the inside pocket of his light blue windbreaker, next to the small leather case containing his gold CID badge. The chits could only be used at Kagnew Station's two enlisted men's clubs. The officers' club had subtly been placed off limits to him. Apparently, Murphy thought, Major Hilton doesn't want to accidentally run into me on post.

Murphy read the 201 file, an outline of Wallace's military life.

From the "US" prefix of the dead man's serial number, he deduced the dead man had been drafted into the Army. In 1950, Wallace had been sent to Korea as a rifleman. Later, after apparently deciding to make a career in the Army, he'd had trained as a military policeman at Fort Gordon in Georgia.

From the thick sheaf of travel orders in the 201 file, Murphy learned Wallace was on his second 17-month tour at Kagnew Station, returning after spending a year in Vietnam. Previously, he'd served at ASA bases in Korea, Germany, and the United States.

According to his records, Wallace had been awarded a Bronze Star during his Vietnam service.

After serving in Vietnam, given his length of service, Wallace could have had his pick of duty stations. Murphy wondered why the dead man had decided to return to Kagnew Station, hardly a garden spot in comparison with some of the other bases he could have requested.

Before moving on to the next item, Murphy caught himself. Remembering Van Dyck's words, he reached for his little ringed note pad. "Don't make a mental note. Write it down," V.D. had harped. "If you get killed investigating something, how the hell am I going to know what you were thinking about."

So, Murphy wrote a note to himself.

According to Smyth's report, Wallace's body was discovered a short time after sunrise two days before. The report suggested the MP may have been killed by elements of the Eritrean Liberation Front. Murphy noticed there was no mention of the caliber of the weapon used to kill him.

The autopsy report said Wallace was killed by a single gunshot to the head, fired from extremely close range.

Again, no mention of the caliber of the bullet.

A part of the Provost Marshall's report referring to an Article 15 Wallace had received a few months before intrigued Murphy. It indicated the dead man had waived his right to court martial and had accepted administrative punishment for violating the Absence Without Leave clause of the military judicial code.

From his experience, Murphy knew senior non-commissioned officers like Wallace seldom went AWOL. Usually, it was an offense committed by much younger soldiers away from home for the first time.

The charge cost Wallace a stripe. He had been busted back down to buck sergeant. Ouch, thought Murphy, calculating the reduction in rank would have cost the dead man thousands of dollars in retirement benefits had he been discharged at the lower rank.

Career soldiers, like Wallace, usually were savvy enough to avoid such pitfalls. Most NCOs knew how to play the game, and Murphy wondered how Wallace, who managed to compile an unblemished record during his first 18 years in the army, had managed to leave himself open to an AWOL charge, and the indignity of receiving an Article 15 at this stage in his military career.

It just didn't add up.

LIEUTENANT LOGAN'S wife, a tall, pretty ash-blonde woman in the later stages of pregnancy, answered the door to Murphy's knock.

V.D. once told Murphy there was something about pregnant women that really turned him on. "They're so genuinely feminine," the unmarried warrant officer confided. "There's a certain glow."

But the bloom had long faded from the cheeks of Lieutenant Logan's wife. This was no longer a blessed event. She just wanted to get it over with. Fast.

After arriving at Kagnew Station, it had taken Murphy less than five minutes to find Logan's quarters.

Murphy's arrival onto the compound had come without fanfare. Neither of the two heavily-armed MPs stationed at the checkpoint at the front gate paid any attention to him, One of the two unarmed Ethiopians, charged primarily with checking their countrymen on and off the post, merely tipped his pith helmet when he walked through their small enclosure, a glass booth erected on the sidewalk leading to the post.

After walking onto Kagnew Station, Murphy headed for the housing complex for company-grade officers Smyth had shown him. It was located in a clutch of duplexes across the street from the playing fields in the southeast corner of the compound. A fast-pitch softball game was in progress when Murphy walked up to the softball field, which reminded him of Fenway Park with its unusually tall chain link fence in left field. A first lieutenant, dressed in fatigues and sporting an Officer of the

Day arm band, had parked his jeep there to watch the game. Passing himself off as an old friend of Logan's on temporary assignment to Kagnew Station, Murphy had obtained directions to his quarters from the young OD.

Despite his excellent physical condition, Murphy felt light-headed after the walk from the St. George Hotel to the main post. Maybe it's the cigarettes, he thought. But the air is a little thinner at seventy-six hundred feet above sea level, and Murphy knew it would take time for his body to become accustomed to it.

Murphy figured Logan would be happy to see him, and he wasn't disappointed. The young lieutenant probably didn't have a clue who Murphy was. But he knew his unexpected visitor was important. To Logan, that was all that mattered.

"Mr. Murphy, this sure is a surprise," Logan had followed his wife to the front door. "Come in. What can I do for you?"

As the two men sat down in the living room, Logan's wife, her bulging stomach pushing against her blue UConn sweatshirt, drifted off to another part of the small apartment.

"I think your wife was hoping I was the stork," Murphy said.

"That's for sure." The lieutenant smiled. "Any time now. It's our first."

Murphy understood Logan's reason for wanting to avoid a trip to Vietnam. And he didn't blame him.

As they took their seats in matching blue swivel rockers with the worn look of furniture from military housing, Logan said: "I wish I could offer you something to drink, but we don't have any water at the moment."

He went on to explain how a rebel squad had sabotaged the pumps at Asmara's water works, located west of the city off the road to Keren.

"They hit the place every few months. After they attack, the

Ethiopian army sends a platoon out there to guard the place. As time goes by, and the rebels don't attack, the Ethiopians start withdrawing men. About a week ago when the guard detail got down to two soldiers, the rebels struck again. It's a game they play."

Murphy thought about his abbreviated shower.

Then, almost as an afterthought, Logan added: "Major Hilton thinks Sergeant Wallace might have run into the same group that hit the water works."

Wrong place, wrong time, thought Murphy. It made sense.

Logan said water use on post was now restricted to four hours daily. "Maybe, in a couple of days, we will have full pressure back."

Then Logan changed the subject. "But you didn't come here to hear about our water problem."

Murphy shook his head. "No, I didn't. But I'm glad you explained it. It solved a little mystery for me. Now, I know why there isn't any water at the hotel."

Both men laughed.

Then, Murphy came to the point of his visit.

"I need to know more about Wallace's Article 15. How does a vet like him manage to get written up for being AWOL?"

"Well, he didn't show up for work one night."

"Why not?"

"Apparently, he'd tried to switch his duty with another sergeant. He told him he had to go down to Massawa. When the sergeant wouldn't switch duty assignments, he went off the mountain anyway."

"What was so important about Massawa?"

"He wouldn't say, and that drove the provost marshal wild," Logan replied. "He wanted the colonel to throw the book at Wallace, bust him all the way down to private. But the colonel wouldn't do it. He'd pinned a bronze medal on Wallace the month before, so he went easy on him. He only took one stripe away."

"What did he do to deserve the medal?"

"He saved the life of his commanding officer in Vietnam."

Murphy had one more question. "You have any idea why Wallace wanted to come back here? After Vietnam, he could have gone anywhere he wanted."

Murphy thought he noted a nearly imperceptible shrug to Logan's shoulders. But U.S. Army officers never shrug.

"No sir," Logan said. "I don't know why he chose to return to Kagnew Station."

When Murphy stood up to leave, he noticed a helmet liner hanging on a hook next to Logan's field jacket near the front door. Emblazoned in white letters across its front were the words "RANGE OFFICER."

Logan followed Murphy's gaze.

"I'm the junior man on post," he explained. "I do a lot of different things."

"I bet you do," Murphy headed toward the door.

AFTER HIS VISIT WITH Lieutenant Logan, Murphy looked for a place to eat.

He avoided the mess hall on the off-chance one of the cooks might want to see his identification card as he trooped through the chow line. In keeping with Major Hilton's directive, Murphy would keep the purpose of his visit to Kagnew Station secret.

A string of broken English greeted Murphy when he down on the stool in the stag bar at the Top Five Club located across the street from the mess hall.

"Hey Joe, you want *speciale.*"

To Murphy, the word sounded like "Spit Charlie."

"Old Milwaukee Beerah. Ten cents."

A small black man stood behind the bar. A white tag pinned to his red waiter's jacket said his name was "Berhani."

Shaking his head at the barman's suggestion, Murphy scanned the long line of beer bottles and cans on the shelf behind the counter and ordered a San Miguel.

After flipping open the covers of the beer cooler located under the counter, Berhani came up empty. "No have herah, Joe," he said. "I go get."

Berhani left, and Murphy thumbed through the menu he found lying on the bar. Except for the roll Waldo had given him, he hadn't eaten since boarding the plane in Athens. He was famished.

The Top Five Club, restricted to the post's non-commissioned officers and their guests, was one of the top two nightclubs in Asmara; the other being the Oasis Club, which catered to the post's lower-ranking enlisted men. Even Emperor Haile Selassie had spent time at the Top Five. To commemorate the occasion, a life-sized photograph of him wearing a white tunic, festooned with medals and ribbons, hung in the club's main ballroom near the spot where it was taken.

Images of burning buildings flickered from the television in a far corner of the small wood-paneled room. It was a summer of race riots and unruly peace demonstrations, and America's inner cities were going up in flames.

"Where are they this week?" asked one of the men playing poker at a table in another corner of the room.

"Who knows?" another card player answered. "Who cares?"

Murphy knew the feeling. After spending most of his Army service thousands of miles away from home, he felt disjointed, out of synch with what was going on back in the United States. The brief glimpses of American life shown on the Armed Forces Radio and Television Service only compounded the problem. From Murphy's vantage, it seemed like another world. He didn't watch much television.

The image on the screen changed to a black man, cradling a television under his arm as he climbed through a broken store-front window.

"Look's like my cousin's got a brand new TV," a black master sergeant quipped. He was playing gin with a white staff sergeant at one of the tables.

Everyone in the male haven laughed.

The two sergeants were the only men in the room in uniform. They wore a shoulder patch Murphy hadn't seen before. It shimmered with patriotic colors. A set of blue antelope horns ran up the sides of the small white badge, and the dark red head of an antelope sat in its center.

For a moment, Murphy wondered if any of the men in the

stag bar knew Wallace. He could flash his gold shield and poll the entire room. But the delicate nature of his investigation, the need for discretion, required a more subtle approach. He would have to be patient.

Berhani returned with a cold can of San Miguel.

Murphy idly sipped his beer while perusing the menu. Then he heard the distinctive sound of the tumblers revolving in the slot machines located in the lobby of the Top Five Club as the door to the stag bar opened. A deep voice said: "The Spirit of Angeles! God, how I love that beer! I didn't think anybody else drank it around here." San Miguel beer was brewed in the Philippines, and a lot of American servicemen had their first taste of it in Angeles, the military town that had sprung up outside the mammoth Clark Air Force Base.

Murphy turned to watch a big man with a round, florid face sit down on the stool next to him. "Hey, Bernie, get me one of those, will ya?" ordered the man, pointing toward Murphy's beer. Dressed liked he was on vacation, the man wore an old fishing hat and a bright floral print shirt.

"Ok. Sergeante K, I go get." The barman rushed back through the swinging doors to the much larger bar on the other side of the partition.

Extending his right hand, the big man introduced himself as Phil Knight. "You new?"

Using his real name, Murphy told Knight he was on temporary duty from his ASA unit in West Germany. "I'm going to be down here for couple of weeks out at Tract C. I'm staying downtown at the King George."

Knight guffawed. "You spooks out at Tract C deserve better than that. You'd think Uncle Sam would spend a little more money and put you guys up at the Nyala or the Imperial. But he can be a cheap sonofabitch."

Murphy's mention of the top-secret ASA site ended discussion of the purpose of his visit. From Knight's reaction, Murphy knew the big man was not cleared to talk about what went on at Tract C. Even if Knight had held a top-secret crypto clearance, Murphy knew he wouldn't talk shop in an unsecured area such as the stag bar.

Berhani returned with a beer for Sergeant K.

As Murphy resumed his study of the Top Five Club's lengthy menu, his stomach emitted an audible growl.

"Just in time for dinner, huh," Knight said.

MURPHY AND SERGEANT K ate dinner in relative seclusion in the upper level of the main ballroom, around the corner and a few steps away from the life-sized photo of the emperor.

Most of the other diners, families and young couples, sat in the club's lower level, where a band was setting up its equipment on a little stage above the dance floor at the far end of the ballroom.

At first, the conversation between the two men revolved around their Army experiences as they searched for common duty stations or perhaps a mutual acquaintance.

Knight had been drafted into the Army during the waning days of World War II. Later, he'd spent time with a training brigade at Fort Ord and a lengthy stint with a transportation unit attached to the 101st Airborne Division at Fort Campbell in Kentucky before discovering Kagnew Station. "I'm on my third tour," he said. "Been here in the transportation section, off and on, the last nine, ten years."

Murphy made sure their careers didn't dovetail. He knew enough about the Army Security Agency to weave a good story. He told Knight he'd trained at Fort Devens in Massachusetts and spent some time at the National Security Agency headquarters at Fort Meade in Maryland before assignments in Vietnam and West Germany.

Like a lot of overweight men, it was difficult to gauge Sergeant K's age. But, after hearing his story, Murphy guessed the big man was well into his forties. Knight kept his hat on during the meal, but Murphy noticed the flecks of gray that peppered his closely-cropped sidewalls. "You must be close to retirement," he observed.

Sergeant K pulled a cigar out of his shirt pocket. "I'm so short I have to stand on a stool to take a piss," he bellowed, biting off the end of his cigar before lighting up. "Three days and a wakeup, and I'm out of this man's army."

The Top Five Club was quite different from the enlisted men's clubs Murphy had frequented in Vietnam. There, the clubs were little more than beer halls, where Slim Jims were usually the best thing on the menu.

For dinner, Murphy had filet mignon with a large baked potato and a salad. Knight had rainbow trout, grilled and served on a bed of rice pilaf. While they dined, Murphy sipped from a glass of French cabernet and Knight downed two San Miguels.

"You guys live pretty good," Murphy observed. His steak had been broiled to perfection; medium well-done, exactly the way he liked it.

Knight chuckled. "Kagnew Station is an American oasis in a sea of barbarism. Some guy from the American consulate told me that once."

Murphy knew who the "guy from the American consulate" was, but he kept it to himself.

At the far end of the club, a band of young American servicemen began to tune their instruments.

Murphy used Sergeant K's Zippo to light his cigarette.

"Kagnew Station seems like a good base for families." he said.

"It's a great place for a single guy like you," Apparently, Knight noticed Murphy wore no wedding band. "But it can be tough on married men."

A melancholy that caught Murphy by surprise replaced

Sergeant K's cheerful mood. "You know, we got a swimming pool, a bowling alley, a movie theater. Up across the street from the Oasis Club, we probably got the only miniature golf course in Africa." He took a puff on his cigar. "We got a lot of things to do, but we got no place to go."

As Knight talked, Murphy thought he caught the hint of a drawl in his voice. He knew the accent didn't mean much. After spending 20 years in the army, a lot of its senior NCOs sounded like they came from south of the Mason-Dixon line. After 10 years in the Army, even Murphy no longer sounded Kennedyesque. His speech had become so homogenized he was no longer chided for "pahhking his cahh in Hahhvahhd Yahhd," by other CID investigators.

Sergeant K went on. "Man brings his family to Kagnew he's got to stay for 30 months, unless he volunteers for Vietnam, and I don't see many of these guys lining up to go over there. Most of the guys work rotating shifts out at the sites. Their wives can get real lonely. Course, everybody gets real lonely five, six thousand miles from home."

A thick column of smoke curled up around the big man's head. "The last time I got orders to come over here it was the last straw. My wife left me. Took the kids and everything."

It was an awkward moment. Murphy looked away. He thought the big man was about to cry, and he grew uncomfortable about that prospect. There were times in Vietnam when some of the men around him lost control of their emotions and bawled like babies. It was especially disconcerting to Murphy. He always seemed under control. He never cried. Only in his dreams.

The conversation stopped. But Sergeant K's comments about his wife and kids made Murphy think of Wallace. The dead man's files made no mention of a wife or a family. He wondered what Wallace did to fill the void. Murphy didn't know a soldier who didn't have someone somewhere. Did Wallace have a girlfriend over here? Is that why he'd come back to Kagnew Station?

Murphy's thoughts were interrupted by a commotion at a nearby table, where a man, with a clean-shaven head, threw his table setting at a waiter. "These are filthy," For emphasis, he mixed in a string of Italian profanity. "Bring me some clean utensils, *subito*."

Sergeant K's mood brightened. "Mr. Clean's been here for almost three years and he's afraid he's going to catch something."

Murphy looked down at his own silverware and glass. "Should he be?"

"You gotta be careful, that's for sure," Knight answered. "There's a French linguist over in B Company who spends so much time downtown the locals call him Pasha Tesfai. When the Turks were around, that was the title their governors used. A while back, he drank water from a well down at the monastery off the Massawa road and got so sick he was laid up in the hospital for a week."

Sergeant K took a long swig from his beer. Then he laughed. "My rule is never to drink anything downtown unless it's in a brown bottle."

The band kicked into the opening bars of "Mustang Sally."

Knight stood up. "Time to leave." He put enough chits on the red table cloth to pay for both their dinners. "Let's stroll downtown."

THEY STARTED at the Awash Bar, a little dive on a dead-end street halfway down the hill between Kagnew Station and Queen Elizabeth Boulevard.

Aside from two bar girls listlessly dancing to the Rolling Stones' "Satisfaction," the place was empty. It reeked of stale beer and fresh urine. After one Melotti, they left.

As they walked down the darkened lane, a man stepped out of the shadows. "You buyah hashish?" he asked them. In his hands he held a large brick of hash. Ignoring the sales pitch, the two men walked on.

Pictures of former winners of the Miss Asmara beauty pageant hung on the wall at the Fiore Bar on the roundabout down the hill from the main gate. There, Sergeant K downed two shots of fiery Ouzo, and Murphy drank another Melotti. An American, one of those clean-cut young men Murphy was sure had flown with him to Ethiopia, got embroiled in a heated argument. He didn't like the price of the champagne his female companion was drinking. Actually, it was flat ginger ale. Knight suggested they move on.

The old sergeant, Murphy noted, had developed a keen sense for avoiding trouble, a valuable asset for long-term survival in the U.S. Army.

Their stay at the San Francisco Bar, located on a side street about a block from the Fiore, was cut short by the arrival of several Saudi Arabian businessmen. "They can't smoke, drink or screw in the Holy Kingdom," Knight complained, "so they come over here and throw their money around. Bunch of friggin' hypocrites."

Next, they took gharry carts, small horse-drawn taxis, down Queen Elizabeth to the Blue Nile, a nightclub near the intersection with Emperor Johannes Avenue. There, a Kagnew Station soldier had commandeered the stage and, accompanying himself on an acoustic guitar he'd borrowed from one of the Ethiopian musicians, crooned a drunken rendition of "Brown-Eyed Handsome Man." His solo came to an abrupt halt when a fight between two Ethiopians erupted and spilled out onto the wide sidewalk in front of the Blue Nile. The club emptied to watch the two men, both bleeding profusely from the nose and mouth, pound each other until a half-dozen mufti-clad national policemen waded in and peeled them off each other.

Finally, Sergeant K took Murphy to Big Rosie's, "to get jumped."

Asmara's high altitude enhanced the effects of alcohol, and the sour-tasting Melottis he'd been drinking had caught up to Murphy. He had a buzz on, but he wasn't drunk enough, not yet anyway, to forget what he was doing in Ethiopia. As he sat across the narrow hallway from Knight, smoking a Marlboro, waiting for their turn with Big Rosie, he decided it was as good a time as any to try to learn more about Wallace, the dead man.

As Van Dyck often said: "If you want to get wet, you've got to jump into the pool." After taking a long drag, Murphy plunged in. "I thought it would be a little quieter around here," he said nonchalantly, "because of the shooting."

"The colonel wants to keep things as usual," Knight said. "Not too many people downtown know about it, anyway."

It was the military way. Dwelling on the loss of a comrade was bad for morale. Murphy remembered the words of a Marine he'd met while working on a case in I Corps in the northern-most provinces of South Vietnam. As a grunt, the young lance corporal had seen a lot of his buddies killed or wounded. "One day they're here, and the next day they're not. If we don't talk about 'em, it's like they never were here."

From his brief taste of combat during Tet, Murphy understood that sentiment. Still, he pressed on.

"Did you know the guy who got shot?"

Knight didn't answer right away. In fact, he seemed puzzled by the serious bent of their conversation. "Yeah, we both lived in the BEQ. I knew him as well as anybody, I guess."

Murphy paused. He waited a few beats. Glancing around the dimly-lit hallway, he asked: "He come downtown a lot?"

Another slight pause.

"Poor old Davy kept to himself, mostly. He spent most of his free time off the mountain in Massawa."

"What's down there?"

"Desert, mostly. We got an R & R Center on Twalet Island, and there's plenty of whores. Nice place to visit, but you wouldn't want to live there, especially this time of year. Hotter than hell."

Massawa. Again.

At this point, Murphy decided not to talk any more about Wallace. Up to now, the tone had been conversational, small talk about a serious subject. There was no reason to probe further. Murphy didn't need to make an old Army sergeant suspicious of him by asking too many questions.

Besides, Murphy already had a lead.

Now, he had to find out what was so important in Massawa for Wallace to risk his military career.

MURPHY LEANED against a wall, smoking a cigarette, waiting for Sergeant K to emerge from Rosie's small stucco house at the other end of the alley.

A few minutes after Knight had gone in for his tryst with Rosie, three young American soldiers came through the front door. Moments after their arrival, Murphy picked his jacket up off the floor, where it had fallen from the back of his chair, and left.

He waited for Knight under a starless sky. A thick cloud, hovering just above the top of the buildings, enveloped Asmara.

While he stood in the shadows, Murphy thought about the last time he'd been with a woman. Nearly a year had passed since he had fulfilled every soldier's fantasy by hooking up with a pretty Pan Am stewardess he'd met on an R&R flight to Taipei. It was lust at first sight. They spent three days together, nearly every minute in bed, before she left to pick up another planeload of troops in Da Nang. They promised to write each other, but never did.

In Vietnam, for medical and professional reasons, Murphy had avoided prostitutes like the plague, and he simply was too busy to take the time to develop a relationship, sexual or otherwise, with the few American women he encountered.

After returning to active duty, following a brief convalescence on Cape Cod, Murphy concluded he really wasn't ready for an intimate relationship, no matter the duration. At Fort Dix, his main tconcerns were getting up to speed in his new duty assignment and an obsessive need to heal and strengthen his body.

Murphy had been burned once. He'd nearly gotten engaged to Michelle, a nurse he'd met through one of his Boston cousins. They started as pen pals, writing to each other during his first tour in Vietnam. Later, during Murphy's brief assignment at Fort Devens, their relationship blossomed into something else. But when he volunteered for another 12-month stint in Vietnam, everything changed. Not long after he returned to Southeast Asia, Michelle stopped writing. In her final letter, she told Murphy it was becoming too difficult to worry about him all the time.

To soldiers, Dear John letters were an occupational hazard. That didn't make it any easier. When Murphy received his, he was devastated. He couldn't believe it. At first, he reread the single hand-written page to see if he had misunderstood it. After a while, he no longer had to do that. He'd memorized every line.

In Vietnam, there really wasn't much time to dwell on such things. Soon, he was too busy to think about Michelle. The natural tension of trying to operate in a war zone demanded he focus on his work. Even for those not pushing a rifle, Vietnam was a dangerous place. You had to pay attention.

Not until after he left Vietnam did Murphy realize no one waited for him. Only then did he truly understand the depth of the void in his life. His relationship with Michelle had been the first he'd had with a woman that wasn't based on sex from the start. Long before they'd become lovers, they'd been friends. Murphy still missed that part of the relationship, the intimacy of the letters she'd written him.

Murphy knew an encounter with Rosie would have been anything but intimate. However, even the thought of sex had rekindled a much stronger need within him. It had reminded Murphy of how achingly lonely he was.

Loneliness, Murphy knew, was a feeling a soldier could ill afford. It was a dangerous emotion for men and women stationed thousands of miles from home. It got in the way of rational thought and dulled the senses, both essential to a soldier's survival.

"I tell you when it's time to be lonely, boy," Murphy remembered one of his DIs screaming at a young recruit who was whimpering one day in the barracks at Fort Dix. "You don't have time to be lonely because you're ass belongs to the Army from 0100 hours in the morning to 2400 hours at night."

Murphy chuckled at the recollection. Leave it to the Army, he thought, to shorten the length of the day to twenty-three hours. After a few moments, he stopped his musings and regained control of his emotions. He lit up another Marlboro and waited.

About ten minutes later, Knight walked out of the alley. Patting Murphy on the back, he laughed: "Hey Murph, Big Rosie was all juiced up for you. What happened?"

"Guess I'm not in the mood."

The two men walked toward Kagnew Station. Far ahead, Murphy could make out the statue of Empress Menon standing under a faint light in the large square at the bottom of the hill leading up to Kagnew Station.

Knight continued in his jovial vein. "There are two ways to get pussy over here. If you're in a hurry, you can come downtown and buy it on any street corner. If you're patient, you can cultivate a relationship."

Knight went on. "A lot of guys come over here. They meet a little girl, and they play house for a year or two. Since my wife left, I'm more like a butterfly. I flit from flower to flower." Then, he laughed. "But I always come back to Rosie."

The two men walked in silence for the next several minutes.

As they neared the street leading to Murphy's hotel, Knight spoke. But his tone had changed.

"By the way, you dropped this at Rosie's," he said coldly. He slapped Murphy in the chest with his little black identification case. "Why didn't you tell me you're a god-damned cop?"

After dropping Murphy's ID case on the pavement, Knight walked off toward Kagnew Station.

The sudden change in Knight's attitude didn't surprise Murphy. CID investigators weren't very popular with the troops. To most of them, a visit from the CID meant trouble, big trouble. "We give everyone the willies," Van Dyck often told Murphy. The old warrant officer had liked that.

"I guess I lost a friend," Murphy muttered to himself sarcastically. Angry at his own carelessness, he watched Sergeant K's large figure recede into the darkness.

Then, Murphy remembered something V.D. told him all the time: "Mistakes can get you killed in this business."

Van Dyck should know. His old partner had made one mistake too many, and he ended up with a knife in his chest.

AFTER KNIGHT LEFT, Murphy stopped at the King George long enough for Waldo to give him directions to Luigi's.

Murphy still had a slight buzz. But, instead of jet lag, he felt energized. Before going to bed, he decided to check out "the little hole in the wall," as Smyth had put it following the discovery of Luigi's business card in one of Wallace's boots.

Waldo said the little bar was less than a klick away from the hotel, no more than a ten-minute walk. He also warned him about straying into the Bosh, the native quarter on the north side of Haile Selassie, which was off-limits to American soldiers at night. "Mr. John," he intoned, in his heavily-accented English. "If you go there, you will get into trouble."

Luigi's was as Smyth described. It consisted of two rooms not much larger than walk-in closets. It was after midnight, and the lights were on, but no one was around. Murphy walked through the two empty rooms to an open doorway leading to a small courtyard. The building surrounding the enclosure climbed three or four stories into the darkness.

Murphy left Luigi's wondering if the walk downtown had been worth it. As he stepped onto the sidewalk, two street boys took him in tow. "You come to Mocambo. You come to Mocambo," they chorused, as they pulled him along. During the short walk up the sidewalk, the boys, both no older than 10, sold him a pair of sunglasses, not unlike Smyth's,

It was a barter deal. As they stood under a street light, one of the boys held up the fingers on both hands, signifying the price. Murphy, playing the game, countered by holding up three fingers. After several moments of this back and forth, they settled on six Ethiopian dollars. The street boys weren't allowed inside the nightclub. But Murphy was sure they'd receive a few cents for dragging a new customer there.

While making his way to the main lounge, Murphy passed through the brightly-lit taproom, where he noticed three well-dressed men among the group of Ethiopians. They stood along the bar running down the left side of the room. Each of the men tried to avoid looking at him, but Murphy knew who they were.

Van Dyck had always been adept at recognizing his peers. "It takes one to know one," he'd say. "They always try too hard to fit in." The three men at the bar didn't try at all. Most of the local men tended toward dark tweed jackets and woolen sweaters. This trio, given a wide berth by the few other men in the taproom, wore nearly identical, well-cut business suits. Murphy assumed they were off-duty detectives stopping for a nightcap before heading home.

Except for a spotlight shining on the small dance floor, there was no light inside the lounge. When his eyes adjusted to the dark, Murphy made out the outlines of a large divan only a few meters away from where he stood. After sitting down on the couch, he noticed sofas and upholstered chairs had been placed in clusters on both sides of the dance floor, which fronted a small stage, empty except for a drum kit and a few chairs.

From the dark inside the big room, a familiar voice said, "They keep the lights down low so you can't see the rats." But Murphy couldn't place it. He turned to see a figure rise from a chair in the shadows next to the door leading to the taproom. In the dim light, he was unable to make out the man's features. The stranger was nearly his height, but with a slimmer build.

The man wore his hair short, in a crew cut, indicating he too was in the military. From the youthful timbre of his voice, he guessed the man was relatively young, maybe close to his own age.

"As soon as I saw you standing in the doorway, I knew you were John Murphy," The man took a seat in the well-stuffed chair at the end of the divan. "Know you anywhere."

Still, Murphy was unable to match a name with the voice. He began to worry his cover was about to be blown again. He didn't say anything.

"You don't know who I am, do you? I'll give you a hint. We used to play a lot of cribbage together at the Rice Paddy Inn."

The Rice Paddy Inn was the EM club at an Army signal battalion in Da Nang. Murphy had spent the better part of a month at the outfit during his first tour in Vietnam investigating the theft of copper wire from the huge spools at the unit's supply depot. Working under cover, he helped signalmen string telephone wire in Da Nang and Pleiku. He told everyone he was on temporary assignment.

Murphy spent a lot of time at the Rice Paddy Inn, one of the best servicemen's club north of Saigon until a VC rocket scored a direct hit, destroying the ornate stonework next to the bar. At the Inn, he'd played marathon sessions of cribbage with the man sitting at the other end of the couch, a fellow New Englander by the name of Billings. He was a prime suspect in the theft of the commo wire until Murphy had discovered how an enterprising group of South Vietnamese had dug a tunnel into the compound through which they had threaded the copper wire one strand at a time. "Probably used it to set up a telephone system on the Ho Chi Minh Trail," Van Dyck surmised.

Murphy was surprised to run into his former cribbage

opponent in this seedy nightclub in the middle of nowhere. "What are you doing here?" he asked. "I thought you were getting out."

Billings moved closer, near enough for Murphy to see his boyish features. "Uncle Sam made me an offer I couldn't refuse." While in Vietnam, Billings had taken advantage of the Army's Variable Reenlistment Bonus program. "I re-upped and picked up six thousand dollars tax-free."

Billings worked in the finance department at Kagnew Station. The conversation was interrupted by a waiter, who came out of the darkness to take their orders: a shot of Johnny Walker Black for Murphy and a glass of ouzo for Billings.

After the waiter left, Ethiopian music blared through the Mocambo's sound system. Moments after the music started, one of the three men Murphy had tabbed as police detectives entered the lounge. Walking slowly, as if he was looking for someone, the man stepped into the darkness on the far side of the dance floor. A few moments later, he reemerged and, with a young woman on his arm, stepped onto the dance floor. The couple tried to waltz to the music. But when the young man pulled at the woman, who wore a blouse and tight skirt, she pushed him away, shouting a few words in Tigrinya. Murphy wondered about the Ethiopian policeman's timing, but he said nothing about it. Instead, he nodded toward the empty stage. "No floor show tonight?"

"It looks like no floor show any night, for a while," Billings lamented. "They quit." For more than a month, an exotic dancer had been performing at the Mocambo, he explained. "She's Lebanese. Her husband manages her, and they've been trying to get out."

"What's stopping them?"

"Money."

The conversation ceased when the waiter returned with the drinks, paid with a $10 Ethiopian note from Billings.

During the lull, Murphy lit a cigarette. "You were saying?"

Billings took a big slug of Ouzo. It went down hard, and it took him a few moments to recover his voice. "They got paid in Ethiopian money," Billings rasped. "The problem is it is practically worthless anywhere but here."

"Why don't they exchange it?"

Billings cleared his throat. "The Ethis won't let them. They like to keep all the foreign currency in the country. It makes it a lot easier for them to shop out of country."

The music stopped. Murphy looked up to see the two dancers part company. The man went into the taproom to rejoin his friends, while the woman retreated into the darkness on the other side of the dance floor. Within seconds, the sound of feminine laughter tittered from the other side of the room as the woman shared her critique of her dance partner's moves.

Billings continued. "You know, the Ethis pull a great scam at the end of every month up on Kagnew."

"How so?"

"Every pay day, we line up to exchange our greenbacks for their money. For every American dollar, we get two-and-a-half Ethi. Anywhere else in the world, you can get eight, possibly nine, Ethi to the dollar."

"How do they get away with that?"

"It's part of the price we pay for Kagnew Station."

Murphy took a sip of his scotch, calculating how the unfair exchange rate dumped thousands, perhaps hundreds of thousands, of more valuable U.S. dollars into Ethiopian treasury each year.

Billings moved onto the couch next to Murphy. Speaking in more conspiratorial tones, barely above a whisper, he said:

"I've been trying to help out the dancer and her husband, but I've been having trouble catching up with them."

Murphy looked toward the empty stage. He didn't say anything. He just let Billings talk.

"I want to do a little banking. I figure I can convert their money on a five-to-one ratio and stretch my money a little."

Even in the dim light, Murphy could see the smile playing on Billing's face, making him appear even more innocent than he really was.

"But you also can get in a whole lot of trouble."

"Only if I get caught."

When Murphy shifted his gaze slightly, he noticed one of the detectives had moved to the archway connecting the lounge with the taproom. He seemed to be staring in their direction.

"I'd be careful. I understand the police are everywhere."

MURPHY AWOKE with a hangover. Too much beer, wine, and scotch. A shower, cut short by the low-water pressure, and breakfast, consisting of a poached egg, hard roll and a glass of freshly-squeezed orange juice, had done little to ease the depressing feeling.

Waldo told Murphy the Littorina was the fastest way for him to make the one-hundred kilometer trip to Massawa.

Under leaden skies, Waldo's friend Tesfai, took Murphy in his gharry cart to the train station, a little more than two kilometers away in Asmara's east end.

During the ride, they rolled past the tall gray walls of the emperor's palace, where three national policemen stood guard near its massive wooden gate, and the cathedral. On Haile Sellasie Boulevard, they went by the provincial headquarters, the municipal hall and courthouse, monumental structures built by the Italians during their 50 years of rule.

Tesfai, a sullen man who apparently didn't speak English, didn't point out any of these landmarks, so Murphy saw some of the most important buildings in Asmara ignorant of what went on inside them.

It was a quiet Sunday morning, and they had the streets to themselves. As the gharry cart had rolled along, the only sound Murphy heard was the clip-clop of the horse's shod hooves echoing off the buildings.

Van Dyck would have liked the quiet of Asmara, thought Murphy, a city of nearly 150,000 people who all seemed to be sleeping in. In Vietnam, the warrant officer often complained about the noise. "Something's always popping off. I can't get a decent night's sleep." Asmara was more his style.

The 50-foot Littorina stood on the track with one of its two diesel engines humming. Elsewhere in the train yard were parked little steam engines, miniature versions of the locomotives Murphy watched switching cars in South Boston's railyards while visiting his cousins when he was a kid. Dozens of tiny flat cars, tank cars, and box cars, all built to run on the Ethiopian Railways' narrow-gauge track, sat on nearby sidings.

Murphy had arrived early. He took a seat at the rear of the empty rail car. He paid little attention to the people, mostly women and children, who climbed aboard the trolley through the door at the opposite end of the car.

In addition to his hangover, Murphy had awakened with doubts about his assignment. He wondered whether he was on a fool's errand. How was he going to find out how the Eritrean Liberation Front had come into possession of ammunition originally issued to the U.S. Army without making some waves? Did anyone really want to know? It seemed an impossible task. The more Murphy thought about it the more his uncertainty grew.

Murphy was not skeptical by nature. But, under Van Dyck's tutelage, he had come to at least entertain some doubts. "Don't believe anything you hear and only half of what you see," V.D. often joked.

From two different sources, Logan and Knight, Murphy had learned Wallace had a reason to go to Massawa so compelling he blemished an unsullied military record. What was it? Maybe, it would help explain what Wallace was doing in the antenna field the night he was killed. Or maybe, Murphy was running up a blind alley. Whatever the case, he had to find out.

Murphy traveled light. He had jammed a change of clothes

and his dop kit into his flight bag. He wore jeans and his windbreaker over a pale yellow knit shirt, and his dark brown boots ran just above his ankle.

His slightly-flared jeans, navy work pants purchased at the military surplus store at Fort Dix, allowed easy access to his small Browning. But Murphy didn't bring his gun. He didn't think he would need it. This trip amounted to a fishing expedition. Besides, it would be one less thing he would have to explain should the Ethiopian police take interest in him.

After the previous night's fiasco with Knight, Murphy also wondered about carrying his CID credentials with him. Then, after recalling Hilton's instructions, he decided to keep the badge with him. The major told him he didn't care how he handled himself with his fellow Americans; he just didn't want him to advertise his presence to the Ethiopians.

The gold shield was a powerful tool, especially when dealing with American soldiers. Murphy thought he could use it without attracting the attention of the local police.

An old Ethiopian soldier was the last to climb aboard the Littorina, a converted electric trolley car. A few moments after the guard settled on his perch on top of the engine cowling at the rear of the car, the doors closed and it started down the track.

For the first few kilometers, the Littorina rolled through lush woods. As soon as it cleared the trees, the track veered sharply to the left, and the trolley began its descent to the valley floor more than a thousand meters below.

The tracks hugged the mountains on Murphy's side. Through the windows on the other side of the car, he saw a deep canyon running for several kilometers between two tall mountain chains.

It was a slow, steady descent. The Italians started building the railway before World War I. In some places, the rail bed was carved out of the rock, and the tracks laid on little shelves hundreds of meters above the valley floor. Elsewhere, stone trestles were built into the side of the mountains to carry the tracks. When those techniques were unfeasible, the Italians built stone viaducts to carry the tracks over narrow gorges or bored tunnels, thirty of them, and ran the tracks through the mountains.

The lingering hangover didn't make the ride enjoyable for Murphy. Within minutes after the Littorina started its long descent, he began to have problems. Feeling the bile rise in his throat, he was sure he was going to throw up. He fought the urge by leaning forward and burying his hands in his face. He hoped breakfast would stay in his stomach.

It took less than twenty minutes to reach the canyon floor, which was nearly devoid of vegetation. Murphy's stomach churned as the car swayed back and forth. Sneaking a peak through his intertwined fingers, Murphy saw the wisps of clouds still visible on the peaks high above the deep gorge. He saw very little greenery.

Most of the trees were stunted. Rocks and boulders filled a landscape where the dominant shades were grays and browns.

Murphy's condition improved as the trolley snaked its way across the valley. He turned his attention toward the soldier sitting about an arm's length away from him, intrigued by the old man's ancient rifle, a British Enfield .303. When Murphy leaned forward to take a closer look at the weapon, the soldier spoke to him in Tigrinya.

"Excuse me." Murphy looked up into the soldier's brown, weathered face. "What did you say?"

The old soldier didn't answer.

Then, Murphy heard a much softer, lightly-accented female

voice. "He said: 'You can look, but you can't touch.'"

The English words surprised Murphy.

As he sat up in his seat, Murphy looked up to see the stern-faced old soldier staring back at him. From the other side of the car, a pretty young woman spoke to the guard in Tigrinya.

While he was battling to keep his breakfast down, Murphy hadn't noticed her sitting across the car from him. She was looked quite different from the Littorina's other passengers. Her skin was much lighter, the color of light brown sugar. Instead of the long floor-length dresses and shawls worn by the other women, she wore a stylish lavender outfit, a knee-length skirt with matching jacket and a white blouse.

"You speak English," Murphy said, after the woman finished talking to the soldier.

She turned her attention to Murphy. "Of course, I do." She favored him with smug grin. "I'm an American." After a slight pause, she added, "Like you." She glanced at the soldier. "I told him you were just looking." Then, she chuckled. "I think he thought you were Shifta."

There was an empty seat next to one occupied by the large cloth bag the woman had carried onto the Littorina, and Murphy moved across the aisle and sat down. "You don't mind if I sit here, do you?"

The woman picked up the book she'd been reading. "As you wish." Then, she resumed reading.

Murphy, rapidly recovering from his hangover, wanted to talk. He was intrigued by the woman, whose short, naturally-curly, jet black hair and small, delicate features made her look so attractive. "Excuse me. I don't mean for this to sound like it does. But what is someone like you doing in a place like this?"

The woman put down her book. Before answering his question she surveyed Murphy with her sparkling hazel eyes.

"I live here."

"But you said you were an American?"

"I am an American. But I'm also Eritrean and Italian."

"That's quite a mix."

Her name was Romana.

She told Murphy her father was an American civilian who had to come to Massawa during the war to help salvage ships scuttled by the Italians when they abandoned the port in 1941. "He died a short time after he married my mother, and she decided to stay. Her family's here."

Romana learned to speak English at the American school at Kagnew Station. At home, and with her relatives, she spoke Italian and Tigrinya, the principal language spoken by the people who lived in the province.

Murphy told her he was on temporary assignment to Kagnew Station and was going to spend his day off in Massawa.

Romana said she worked as a nurse at a hospital in Asmara. "I'm going to mass in Massawa. The priest there married my mother and father."

It took about twenty minutes for the Littorina to cross the valley. Then it climbed for a few minutes more before gliding down into another valley where the foliage was thicker and greener. Five minutes later the trolley stopped. A faded sign announced the Littorina had arrived at Ghinda.

No one boarded. But a few of the women picked up their bundles, gathered their children, and climbed down from the car. After they disembarked, the soldier climbed down to stretch his legs.

The temperature had warmed. Murphy removed his windbreaker and stuffed it into his travel bag.

"Why is he on the train?" He nodded toward the soldier.

"Sometimes the Shifta attack," Romana had donned sun glasses. "A few months ago, they stopped a passenger train and took everyone off it. The empty train rolled through Asmara and halfway to Sudan before anyone could stop it."

A few minutes after the trip resumed the Littorina began to roll down the foothills. The descent was sharp and brief. At the base of the hill, the single set of tracks ran through a dry riverbed. The landscape grew barren as the relative lushness of the highlands gave way to desert acacias, cactus and scrub grasses.

Moments after reaching the coastal plain, the trolley slowed for a tethered line of a dozen camels moving up the side of the track from the direction of Massawa. As the car slowly rolled past the heavily-laden animals, Romana explained some caravans travel through Eritrea between Somalia and Sudan. "We have few roads here. The camel drivers have their own highways."

The Littorina picked up speed as it rolled through arid wasteland the final twenty-five kilometers across the desert. Ten minutes after passing the caravan, the Littorina rolled past a rail siding, where Murphy noticed a number of conexes, huge metal boxes used by the U.S. Sealift Command to ship materiel. The containers were stacked on several small flat cars or sitting on the desert floor. In Vietnam, U.S. troops converted the large metal boxes into hooches, places where they could stay dry and maybe catch up on their sleep.

A few minutes later, the tracks went under a stone trestle, veered to the right and ran parallel to a paved road.

Romana glanced at her watch. "We're coming to Massawa now. I think I will be on time for mass."

Rows of low-slung buildings appeared on both sides of the trolley. Most were a faded, sun-bleached yellow. The few people who were out, mostly men dressed in long, flowing *ghebellas* strolling along the dusty dirt path next to the tracks, stopped to watch the Littorina roll past. The tracks ran over a long causeway and curled toward the north end of Twalet Island to a small train station at the water's edge.

While the trolley was moving, Murphy hadn't noticed the heat. But he began to perspire as soon as it stopped. The sun beamed down through a cloudless sky, and a warm blast of hot air seemed to rise from the ground as he stepped down from the car.

Murphy wished he'd brought the sunglasses he'd purchased from the two street boys with him. When he looked up at Romana, she looked cool and composed in her shades. Murphy took her hand to help guide her down from the trolley. As soon as her feet touched the ground, she let go.

Cold shoulder, hot climate, Murphy smiled to himself.

Romana led him around a large brown-stoned building, surrounded by a tall wall. "That's the emperor's palace," she said. "He has them all over the country." This imperial compound was much smaller than the one in Asmara.

They crossed a paved road leading to the low stone bridge running to the old port on Massawa Island and walked along the sidewalk. Romana pointed to a three-story, white-brick building, which looked much newer than the neighborhood's other sun-bleached buildings. "That's where you want to go."

It was the U.S. Army's Red Sea Rest Center, the first stop for most American soldiers visiting Massawa. Without another word, Romana kept walking down the sidewalk. Less than a hundred meters away, on the opposite side of the street, the vaulted roof of a brown-stoned church towered over the other buildings.

"Maybe I can see you again some time?" Murphy asked.

"Maybe." Romana turned to look back back while continuing to walk down the sidewalk. "Ciao."

Murphy doubted it.

After crossing the street, he turned to watch her as she stepped through a gate in the wall surrounding the church.

MURPHY ENTERED the rest center through a door near the dining room, which had a panoramic view of the channel between the two islands.

All of the tables were full, so the maitre'd directed him to the stag bar on the third floor.

The air conditioner in the stag bar was on full blast, and Murphy felt like he had stepped into a meat locker. It must be the coolest room in Massawa. At the other end of the bar which ran the length of the long, narrow room a big, gray-haired man sat alone. "Take a seat," he said, pointing to the stool next to him.

As he made his way down the bar, Murphy noticed the red-and-gold MACV shoulder patch the man wore on his right sleeve. When he sat down, Murphy also noticed the camouflaged CWO bars pinned to the collar of the man's sweat-stained fatigue blouse.

"Abdi, get this man whatever he wants." The warrant officer looked old enough to be Murphy's father. "And get me one more of these." He downed the contents of his glass and set it back on the bar. "Name's Stetson." He offered a meaty right hand for Murphy to shake. "Just like the hat."

After he finished making another gin and tonic for Stetson, Abdi, the small black bartender, asked Murphy what he wanted.

"Kind of early in the day for me," he said, glancing at Stetson's drink. Murphy ordered an iced tea.

"I get from dining room," the barman said. He reached under the bar, picked up a telephone and yelled a command in Tigrinya.

Murphy pulled his cigarettes out of his shirt pocket and placed them on the bar in front of him. "Tell them to send up a hamburger and fries, too." He lit up his first cigarette since breakfast. The heat had cured his hangover, and he now had the urge to smoke.

Before hanging up the phone, Abdi yelled a few more phrases into the telephone. He then brought Murphy an ice-filled glass of water.

Murphy took a long drink. "Boy, is it hot."

Stetson smiled, deepening the furrows on his brow. "Going to hit the big one two zero, this afternoon. Another day in paradise."

"Hotter than Vietnam?" Murphy asked.

"Nowhere's hotter than Vietnam. It's the humidity. You been there?"

"I pulled two tours," Murphy answered. "Saigon. Da Nang. I spent a lot of time in I Corps, up around Hue."

Stetson took a sip from his drink. "Never left Cam Ranh Bay. Spent most of my time unloading ships."

Murphy considered flashing his CID badge. But the old warrant officer seemed talkative enough. He kept his gold shield in his pocket. Instead, he repeated the lie to Stetson he'd told Knight and Romana. "I'm TDY from Germany, and I took the Littorina down to Massawa for the day."

Stetson worked at the American port facility on the Gerar Peninsula on other side of the harbor. It was his job to make sure the ships cleared port on time. "Right now, it's all assholes and elbows," he said. "Started at three o'clock this morning. Knocked off about an hour ago. When it cools down, I'll get the work gang going again. Got to get the ship out of here by the end of the week."

A waiter entered the bar carrying Murphy's iced tea,

hamburger and fries on a tray. Stetson handed him his chit book, and the waiter tore off enough chits to cover the meal.

"Since the Egyptians closed the canal last year, things are all screwed up down here," Stetson explained. "It takes a helluva lot longer for a ship to get here, and we got stuff all over the place. Don't know where half of it is."

Murphy, taking a bite out of his hamburger, recalled the abandoned conexes he'd seen out in the desert.

The door opened. Two crew-cut young men in civvies, walked in, sat down at the other end of the bar, and began to peruse menus.

"The dining room always this busy?" Murphy asked.

"Gotta-go day for a lot of these people," Stetson answered. "Most of them bugged out of Kagnew Station Friday afternoon to come down here. Now, they've got to get back up the hill."

On the way in, Murphy had noticed the gravel parking lot was filled with cars and motorcycles. An Army jeep, which he now assumed belonged to Stetson, was parked at the main entrance to the hostel. Murphy looked at his Seiko. It was a little after 11 o'clock. "It's kind of early to start worrying about getting back home, isn't it?"

"Every afternoon at one o'clock, the Ethis close the road to Asmara," Stetson explained. "Got four hours to get up the hill before they close it at the other end." The 105-kilometer trip up the mountains to Kagnew Station could be made in under two hours by car. "But the going's much slower for trucks, especially climbing through the switch backs above Nefasit. There, the guys who drive the reefers and tandem rigs spend most of the time in low gear."

Murphy finished taking a bite out of his hamburger. "Why shut down the road?"

Stetson swirled the ice in his near-empty glass. "Around

here, the night belongs to the Shifta." He finished his drink. "Don't worry. They usually don't bother us Americans."

That's a switch, thought Murphy. In Vietnam, the night belonged to Charlie, and he definitely went out of his way to bother Americans.

Murphy thought about Wallace, the dead MP. "What about the guy up at Kagnew Station? Everybody says the Shifta got him."

"Must have been in the wrong place at the wrong time," Then, pointing to his glass, Stetson called to the bartender: "Abdi, one more time."

Murphy took a few more bites out of his hamburger, waiting until the bar man brought the warrant officer another drink to continue the conversation: "I heard that guy spent a lot of time down here. Did you know him?"

"Not really," Stetson answered. "Saw him sometimes when he come in here for a drink or to buy smokes. Spent most of his time over at the Four Floors of Whores. Shacked up, I guess."

Murphy took another bite from his hamburger, washing it down with a big slug of iced tea. "Four Floors of Whores, huh. Sounds interesting. Where's it at?"

Stetson smiled. "Hotel Torino. Big white building right in the middle of the fork in the road on the other side of the bridge. Can't miss it."

STANDING IN THE SHADE of a large date palm outside the church compound, Murphy smoked a cigarette while he waited for Romana.

Murphy was going to need her help at the Hotel Torino. She spoke Italian and Tigrinya, and her language skills would be essential in finding Wallace's hangout.

While he waited, several cars left the parking lot at the rest center, heading toward the causeway back to the mainland and the road to Asmara. Five minutes went by before a small group of people, mostly old Italian men and women, stepped onto the sidewalk through the church gate. A minute later, Romana followed.

"Well, hello there," she said, with a slight smile as she noticed Murphy standing on the sidewalk. "I'm surprised to see you so soon."

Murphy stopped smoking. He dropped his cigarette on the ground, stubbing it out with his boot. "I need your help."

"And I need to go back to Asmara." She glanced at her watch. "The Littorina leaves in about an hour."

Romana started walking down the sidewalk. Murphy fell into step beside her. "This won't take long." He gently put a hand on her arm. With his other hand, he handed her his CID credentials. "I need you to help me talk to someone."

After glancing at his CID shield, Romana handed it back. "I see. You're here on business."

Romana resumed her walk. "I need someone to interpret for me." She stopped to listen. "It's just over the bridge. It will take less than an hour. I'll make sure you catch your train."

Romana began to walk. Then, she turned. "Come on, let's get this done. I don't want to be late."

During the walk, Murphy told her he was investigating the death of a military policeman at Kagnew Station. Officials at the base had kept a lid on the shooting. Romana, because of her ties with Asmara's American community, knew a soldier had been killed at the base. But she didn't know any of the details, and Murphy didn't fill her in.

It took five minutes to reach the Hotel Torino, an imposing structure with a rounded stone facade facing the bridge.

Romana stopped at the door. "I can't go in there. Don't you know what kind of place this is?"

Murphy understood her reluctance. But he needed her help. He was insistent. "You said you'd help me. I'll make sure nothing happens to you. After this, you won't have to deal with me."

There were no pedestrians in front of the tight cluster of buildings on the street, which cut through the heart of the small island. It was noon, and all the windows and doors were shuttered.

"Look, there's nobody around. No one's going to see you."

Murphy opened the door and Romana, after looking both ways to check whether anybody indeed was watching, slowly walked through it. They stepped into the vestibule. A narrow stairwell ran up the inside of the large stone building, which remained relatively cool despite the torrid temperature outside. "We'll start at the top and work our way down," he explained.

They took the stairs to a roof-top bar. It was empty. Strands of colored party lights, strung from posts, crisscrossed the open-air lounge. Looking across the harbor, perhaps two kilometers away, Murphy saw the huge mountains of salt stockpiled at the Salina salt works.

They came down one flight of stairs and started to knock on doors. Murphy kept it simple. "I'll knock. You ask if they know David Wallace."

It was the same at every door on the fourth floor. Murphy knocked. When a muffled voice responded, Romana shouted her question in Tigrinya and put her ear to the door to listen to the answer. Then, she'd look up at Murphy and say: "They don't know him." After that, Romana walked to the next door and waited for Murphy to knock again.

The search ended at the first door on the third floor.

FATIMA, A ROBUSTLY-BUILT black woman nearly as tall as Murphy, had been waiting for Wallace all weekend.

Greeting them warmly in Tigrinya, she opened the door and ushered them into her one-room apartment.

Once inside, Romana talked with the girl for a few moments. Then, in English, she spoke to Murphy in a low voice. "She doesn't know what's happened to him. She thinks we're his friends."

Murphy unslung the travel bag from his shoulder and placed it on the queen-sized bed that dominated the room. "Tell her I'm from the military police. Tell her what happened to him."

Romana took off her glasses. Looking up to Fatima, she spoke in a soft voice. Murphy watched as Fatima's smile slowly faded. Soon, tears rolled down her seamless face. Murphy guessed she was not much older than twenty. As the two women sat down on the edge of the bed, Fatima began to weep, a soft whimper. Romana turned and tried to put her arms around the big girl. Failing that, she tried to console her by stroking her back.

Murphy surveyed the room.

A naked light bulb hung from the ceiling over the bed. An air conditioner, in one of the two small windows, cooled the room. Two folded lawn chairs leaned against the wall underneath the other window, which was shuttered. On the opposite side of the room, in a little alcove, a hot plate and a small refrigerator stood on a side board next to a sink. On one side of the door, three large framed photographs were lined up on top of a small chest of drawers. In the shadows on the other side of the door stood a small gun cabinet. Several pieces of men's and women's clothing hung on hooks on the wall near the cabinet. Next to the bed stood a small night stand, the only other piece of furniture in the room.

Home, sweet home, thought Murphy. This is where Wallace hung his hat when he wasn't at Kagnew Station.

Murphy walked over, picked up one of the photographs, and moved to the center of the room so he could view it in the light.

It was a photo of Wallace and Fatima cuddling on a settee in the roof-top lounge. The colored photograph had been taken at night. Murphy could see the party lights in the background. Wallace wore his blonde hair in a crewcut and held a protective arm around the girl.

Before picking up another of the framed photographs, Murphy checked on the two women. Romana no longer held Fatima. As the girl sat on the bed staring blankly, Romana sat next to her, daubing at the bigger girl's tears with a cloth hankie.

The second photograph also was in color. It showed a sunburnt Wallace posing with a dead antelope, a yellowish, gray-colored animal. Kneeling on one knee behind the carcass, Wallace held a horn in each hand, lifting its expressionless head for the photographer. A broad smile played across Wallace's face..

The third photograph, in black and white, showed a full-bird colonel pinning a medal on Wallace's chest. He was dressed in khakis, and the officer pinned the medal on the left breast pocket, next to an expert marksmanship badge and below three rows of service ribbons. In the background, men stood in formation.

Murphy looked toward the bed. Now, Fatima held the hankie

and wiped her own tears. Romana stood next to her. Both had their eyes on him.

"Please tell her I'm sorry about what happened to her friend. But I must investigate. Ask her if I can look around."

A few moments later, after Romana translated, Fatima nodded.

Murphy looked inside each one of the drawers. The top drawer contained women's lingerie. The other two drawers contained rolled-up sweat socks, and neatly-folded men's briefs and t-shirts.

The door to the gun cabinet was locked.

Murphy looked toward Romana. "I want to look at the guns."

Romana spoke a few more words of Tigrinya to Fatima, who answered in a barely audible voice. Romana translated: "She says the key is hanging on the side of the cabinet."

Murphy found the key and opened the glass door. The small, narrow cabinet had space for four rifles. It contained three guns — a 30.06 caliber rifle, a seven-millimeter Rigby and a .416-caliber Rigby. Wallace also kept a 35-mm Nikon camera inside the cabinet.

Murphy took one of the Rigbys out of the cabinet. He slid the bolt back. Rubbing his index finger along the inside of the chamber, he could feel a light coat of oil. Wallace kept the rifles clean and ready for use. Murphy put the weapon back.

Then, Murphy knelt down to open a drawer at the bottom of the cabinet. It contained several boxes of ammunition. In the bottom of the drawer, he found a bullet rolling loose. Murphy stood up to the light, studied the live round for a moment and then slipped it into the front pocket of his jeans.

Closing the cabinet door, he turned his attention to Fatima.

"Can you ask her where Wallace hunted."

Murphy kept his eyes on the girl as Romana translated the

question. "In the desert."

"Who did he hunt with?"

Fatima looked away for a few moments before answering the question.

"No one," Romana translated. "She said he went hunting alone."

Murphy walked over to the bureau. He picked up the photo of Wallace with the dead antelope and showed it to Fatima. "Who took this?"

She averted her eyes. She was slow to respond. When she did, her voice was barely audible. Romana spoke to her in Tigrinya, and the girl repeated her answer in a louder voice.

Romana seemed surprised. A few moments went by before she repeated what she had been told. But Murphy had heard Fatima's reply the second time. He knew the answer to his question even before Romana translated.

"Shifta," Romana repeated. "She said the Shifta took the picture."

MURPHY AND ROMANA missed the Littorina and had to take a bus back up the mountain to Asmara.

If it hadn't been for Stetson, who drove them in his jeep across the causeway to the mainland, they might have missed the bus as well.

As it was, Murphy had to hand the ticket agent a twenty-dollar bribe to secure two seats on the old Renault. "That's way too much," Romana chided as the old man climbed aboard and used his Shifta stick to create space for the late arrivals.

Romana was mad at Murphy. She'd let out a stream of Italian expletives when they arrived at the train station too late for the trolley. As the bus rolled through the flats outside Massawa, she sat next to him silently fuming.

Murphy decided Fatima had nothing to do with Wallace's death. But the revelation the dead man had spent time out in the desert with the Shifta intrigued him. Murphy didn't know whether the man who'd taken Wallace's picture with his dead trophy was a bandit or a member of the Eritrean Liberation Front. Then, he recalled what Smyth said about the Ethiopians' refusal to officially acknowledge the ELF's existence. The government referred to the freedom fighters as Shifta, common bandits. Apparently, common folk, like Fatima, also used that term.

As the bus barreled down the long straightaway through the desert, the driver talked in Tigrinya to the two Ethiopian soldiers sitting in the seat in front of Murphy and Romana. "He's telling them they left Massawa too late to go with the convoy," she translated. "He's hurrying to catch up before it gets into the mountains." The Ethiopians ran armed convoys between Massawa and Asmara to protect trucks and buses from the officially unacknowledged liberation front.

In the back of the bus, someone tuned a transistor radio to a station in Cairo. A woman sung in Arabic accompanied by a host of woodwind instruments. Her high-pitched wail soon flooded the bus, which stank of unwashed bodies and clothes.

Murphy stared out the window and watched the landscape roll past. It was a desert, a flat, lifeless wasteland, but with no sand dunes. Not at all like the Sahara he always imagined.

Before leaving Fatima, Murphy had given her 100 Ethiopian dollars and instructed Romana to tell her to move out of the apartment she'd shared with Wallace. "Tell her I don't want her to get into trouble with the police."

Murphy was satisfied Fatima had told him all she knew, but he sensed the Ethiopian police would treat her rough, especially if they found out Wallace had spent time with the Shifta. "Tell her the American MPs will come to take Wallace's things away. She can take what belongs to her, but she must leave all of his things here."

Murphy already had removed a few items from the apartment: the .30 caliber round he found inside Wallace's gun cabinet, a roll of exposed film from the Nikon and the picture of Wallace and Fatima sitting together in the Hotel Torino's roof-top lounge.

The shell was a tracer round similar to the one Hilton had shown him the day before.

Murphy took the other items from the apartment because he didn't want other investigators to find anything linking Wallace to Fatima. "The girl has enough problems," he told Romana. "She doesn't need the Ethiopian police beating on her trying to get her to tell them something she probably doesn't know.

About thirty minutes into the trip, the bus crossed a large steel span over a dry wash. Not far from the bridge stood the bombed-out shell of a large stone building.

"Shifta?" Murphy asked, giving Romana a gentle poke in the ribs.

"No," she said. "Some Americans call it the Italian War Memorial. The British artillery knocked it down during the war."

Five kilometers beyond the bridge, the landscape began to change as the bus started the ascent into the foothills. The brush along side the road became denser. The incline steepened, and the driver geared down. He would not catch up with the convoy today. Soon, the bus slowly crept toward the brow of a hill. After crawling over the top, it picked up speed heading down the other side toward a bend in the road.

The jolt came without warning.

Murphy slammed into the seat in front of him as the driver suddenly braked after rounding the bend. Screams and angry shouts filled the bus as he wrestled with the steering wheel to keep the vehicle on the tarmac while trying to stop the bus. One passenger rolled down the aisle past Murphy and slammed his head into the metal post behind the driver.

The bus stalled out as it came to stop at an angle in the road about ten meters shy of a line of tethered camels. It looked like the same caravan Murphy had seen from the Littorina that morning. The heavily-laden animals apparently had refused to budge when they heard the bus approach. The four men leading the camels strenuously pulled on the lines in an effort to get them moving again.

The driver tried to restart the bus. Turning to the two soldiers sitting in front of Murphy, he pointed at the camels while jabbering away in Tigrinya.

"He wants them to move the camels," Romana explained. She also had hit the back of the seat in front of her. She rubbed her nose as she looked for her sunglasses, which had fallen off when the bus suddenly stopped.

As the two soldiers moved to get off the bus, Murphy leaned forward and picked up Romana's sunglasses from the empty seat in front of him. He was handing them back to her when shots rang out.

THE CRY OF "SHIFTA!" echoed through the small bus. Murphy looked out the side window beyond Romana and saw nearly a dozen men standing in the scrub brush, perhaps twenty five meters off the road, firing weapons into the open area between the bus and the caravan.

He looked in the direction of the camels and could no longer see the two Ethiopian soldiers. Within seconds, the shooting stopped. Two of the attackers quickly moved to the side of the bus. Hitting the side of the bus with their rifle butts. They screamed at the passengers in Tigrinya.

"They want us to get out," Romana said in a calm voice.

As the passengers stepped off the bus, some of the gunmen took up positions around the vehicle. Others helped move the camels off the road. One man led the passengers around the front of the bus.

When he passed by the front bumper, Murphy noticed one of the fallen soldiers was still alive, crawling along the tarmac. Romana also noticed the man, who was only a few meters away, and she took a step toward him. But Murphy took firm hold of her wrist and pulled her with him. "It's too late to help him," he muttered.

Moments later, one of the attackers walked over to the fallen soldier and finished him off with a shot in the back of the head. Close by, another man searched the body of the other soldier.

This is war, thought Murphy. No quarter asked. No mercy given.

He'd had a taste of combat during the Tet Offensive when

he had joined a group of U.S. Marines, American and South Vietnamese Army soldiers in a bitterly-fought battle against a reinforced Viet Cong battalion. The VC advanced down Highway One intent on capturing the airfield at Phu Bai. Very few prisoners were taken by the desperate defenders.

It was an experience Murphy was still trying to come to grips with, and one he'd rather not repeat. He'd gotten his fill. After two trips to Vietnam, he now knew what war was all about.

All the marauders looked dusty and dirty, their hair unkempt and faces unshaven. Wearing no common uniform, they were dressed in shorts or long pants, topped with tee-shirts, sweaters or jackets. Ragged head-dresses protected them from the sun. They didn't look like soldiers. They looked like Shifta, the bandits the Ethiopian government said they were.

After the passengers lined up along the side of the road, two of the raiders walked down the row and inspected them. They didn't stop until they came to Romana. One of them said something to her in Tigrinya. She responded by slapping the man hard across the face. Startled, he took one hand from his rifle and cocked his arm to answer the blow. But Murphy struck first. He lunged forward and drove his right fist as hard as he could into the rebel's chest. The man gasped, reeled backwards, and dropped his rifle in front of Murphy. It was an M1 carbine.

The weapon looked liked it was brand new. When he stooped to pick it up. Murphy caught the faint whiff of oil, the smell a weapon has when it's first issued.

Murphy then heard a rifle bolt slide forward. He stopped and left the rifle where it lay. He gritted his teeth. The man he'd hit rolled on the ground fighting to catch his breath. Seconds ticked by, and nothing happened. Murphy looked up to see two Shifta standing pointing bolt-action Enfields at him. Slowly,

Murphy rose and raised his hands high above his head. He tried to appear relaxed and unafraid.

Romana shouted a few words of Tigrinya, and the two men slowly lowered their weapons. Then, another armed man came around the back of the bus. His head-dress covered most of his face. He spoke to the man lying on the ground in harsh tones and kicked him hard in his side. The man in the mask was tall, as tall as Murphy. He spoke to the two other men, who quickly moved to help their fallen comrade to his feet. Then, the tall man gave Murphy a gentle poke in the ribs with the barrel of his rifle and said in slightly-accented English, "You Americans should keep your noses out of other people's business."

Murphy was struck by the intensity of his stare. His eyes were cold, hard. When the man turned to say something in Tigrinya to Romana, the look seemed to soften. They exchanged glances, and, for a moment, Murphy thought he detected a hint of recognition between them. A few seconds later, the man began to bark out orders to his men.

The camels were on the move, driven down a track leading into the underbrush on the far side of the road. Most of the attackers accompanied the animals, but one man went around the bus to shoot out the tires. The leader walked quickly across the road and into the bush. Two men followed him. When they got to the other side, they stopped and turned, keeping their eyes and their guns trained on the passengers and waited for their comrade to finish with the tires. When he was done, all three quickly disappeared into the underbrush.

The entire incident lasted less than five minutes.

"**HIS NAME IS MEKELE**," Romana said, struggling to remove her nylons while she leaned against Murphy's hip.

The revelation came nearly a half hour after the couple began their trek up the highway into the mountains.

"He was from Asmara. He left a long time ago. Everyone thought he was dead."

Romana hadn't bothered to take off her stockings when she had changed into her deck shoes at Fatima's apartment. Now, unwilling to sit on the hot tarmac, she used Murphy as a support to help her remove her nylons. "They are like gold." She carefully rolled up each stocking before putting it into her large cloth bag. "I have some American friends who buy them for me at the PX."

Murphy didn't want to be around when the Ethiopian army came looking for the bus. It had become mired in the soft sand next to the road when the driver tried to turn around and drive back to Massawa on its flattened tires.

No, Murphy didn't want the local authorities to take an interest in him. Maybe, they'd take a closer look and discover he was CID. When Romana told him she thought it was six or seven kilometers to Dongolo, the next town, he decided to walk. "Maybe there's a telephone. I have a friend who I can call."

Since leaving the marooned bus, Murphy and Romana had barely spoken to one another. And now, without his prompting, she'd given him the name of the leader of the rebel band.

The air was cooler a few hundred meters above the desert

floor. As Romana leaned against Murphy, who had been ordered to look the other way, he took out a cigarette. When he lit up and took his first deep drag, a shadow ran across his face. He looked up to see a large bird in the cloudless blue sky moving through the air a few hundred meters above him. Its wings fully extended, the bird rode the thermals rising from the desert. It hovered for a moment before tipping a wing slightly and moving to another place in the sky.

Murphy could overhear Romana muttering to herself in Italian, as she tried to keep her balance while leaning against him and tying her laces.

Later, while they walked, Murphy asked: "Why did you hit that man back there?"

Romana was slow to answer. Finally, she said: "He asked if I was your *sharmuta*, your whore." Then, after another pause, she added: "You didn't have to hit him."

"I was trying to help." Finished with his cigarette, Murphy flipped it onto the pavement and stomped it out with his boot. "That guy would have knocked your pretty little head off."

Romana picked up her pace as they climbed the hill. "I can take care of myself."

Murphy, who had labored to keep up with her at in Massawa's heat, was able to match her stride in the cooler highlands above the desert. "I feel responsible for you."

"That's a national trait, isn't it?"

"You're an American, too." He was taken aback.

"Not that kind of an American." With that, Romana, who barely came up to Murphy's shoulders, picked up the pace again.

As the two walked in silence up the steep incline, Murphy wondered what Van Dyck would make of the meeting between Romana and Mekele. "What a small world," V.D. would say, his eyes wide in wonderment. "Everyone knows everyone else. Amazing."

But Murphy did believe the meeting had been coincidental. Besides, he was the reason they were on the bus in the first place. If he hadn't made Romana miss the Littorina, she would never have been caught in the ambush. And there would have been no reunion.

Eritrea, which had a population of about a million and half people, was a relatively small place, and Asmara was not a large city. It appeared Mekele and Romana were nearly the same age. Why shouldn't they know one another?

Just the night before, in the Mocambo, Murphy had run into Billings, someone he'd known half a world away in South Vietnam.

It was a small world, Murphy thought as he kicked a stone, and Romana's world was even smaller.

About an hour after starting their hike up the road toward Asmara, Murphy and Romana found Petros, a tall black man, standing next to a faded green Opel.

The car was parked in a turnout near the brow of the last hill before the road from Massawa dipped into Dongolo. Nearby, a Moslem, an elderly white man, knelt on a cloth mat saying his afternoon prayers.

Petros spoke to Romana in Tigrinya and told her he was the driver for Ahmed, a salt trader from Yemen who had rented his Opel to visit some business associates in Massawa. In Islam, Sunday was not the sabbath, just another day for business.

"I told him our bus was attacked by the Shifta," Romana explained to Murphy. "I said we were going to Dongolo to find a telephone to call a friend in Asmara for a ride."

When Petros told Ahmed their story, the old man instructed

the driver to make room in the backseat for the young couple.

But the car didn't stop in Dongolo. Instead, Petros drove on to Ghinda, the largest town between Asmara and Massawa, to report the attack. He left his three passengers at a small country inn, the Halfway House, a popular stop for Americans traveling along the road. While they sipped on tall, cool glasses of iced tea, Petros drove to the local police station. He didn't want to involve his passengers with the police.

Moments after resuming their trip, they encountered a small break in the line of the hills behind the town's small stone houses. Romana pointed to an earthen dam, which provided water to irrigate the crops at several large farms in the area. The reservoir was dry. "The rains are late this year. Sometimes, they don't come at all."

It was difficult for the four people in the car to converse.

Ahmed spoke only Arabic. Petros spoke Arabic and Tigrinya. In order to talk to Ahmed, Murphy had to first speak to Romana. She, in turn, translated his English into Tigrinya; Petros then translated into Arabic. It was a cumbersome process. So, aside from exchanging a few pleasantries, little conversation transpired among the car's occupants.

After Ghinda, the road ran on a slight incline across the base of a large mountain. There, Petros stopped the car long enough for Ahmed to drop a few coins into a cup held by an old man dressed in rags. He leaned on a Shifta stick and stood on the side of the road. As Petros drove off, the old man, his head bobbing up and down, shouted up at the mountain. Romana told Murphy the beggar was exhorting God to grant them safe passage. It didn't work. Less than five kilometers up the road, a group of baboons, perched on a cliff, pelted the Opel with rocks.

Murphy chuckled. "I guess he didn't give the old beggar

enough money." Then he became serious. "I need to know more about Mekele."

Romana started with a history lesson. She explained how Ethiopia annexed the province more than five years before by simply marching in and dissolving the Eritrean parliament.

"Mekele's father was one of the few members of parliament who resisted. Mekele was in California studying to be a doctor. After the Ethiopians took over, they arrested his father and confiscated the family's property. They took everything. Mekele had to stop his studies. He came home and joined the Shifta."

A man with a score to settle, thought Murphy.

"Do you see him often?"

"No. Until today, I hadn't seen him for years. Like I told you before, everyone thought he was dead."

From Ghinda, it took a little more than an hour to complete the trip to Asmara.

At Nefasit, Petros had to negotiate the fifteen switchbacks up the face of a mountain. Halfway up, during one of his full-speed turns through a switchback, Murphy and Romana got entangled on his side of the car. As the couple unwrapped their arms and legs from around each other, Murphy saw Romana smile for the first time. During the pileup, he had inadvertently touched one of her breasts. The smile followed. Was it an invitation? Or did she find humor in his utter embarrassment? He didn't know. All he did was apologize profusely.

From the top of the switchbacks, the road hugged the side of the mountains all the way back to Asmara. There was no traffic in either direction, so Petros put his foot down. It took the little sedan less than fifteen minutes to cover the final twenty kilometers.

Along this stretch the cliffs rose several hundred meters

above the road on Romana's side of the car. On Murphy's side it ran next to a drop off of more than 1,000 meters. Instead of guard rails, little blocks of stone had been placed every few meters along the side of the road as barriers. In some places, small monuments, obelisks or stone crosses, had been erected to mark the place where motorists had driven off the mountain to their deaths. In one spot, four monuments were clustered.

Romana pointed toward the stone markers as the Opel sped past. "One of those was put up by the family of an American soldier. They used to raffle off cars every month at the Oasis Club at Kagnew. Sometimes, they would give away an Alfa Romeo. But they stopped after an American soldier drove one off the road here."

What a waste, thought Murphy. In Vietnam, dozens of our guys died every week for no good reason. Here, our guys died for no reason at all.

As the road pulled away from the canyon and headed toward a tree line, Murphy noticed a tall white cross standing on heights overlooking the valley. Soon, the road snaked through a large grove of trees, where a thick canopy of leaves and branches blocked the late afternoon sun. As they approached a raised wooden barrier, Petros slowed the car. A quarter-ton truck blocked the opposite lane of the road, closing it to Massawa-bound travelers. As the Opel slowly rolled past, Murphy saw a squad of soldiers lounging under the trees on both sides of the road. Less than a kilometer ahead, not far from the entrance to the train station, the road broke out into the open.

"Do you want to go back to Kagnew Station?" Romana asked.

"No. I want to go to my hotel, the King George."

Romana leaned forward and instructed Petros in Tigrinya.

Shortly after turning onto Haile Selassie Avenue, Petros made a left turn, drove past a little park and headed up a steep hill through a residential neighborhood. All the houses were surrounded by tall stone walls, and branches from trees growing behind the walls drooped over the narrow street, providing a leafy canopy. To discourage intruders, shards of broken glass had been embedded into cement on the top of the walls.

The little Opel shot through a narrow street into a small roundabout, which had five streets radiating from it. When Petros paused to look for oncoming traffic, Romana pointed out her street, and the car rocketed straight across the intersection and up another steep incline. Petros drove for less than twenty meters before coming to a stop in front of a small stucco building on her side of the car. She opened the door and slid out of the car, hauling her large cloth bag behind her. "It was nice to meet you, John Murphy." She held the door open for a moment. "It has been an interesting day."

He smiled "Maybe, we can do it again sometime."

"Maybe." Another smile. "Ciao." Then, she closed the door.

Romana lived on a cul de sac. A service road for the large houses located on top of the hill, it ended less than fifty meters beyond her house. The turn-around was large enough for Petros to make a u-turn. By the time the car passed Romana's house, a small single-story structure with a flat roof, she had closed its large green wooden door behind her.

AFTER PETROS dropped him off at the St. George, Murphy waited about ten minutes before walking up to Kagnew Station. First he stopped at the Logans, but no one was home at the young lieutenant's quarters. Then, Murphy walked up to the arsenal at the north end of post. The two large bunkers, built into a grass-covered, man-made berm, were unguarded. But their metal doors were locked, and the iron gate in front of each door was secured by a padlocked chain. Murphy had wondered whether the mint-condition carbine the Eritrean rebel had dropped on the ground could have come from the weapons cache. But, after inspecting the post's magazine, he doubted a group of Eritrean rebels could have come onto Kagnew Station and broken into bunkers unnoticed.

At the nearby Oasis Club, the Sunday afternoon dance was in full swing. On Sundays, the young women of Asmara flocked to the sock hop in the club's grand ballroom. "Pig push," he heard one of the card players at a nearby table call the dance after he'd taken a seat in the club's dining area. It was a spacious room with the look of a '50s-style soda fountain.

Murphy hadn't eaten since that morning, and he was famished. He rummaged through a large garden salad and cut into an inch-thick prime rib while downing a couple of Heinekens.

After blowing his cover the night before, Murphy avoided the Top Five Club. NCOs were not allowed in the Oasis Club. It was restricted to enlisted men, pay grades E-1 through E-5.

He doubted Knight, or any of his friends, would be at the club. Technically, his rank, Sergeant First Class, E-7, should have kept Murphy out of it, too. But he looked young enough to pass for one of the low-ranking soldiers who belonged there.

After dinner, Murphy phoned Smyth. Then, he walked to meet him near the Empress Menen Statue in the large square down the hill from Kagnew Station. They drove in the Rover to the soccer stadium on the road to Keren less than a kilometer west of the King George Hotel.

A few months before, more than thirty thousand soccer fans had jammed the arena's stone benches to watch the Africa's Cup soccer tournament, Smyth told him. Tonight, less than five thousand people turned out to watch two local sides play each other under the lights in an early-season match.

The two Americans found seats in the nosebleed section. It was a secure location. Nobody was within thirty meters of them.

Smyth didn't start talking business until they sat down. "Well, what have you been up to today?"

Murphy reached into the breast pocket and pulled out the bullet he found in Wallace's apartment. "I think this came from the same lot as the round that killed Wallace."

He told Smyth where he'd found it.

Smyth studied the round. "Interesting."

Murphy went on. "His girlfriend said Wallace met some Shifta while hunting in the desert near Massawa."

"Now, there's a couple of no-nos," Smyth said. "Our boys aren't supposed to hunt in this province any more. The Ethiopian government doesn't want a bunch of armed Americans running around Eritrea. They're afraid someone will take their weapons away from them, I guess. And they're definitely not supposed to talk to Shifta."

Before continuing with his report, Murphy handed Smyth the key to the rifle cabinet and gave him directions to the apartment. "Ask the provost marshal to send a detail to clean out the place and get Wallace's personal effects."

Murphy expressed surprise at how easy it was for him to find Wallace's pad in Massawa. "I was in town less than five minutes, and I was able to learn where he'd shacked up."

"You got lucky," Smyth said. "Most of the guys at Kagnew let only their closest friends know about their off-post residence. The colonel doesn't want his unmarried soldiers living off post."

Smyth said the ASA didn't mind one-night stands. "But the colonel doesn't want any of his boys playing house with some Eritrean cutie. If he catches them living downtown, he'll throw the book at them."

Murphy described the ambush by the Shifta. When he explained his rationale for knocking down the Eritrean rebel, Smyth interjected: "It's good to know the age of chivalry isn't dead."

Murphy said he was surprised the rebels hadn't shot him after he had leveled one of their comrades.

Oddly Smyth didn't seem surprised. "Usually, the liberation front seems to avoid hurting Americans." He brushed a lock of wispy blond hair from his forehead. "They seem not to want to antagonize us, and we've gone to great lengths not to antagonize them."

He told Murphy the U.S. Army pulled its military advisors out of Eritrea two years before and sent them to Galla province in southern Ethiopia and the Peace Corps was restricted to working on projects in neighboring Tigre province. "We're doing our darndest to stay out of their way. That's why it's difficult to believe the ELF killed Wallace. But stranger things have happened."

Then, Murphy told Smyth about the carbine the rebel

carried. "Looked like it had come right out of the box."

Smyth pursed his lips. "Now, that's very interesting."

Murphy described the precision of the attack on the bus. "These guys didn't waste any time. It was a classic ambush. They used the camels to stop the bus. After isolating the soldiers, they took them out quickly. They moved out in an orderly fashion. I'm impressed — they know what they're doing."

Murphy's words came in a torrent. He was surprised how easy it was for him to share his information with Smyth, someone he hardly knew. In the past he'd have shared what he'd learned only with his partner. But Murphy had no partner, so Smyth would have to do. Someone had to be told about what he'd found. If anything happened to him, another CID investigator would have an easier time picking up where he'd left off.

For a while, Smyth, who continued to wear his dark glasses in the fading light, didn't say anything. Then he asked for Murphy's opinion. "Still think Wallace knew the person who killed him?"

Murphy looked down at the soccer field, where one of the teams was setting up to take a corner kick. "I don't know what to think. But it seems plausible."

During an investigation, Murphy tried to keep an open mind. Other investigators formulated theories early in their inquiries, then they searched for clues to support them. But Van Dyck had taught Murphy to collect as many details as possible, then sift through them until he found a solution. "Put it together like a puzzle," the old warrant officer told him. "Find where the pieces fit. Don't trim the edges to make them fit."

Smyth wasn't done. "You say the Shifta shot out the tires before they left?"

Murphy nodded.

Smyth pushed his glasses above his forehead. "That's odd.They've usually blown up the trucks and busses they've stopped."

THE NEXT MORNING, the knock on Murphy's door came before seven o'clock. It was Smyth. "The major wants to see you and he wants to see you now."

No shower. No breakfast. Just enough time to slip into a tee-shirt, a pair of jeans and boots, and head out the door.

Smyth drove to the Prince Makonnen Golf Course less than a kilometer away near an Ethiopian fort. The military installation, a huge dirt mound built into the side of a hill by the Italians, was the headquarters of the Ethiopian Army's Second Division.

By the time Smyth and Murphy arrived, Hilton was teeing off. Except for the little Eritrean boy serving as his caddy, no one else was on the course.

Murphy stood next to the sparsely-grassed tee box as the major swung his one iron, sending the Titlist into a low trajectory down the fairway of the tenth hole at Kagnew Farms. "Where is everybody?" he asked after the shot.

Hilton watched his ball bound off the hard pan and roll to a stop in a swale at the bottom of the hill within 100 yards of the 325-yard hole before answering. "During the week, the course doesn't get much play this early in the morning. The men who work eves or mid tricks don't show up until later."

"You're all by yourself, sir." As the three men started down the rocky fairway, the little caddy, who was barely as tall as the bag he carried, raced ahead to the ball. "Aren't you worried about security?"

The major chuckled. "There's a full regiment of Ethiopian soldiers less than a half klick down the road. I don't think the liberation front really wants to tangle with those boys."

Then, as the three men slowly walked along, the major got down to business.

"Smyth tells me you think Wallace knew the person who shot him. He also tells me you found evidence Wallace had been in contact with the Shifta, I mean, the Eritrean Liberation Front, and that you saw a new carbine in the hands of one of the rebels." A slight pause. "What do you think all that means, Mr. Murphy?"

Murphy didn't have an answer. "I wish I knew, sir. I don't know if there is any connection between Wallace's death and his contact with the Shifta. And I don't know how the rebel came to the have that new carbine."

The conversation stopped when the trio arrived to where the little caddy hovered over Hilton's ball, which had come to rest on the downward slope, just short of the bottom of the swale.

From where they stood, none of the them could see the flag marking the hole. However, they could see the two large radio telescopes at the U.S. Army's Stonehouse facility, located across the dirt road behind the back nine, and the major lined up his next shot using one of the two white antennas. The dishes, which stood several stories high, looked out of place on the African plain.

Despite the down-hill lie, the major used his six iron to punch the ball. "Can't get any loft off these fairways. There's been no rain, and the grass is short. Besides, you get absolutely no roll when you fly the ball into these greens. So it's best to bump and run."

Setting up with the ball back in his stance, Hilton took a half-swing and sent a shot toward the big dishes. "That should get it there." The ball never traveled more than ten yards above the ground as it headed over the rise toward the antennas.

Following the ball, the young caddy ran off ahead of the threesome. As soon as the boy was beyond earshot, serious talk resumed.

"Our ability to continue to operate the facilities at Kagnew Station must not be jeopardized," Hilton told Murphy. "Earlier this year, the North Koreans captured the Pueblo, a U.S. Navy ship doing the same kind of business as our people out at Tract C. That was embarrassing, to say the least. If we were to lose our facilities here, it would be devastating."

Hilton's pace quickened as they reached the top of the knoll. The ball had stopped ten feet short of the cup on the hard-packed brown earth which served as a green.

"We have been able to set up shop here as guests of the emperor," the major continued. "We pay a lot for the privilege, and we've invested more than fifty million dollars on our facilities here during the past twenty years."

Hilton paused, as if to reload, and Murphy sensed the major was about to get to the main point of their meeting.

"The Ethiopian government may not be as cordial to us if it knew some of our soldiers were dealing with the liberation front. If the Ethiopians believed some of our men were supplying the rebels with weapons, they'd probably show us to the door, and it's my job to see that doesn't happen."

Murphy hadn't considered such a scenario. But now he could see how the evidence he'd found—the bullet, the picture of Wallace allegedly taken by a member of the liberation front and the like-new carbine in the wrong hands—could be construed in such a way. Wallace could have been helping the rebels, and he could have ended up dead for his trouble.

Hilton walked up to his ball, where the young caddy stood waiting to hand him his putter. After sliding the major's six iron back into the bag, the young boy slowly walked across the brown earth to pull the pin. The major's putt stopped about a foot short of the hole. "Slowest greens in the world." He stepped forward to tap the ball in for his par. "But there's absolutely no break on them."

The caddy ran off to the next tee, but Hilton lingered near the tenth hole. Wearing the satisfied look of someone who had arrived at a right decision, the major told Murphy he'd fulfilled his mission. His services were no longer needed.

"I really think, you've done enough. But it's kind of dangerous having you run around. If the Ethiopians learn about you, and what you've turned up, we'd have another problem."

Then, almost as an afterthought, Hilton added: "You can stand down until transportation can be arranged for you."

With that, the major strode off to the next tee.

BEFORE GOING BACK to Kagnew Station to arrange transportation home for Murphy, Smyth made his rounds, trying to cultivate friends among the local populace.

First, they visited Yohannes, a silversmith, in his little shop off the treeless boulevard which ran for nearly a kilometer through the heart of the Bosh.

"One of our spooks thinks he has links to the liberation front," Smyth explained before they went in. "But I think he's leading us on."

Smyth used a mixture of Arabic and English to talk to Yohannes, a thin brown man with a growth of stubble. It was difficult for Murphy to follow. Before they left, Smyth paid seventy-five dollars Ethiopian for the Star of Mogadisio, a stylized crucifix Yohannes had made for him in silver.

The sun had burned off the early-morning overcast. Fumbling with the steering wheel as he pulled his sunglasses out of his breast pocket while turning onto Haile Sellasie Boulevard, Smyth told Murphy what had happened. "Normally, all we talk about is the weather. This time, he complained about his little brother. He's making a ton of money working in the oil fields in Bahrain while Yohannes is nearly starving here trying to live on the few trinkets he sells. Ah, sibling rivalry."

During the drive across town, Smyth briefed Murphy on etiquette before they visited Mahmed at his doucan in Ghezabanda, a residential neighborhood built on the height of land in the east end.

"It's bad form to take advantage of a Moslem's hospitality,

no matter how cordial the invitation," Smyth explained. "And whatever you do, don't use your left hand to do it. They're very distrustful of southpaws."

At the doucan, Murphy was kept out of the conversation. It was held entirely in Arabic. But he followed Smyth's instructions. When Mahmed insisted he accept a fourth cup of the sweet-tasting tea, one of several mixtures the Arab sold from small wooden bins in his store, Murphy declined. Mahmed, a stout, olive-skinned man, dressed in a flowing gray burnoose, didn't understand a word Murphy said, but he smiled in appreciation of the young American's politeness.

In between visits, Smyth tooled around the back streets trying to gauge whether he was followed. Murphy thought it easy to pick out a tail, especially in the wide empty streets of Ghezabanda, but he appreciated the trade craft.

"The spooks like to play games, so I try to indulge them," Smyth explained. "Sometimes, they follow me. It keeps them sharp."

But it was serious business. While trying to lose his imaginary tail, Smyth talked.

He told Murphy the CIA was concerned the Eritrean liberation movement was communist-inspired. It was worried another hot round in the Cold War was about to start in the Horn of Africa.

"Last year, the British consul went for a walk in the bush around Keren, and he was a guest of the liberation front for six months. He didn't learn much. But there is evidence a number of rebel groups have banded together to throw the Ethiopians out.

Communists, Moslems, any Eritrean with a score to settle, have apparently joined together in common cause."

Murphy thought about Mikele, the rebel leader, and what

Romana had said about him.

Smyth said tensions were developing in the cozy relationship between the United States and the Ethiopians.

"Right now, we're involved in negotiations concerning our future here in Ethiopia. It's a rather touchy situation. That's why Major Hilton doesn't want you to probe any further. It's a case of the less we know—the better."

Smyth said the Ethiopians had upped the ante on extending the lease on the U.S. installations in Eritrea.

"In addition to everything else we give them, the Ethis want us to outfit another brigade so they can chase the liberation front around the countryside. It's a pretty steep price. Besides, there's a clique within the Ethiopian military who don't want us here at all. They'd rather cozy up to the Soviets."

Geopolitics meant little to Murphy, but he listened.

Always, his main concern was the case he was assigned to investigate.

His removal from the investigation didn't sit well. The case had become interesting. But Murphy could do nothing about it. A superior officer had ordered him to cease and desist.

If he made a stink, the Ethiopians would get wind of it.

Murphy had to keep quiet.

ON THE WAY to Kagnew Station, Murphy and Smyth witnessed a traffic accident.

After driving around Ghezzabanda trying to shake his imaginary tail, Smyth stopped at a wide intersection near one of the steep hills leading down from the neighborhood. He idled while a large truck came barreling straight through it.

Sheets of used corrugated steel were stacked high in the truck's rack body. Several men sat on top of the pile trying to keep the sheets from blowing away. As the truck headed down the incline, less than twenty meters from where Murphy and Smyth waited, a motorcyclist started to pass it. A little further down the hill, one of the sheets of corrugated steel went sailing into the air. It came down and hit the motorcyclist as he pulled even with the truck.

Immediately, the man and his bike went down.

The man struggled to stand up. When he did make it to his feet, he stood unsteadily in the middle of the road. His face was missing. The jagged edge of the metal sheet had cut clean as a meat cleaver.

Smyth covered his mouth with one hand while reaching to open his door with the other. His sunglasses fell into the street as he leaned through the partially-opened door and retched on to the pavement.

Murphy watched as the stricken man fell back to the pavement.

A large gray Mercedes, which had pulled up behind Smyth's car, moved around and stopped next to the man. Three men, dressed in business suits, climbed out of the car to look at him. After a brief inspection, two of the men picked the man up and carried him to the back seat of their sedan. Then, all three men climbed in, and the car roared off.

Nothing was said during the ten-minute ride to Kagnew Station.

Smyth broke the silence when he parked his car in the large square between the commissary and the post exchange. "I've never seen anything like that before."

"Neither have I." Then, remembering the coup de grace he saw delivered to the Ethiopian soldier the previous day, Murphy added: "At least not until I came here."

Smyth seemed surprised. "But I thought you were in Vietnam."

Murphy stared out the windshield. "Over there, I usually dealt with the aftermath. I've seen my share of dead and wounded. But I never saw anyone get it like that. The few times I was involved in a firefight, I was too busy to really notice what was happening to the people around me. Only after." His voice trailed off.

"You think he's going to die?"

"I doubt there's anything anyone can do for him."

While Smyth was off arranging his transportation back to the states, Murphy dawdled at the snack bar next to the PX. While waiting, he picked at his breakfast of ham and eggs, smoked three cigarettes and downed two cups of coffee.

About a half-hour later, Smyth returned to announce he'd booked a seat for Murphy on an U.S. Air Force transport scheduled to leave Asmara in three days.

Murphy whistled. "Three days?"

"It's the soonest I could get you out of here. You'd have to wait a week to get a seat on a commercial flight."

It's a hell of a lot easier to get into Ethiopia then to get out of it, Murphy thought.

Smyth had calmed down. He was all business as he described the Air Force flight. "It's a milk run. Across the continent to Dakar on the west coast in Senegal, a brief stopover on Ascension Island in the South Atlantic, another night in Recife on the coast in Brazil, then into Homestead Air Force Base in Florida. Should take about three days."

Murphy had hoped to get back to the United States sooner than that, but Smyth softened the blow.

"A friend of mine has got a motorcycle he can lend you. You can ride around and play tourist for a couple of days."

Smyth was driving toward the back gate to visit Tomasso, an old Italian who had the motorcycle at his auto repair shop off the airport road, when Emperor Haile Selassie made his entrance onto Kagnew Station.

As he drove down the straightaway near the BEQ, Smyth noticed the emperor's entourage cueing up at the backgate.

"Jesus," he whined. "Must have been a change of plans. The old bugger was supposed to come through the front gate."

Smyth turned off the road and parked his car in the open area between B Company and the BEQ.

The emperor's arrival was reminiscent of the Oklahoma Land Rush. About a dozen vehicles, traveling three and four abreast, charged down the road from the back gate.

In the back of four Land Rovers, members of the imperial guard, wearing large plumed hats and carrying spears, stood shoulder to shoulder. Those vehicles took up positions at the point, flanks, and rear of the fast-moving procession. The road was so narrow the driver of one Land Rover had to make his way through the shallow ditch next to the road to maintain his position.

Right behind the emperor's black Rolls Royce, two squads of Ethiopian soldiers, armed with automatic weapons, sat in the back of two open three-quarter ton trucks. The rest of the emperor's retinue traveled in two Mercedes Benz sedans and three military jeeps.

Except for the two military policemen on duty at the back gate, no other American soldiers were present when the emperor made his entrance onto Kagnew Station.

Smyth looked at his watch. "His imperial majesty is a little early." He knew the timetable. "First, tea with the colonel. Then, a visit to the dentist for his annual checkup." Kagnew Station had the best dental facilities in the country, he explained, and Haile Selassie visited the post at least once each year to have his teeth cleaned.

As they drove through the back gate, Murphy commented about the emperor's entrance onto the post. "Came in like he owned the place."

Smyth chuckled. "He does." Then, after a slight pause. "At least, for now."

"What do you mean?"

Smyth turned left onto a shady street. "The old boy has sat on his throne for nearly fifty years, but I'm afraid his days are numbered. A few years ago, he took a trip to South America. While he was gone, several young officers tried to pull off a coup. The old man came back and regained control. Soon afterward, his Army marched in and took over Eritrea. I guess he wanted to keep his boys busy."

Smyth was his old self. As they drove to Tomasso's garage, he continued the briefing.

"The Ethiopians live in a pretty dangerous neighborhood."

As Smyth drove, he glanced out his side of the car for a moment. "North of here, in the Sudan, perhaps a hundred thousand people have died in a civil war between north and south that has been going on for five years. Historically, the tribesmen in the south have provided a buffer between the Moslems in the north and Christian Ethiopia."

Next, he took his right hand off the wheel and pointed toward Murphy's side of the car. "To the south, a military coup in Somalia has created some concern. The Ethiopians are worried the new leaders may go to war over the Ogaden, a desert area which has been a point of contention between the two peoples for centuries."

Then, Smyth pointed straight ahead. "To the east, across the Red Sea, it appears the Russians, through their Egyptian surrogates, are trying to fill a vacuum created when the British pulled out of Aden last year. Nasser has sent fifty thousand troops into the Yemen, where a civil war is brewing, and that's given the House of Saud great cause for concern."

Smyth paused to check the traffic before turning onto the airport road.

"In this part of the world, Nasser wrote the primer on palace coups. We're worried some of the young Turks in the Ethiopian army will get ideas and will try to bring the old man down again. But, as you can see, he does a pretty good job of watching his back."

Smyth said very few Americans were aware of what went on in this part of the world.

"All of this a sideshow to what's going on in Vietnam," he said. "Most of our fellow countrymen don't know about any of this, and those who do don't really care."

Most Americans don't really know what's going in Vietnam, Murphy thought to himself. It seemed no one, not even the people who were running the war, had a handle on it.

Even Van Dyck, who usually found a good rationale for just

about anything the Army did, never really understood what it was supposed to be doing in South Vietnam. But the warrant officer never questioned the orders sending him there. "I just go where they send me. I just pray the quartermaster has gotten there before me, and I've got a decent place to sleep and something to eat."

Smyth's friend, Tomasso, loaned Murphy a 175cc Honda Scrambler.

It wasn't as big a bike as Murphy would have liked, but it was enough to get him around until it was time for him to leave.

The little motorcycle's owner was laid up with a broken leg in the post hospital. "He won't be needing the bike for a while," explained Smyth. "Besides, he still owes Tommy for fixing it."

Tomasso was a squat man with a mane of snow-white hair. Smyth said he'd come to Eritrea during the '30s with the Italian Army. Unlike most of the soldiers who invaded Ethiopia, he never went home. His garage, actually six open-air stalls attached to the side of his house, was located inside the walls of a compound on a quiet street off the airport road.

In his broken English, Tomasso showed Murphy the location of the front and rear brakes, the throttle and the clutch. Pointing to the gear shift near the foot peg on the left side of the bike, the old man said: "One a down and three a up." Murphy gave a thumbs-up sign to show he understood.

But Tomasso was unable to fire up the little motorcycle by using the kick starter. The old Italian straddled the bike, stood up on the pegs, and came down hard on the kick starter with his right foot. The engine sputtered, but it didn't catch. Two more times, Tomasso tried to kick the engine to life without success.

His Eritrean workers lined up in front of the repair stalls to watch. Each time their boss failed to get the motorcycle's engine to turn over, the bantering among them grew. When their murmurings escalated to light-hearted chuckles, Tomasso had had enough. Out came a stream of rapid-fire Italian. Most of the words meant nothing to Murphy. However, Tomasso's tirade ended with one word he did know. "*Silencio*," the old Italian bellowed. One of Murphy's uncles had married an Italian from Boston's North End, and she frequently used it to quiet her boisterous nephews and nieces before grace at Sunday dinner. Turning in the long black banana seat, the old Italian stared intensely at his employees and made sure they felt his displeasure. Without his having to say another word, each one of the Eritreans stopped talking and returned to his work area.

"*Aspetta*," said Tomasso, holding one finger in the air while astride the motorcycle. "Wait." He turned the ignition key off. After about a minute's wait, he switched it back on and pressed the electronic starter button on the right handlebar. Immediately, the bike came to life with a high-pitched whine. A few seconds later, Tomasso throttled down, and the bike's engine settled into a never-ending series of burps.

MURPHY HADN'T RIDDEN a motorcycle in more than two years. But it didn't take him long to regain the feel of it.

After tooling through the side streets around Kagnew Station, he headed for the trails near the antenna field. At this time of day, there was no traffic on the long straightaway leading to Tract C, so he opened up the throttle. Nearing the top end, Murphy felt a slight jerk when he shifted from third to fourth gear. When he shut the bike down to investigate, he heard a volley of gunfire.

Murphy always ran toward the sound of guns.

"Some day, it's going to get you killed," Van Dyck warned. His former partner kept his head down when gunfire erupted. "It's a bad habit. Find another one."

Once, while investigating a fragging incident on the Bong Son Plain, Murphy and his mentor got caught in the middle of a fire fight between a platoon from the Seventh Cav and a main-force Viet Cong outfit. "You've got to find another hobby," the older man said. As the two men hunkered down in the ditch next to their jeep, Murphy kept his finger on the trigger of his .45 caliber automatic waiting for a target. He never got off a shot.

Another time, Murphy tried to help out a South Korean Army unit during a skirmish near Nha Trang. On this occasion, he did manage to squeeze off a few ineffectual rounds from his pistol. On later trips into the field, Murphy carried a sawed-off carbine, with a long banana clip, to provide himself with more firepower.

V.D. was no longer around the last time Murphy ran toward

the sound of guns during the Tet Offensive, near Hue, when he collected the large chunk of shrapnel in his back during a firefight.

This time, it was different. This was no fire fight. This time, it was a training exercise at the post's firing range.

About four hundred meters from the road, behind a thin line of trees, Murphy found a platoon of troops from Kagnew Station practicing their marksmanship with the M-14 at the post's firing range.

Murphy found Lieutenant Logan sitting in the front seat of a jeep parked about twenty meters behind the firing line, where about fifteen riflemen lay in the prone position firing at the large white targets about a hundred meters away. Behind each shooter stood a soldier, clipboard in hand, jotting down his partner's score.

Another soldier wore a large red arm band and walked down the firing line. Murphy thought the soldier, who had stopped to say something to one of the shooters, looked out of place. He wore the same camouflaged outfit Murphy sometimes donned when he went into the field in Vietnam. The rest of the men, including Logan, were dressed in olive-drab fatigues, the Army's usual work uniform.

The firing range was quite different from the facilities Murphy had seen at Fort Dix.

Here, each shooter had another partner stationed down range in a deep, slit trench below the targets at the base of a tall, steep hill. After each rifleman fired off a twenty-round magazine, the targets were lowered into the trench for inspection, and hits were marked. When the targets were raised, the men in the trench used long sticks with black or white dots, depending on the location of the holes on the target, to show the riflemen where their bullets had struck.

This was the kind of target Murphy had trained on when he joined the Army nearly ten years before. At most of the Army's major training facilities, like Fort Dix, pop-up targets, which didn't require anyone to be stationed down range were now used for live-fire training.

But Murphy knew rifle marksmanship was not a high priority with ASA units. Agency personnel had better things to do with their time at Kagnew Station than learn to shoot straight, so the Army wasn't in a rush to up-grade the shooting range at its Ethiopian base.

Murphy caught Lieutenant Logan by surprise. He got the impression the young lieutenant had apparently been sneaking a nap in the jeep when he drove up on his motorcycle. He seemed a little worn and haggard.

"You look a little under the weather, sir. Everything all right?"

The two men had to raise their voices to be heard over the gunfire.

"Everything's fine, Mr. Murphy," Logan put his sunglasses back on. "I was up all night with my wife at the hospital. We had a baby girl at five this morning. I barely made it out to the range on time."

"Congratulations, sir."

Suddenly, the gunfire stopped. When Murphy looked up, he noticed the camo-clad soldier was walking in their direction carrying an M14. As he got closer, he picked out staff sergeant tabs on the collar of his uniform. The soldier walked to the rear of the three-quarter truck parked next to the jeep and set the rifle down on the tailgate.

Logan turned in his seat. "Got a problem, Sergeant Turgeon?"

Turgeon looked up. He spoke in a slow Southern drawl. "The action on this weapon don't seem to be workin' raight, sir. Thought I'd take a look at it."

Logan climbed out of the jeep and moved to watch Turgeon work on the M-14. Murphy got off his motorcycle and followed. It took the staff sergeant just a few seconds to break the rifle down to its eight major components. Now, he inspected its inner workings.

As Turgeon examined the rifle, Murphy noticed the 25th Infantry Division shoulder patch on the staff sergeant's right sleeve and the cloth Combat Infantryman's Badge sewn onto his uniform above the left-breast pocket. "Been in some shit, huh, sarge? "

"Not lately. Not around here." Turgeon never looked up from his work. "Been too busy taking care of these kaids."

Once, the CIB, with its depiction of an old long rifle, had been every infantryman's goal in life. Now, with the U.S. body count starting to mount in Vietnam, Murphy wondered if that was still the case.

"Sergeant Turgeon would like to get into the fight," Logan interjected. "But he came into the ASA about ten years ago. He's got a Top Secret Crypto clearance and he's worked in an operations site. He'd like to go to Vietnam and push a rifle again. But the Army won't let him. He knows too much."

Murphy figured the slightly-built NCO must have earned his CIB while serving with the Tropic Lightning Division in South Korea.

"The gas cylinder's shot, sir," Turgeon wore his helmet liner low, nearly covering his eyes. "I got a spare in the back of the truck." He'd laid the pieces of the M-14 on a greasy towel on one side of the tailgate. Reaching into the truck bed, he pulled a small wooden box onto the other side.

"Sergeant Turgeon is our small-weapons' expert," Logan explained. The grimace on Turgeon's thin, weathered face gave way to a slight smile. After pulling a new gas cylinder out of the wooden box, he reassembled the rifle. "He was assigned here to help reacquaint our men with the M14 rifle."

"Really?" Murphy looked toward the firing line. "I assumed this was the annual shoot."

"It is," Logan commented. "But some of these guys haven't picked up an M-14 in two, three years."

Army regulations required every soldier to demonstrate their proficiency with their assigned weapon. Every year, they must certify their shooting ability at one of the Army's three levels—marksman, sharpshooter or expert. Like all CID agents, Murphy had become proficient with a variety of small arms used by the U.S. military. Just prior to coming to Ethiopia, Murphy had requalified with the .45 caliber automatic pistol, the only sidearm the Army issued him. He didn't have to prove his proficiency with the Browning automatic he carried in the holster strapped to his right calf. No one knew he carried that weapon.

"This morning, all of these men drew their weapons from their company armory," Logan explained. "At Kagnew Station, the MPs are the only American soldiers who carry weapons when on duty." The young lieutenant glanced at the firing line. "These men spent the first part of the morning zeroing in their weapons. Now, they're about to shoot for certification."

Murphy glanced at the men on the firing line.

"What were they using before they were issued M-14s?"

"Until this year, the men at Kagnew Station used M-1 carbines.".

Now, the Army was replacing one obsolete weapon with another one, thought Murphy. Then, another thought came to his mind.

"What happened to the carbines?"

"They were shipped back to the states."

"When?"

"Back in January," Logan answered. "We began issuing the M-14s just after New Year's." Logan looked toward the firing line. "This is the last group to go through the training."

Turgeon had finished with the M-14. To test the action of the semi-automatic weapon, he cleared the chamber by pulling back on the operating rod handle with the edge of his right hand and pulled the trigger of the empty weapon. There was a solid click.

"Everythin's fine now, sir," Turgeon reported.

Logan smiled. "Carry on, sergeant."

Turgeon carried the rifle back to the firing line.

A nineteen-year-old, bespectacled Spec Four lay waiting for him. The staff sergeant handed the weapon to the soldier, who had never moved from his prone firing position. After receiving the M-14, the boy-soldier slapped the twenty-round magazine into the rifle.

Moments later, the gunfire erupted again.

MURPHY RODE the motorcycle for about an hour, following the trails crisscrossing the plateau above the antenna field.

He stayed as far away from the firing range as possible.

Twice when Murphy stopped to get his bearings, he heard the soft crackle of gunfire in the distance. Now, as he stopped for a smoke near a large rock on the edge of the plateau, he heard nothing.

Nearly a hundred meters below, the antenna field stretched out across the valley. It was an impressive sight. Dozens of the hundred-foot radio towers extended into the western horizon.

Murphy, who wore no helmet, had pushed his sunglasses above his forehead to take in the view. Somewhere to his right, from the antenna field below, his eyes caught a glint of light. As he started to lean over the Honda's handlebars to get a better perspective of the reflection, he heard the unmistakable snap of a bullet as it passed close to him before ricocheting off the large rock, inches from his head.

Murphy didn't wait around. Immediately, he dropped the bike into gear, released the clutch, and headed down the steep embankment. Using his left foot to brace himself, he leaned into the hillside, angling the motorcycle away from the antenna field, the direction of the shot.

Murphy didn't know what had happened. His first thought was that an errant bullet from the firing range had come to earth on the large rock. The 7.62-mm round fired from the M-14 had an effective killing range of up to a mile. Maybe, he'd strayed closer to the range than he had thought. Then, Murphy remembered he'd heard no shooting from the direction of the range before the bullet buzzed past his head.

If someone had shot at him, Murphy hoped the dust thrown up by the motorcycle would make it difficult for the shooter to zero in on him. The deep-throated roar of the motorcycle made it impossible to hear another shot.

It took only a few seconds to get to the bottom of the hill. But Murphy didn't stop. He bounced across nearly two hundred meters of rock-strewn terrain at a fast clip before he came to a dirt track. After a slight pause, he pointed the motorcycle toward a grove of trees a kilometer away at the opposite end of the valley from the antenna field. As he drew closer to the trees, he could see the tops of thatched roofs in a village, located on the edge of an embankment. He didn't stop his dash across the valley floor until he reached the base of the knoll.

When he did stop, Murphy carefully laid the motorcycle on its side. Then, he crawled to a mound a few feet away to see if he'd been followed. He stayed low and watched the plumes of dust he'd stirred up settle to the ground. There were no signs of another vehicle. His heart pounding, Murphy waited.

As he lay against the mound, Murphy reached down into his boot for his small Browning automatic pistol. He pulled out the magazine, quickly inspected it, and jammed it back into the handle. After chambering a round, he laid the gun down on a small flat rock in front of him.

"A lady's gun," Van Dyck had called the Browning. "You're not going to hurt anyone with that, Alice."

It was Murphy's weapon of last resort. The pistol, which fit snugly into his right hand, was no match for someone with a rifle. If there was a gunman, Murphy hoped he would make a mistake and get close enough for the little automatic to be useful.

Murphy felt on top of his head for his sunglasses. They were gone, lost during his wild ride down the hill.

Slowly, Murphy raised himself into a crouch and peered over the mound. He saw nothing. After taking a quick look, he ducked back down. His heart rate had slowed. He felt exhilarated, still in control.

Murphy took out a cigarette. He started to light up. Then, after considering how the smoke could betray his position, he threw the unlit cigarette on the ground. He continued to scan the valley he'd just driven across.

Murphy heard a sound. A thud. Something had landed on the ground next to the mound. His heart rate quickened. He whirled around, sweeping the automatic in a wide arc to his left. Behind him, several small boys stood on top of the embankment. All of them held rocks in their hands. Hollering something unintelligible to Murphy, two of the boys threw stones in his direction.

Murphy moved quickly. Slipping the Browning back into his boot, he bounded to the motorcycle. Just as he was about to pick up the Honda, a rock plinked off its gas tank. As he turned the ignition key, Murphy could hear the boys' voices grow louder. Then their shouts were drowned out by the whine of the motorcycle's engine. Moments later, Murphy was whizzing over the dirt track through a wheat field. After less than a kilometer, he came to the airport road.

Murphy took his time driving back to town. The afternoon siesta had started, and there wasn't much traffic. Twice he pulled off the main road onto a side street, doubling back to see if he'd been followed. Satisfied he wasn't followed, Murphy cut across the tree-shaded street which ran past Kagnew Station's back gate and headed back out toward Tract C.

Before going into the antenna field, he stopped at the firing range. It was deserted. The area had been thoroughly policed by the troops before they left. Not so much as a gum wrapper had been left behind. There was no evidence fifty soldiers had spent the morning shooting at paper targets.

A few minutes later, after climbing back to the top of the plateau, Murphy returned to the big rock he'd stopped at less than an hour before. While standing next to it, he noticed a rutted road. It angled through the antenna field before hooking up with the dirt track he'd taken across to the wheat field. A section of the road came within three hundred meters of the spot where he stood, close enough for a good marksman to risk taking a shot at him.

Murphy then found a safer way to ride down from the plateau than the route he'd followed earlier. Five minutes later, he was walking along the stretch of road calculating where a shot might have been taken. When he was able to catch sight of the big rock, he got off the bike and walked slowly down the road between the two ruts. As he walked, more of the rock's surface became visible. When the road jogged to the right, however, it receded from his view.

Murphy focused his attention on a twenty-foot stretch of the dirt road. While slowly walking, he kept his eyes locked on the gravel on both sides of the track. About ten minutes later, when he was just about ready to call off his search, he found two spent rounds lying less than two feet apart on the ground in an opening in the scrub brush next to the rutted road.

In a way, Murphy was not surprised to find two .30 caliber shell casings lying on the ground. The shot that ricocheted off the rock was too well-placed to be an errant round from the firing range. Apparently, the shooter also had taken a second, poorly-aimed shot into the cloud of dust Murphy created during his desperate plunge down the hill.

Murphy felt the anger well up inside.

It was similar to the feeling he had when he saw Van Dyck's body in Vietnam.

It had become personal.

Officially, Murphy had been taken off the case.

Unofficially, he was still very much on it.

MURPHY SPENT the rest of the afternoon holed up in his room at the King George Hotel.

It seemed a safe place. From his window he could look out onto the street and see anyone coming into the three-story building through the front entrance.

His little automatic pistol lay on the nightstand less than an arm's length away from the bed, where he lay wrapped in a large white bath towel smoking a cigarette. Despite its alleged shortcomings, he was sure the Browning was just enough gun to stop anyone who came through his door.

Murphy would much rather be outside on the street. From experience, he knew there was safety in open, crowded places. Murders tend to occur out of sight, away from the view of witnesses. They tend to occur in hotel rooms, he thought wryly.

But Murphy locked himself in his hotel room out of necessity. He had nothing to wear. The last three days of hectic activity had wreaked havoc with his wardrobe.

On the trip to Ethiopia, Murphy had brought three changes of casual clothing: the Levis jeans and the opened-neck, short-sleeved shirts he favored, and a light-weight Botany 500 suit. His mother bought it for him during a shopping foray at the Puritan Clothing Company on Main Street in Hyannis when he first joined the Criminal Investigation Division three years before. Van Dyck called it his cop suit. "You might as well print CID in big letters on the back of your jacket," he said. But Murphy kept the suit, which, depending on the light, looked metallic blue or dark green.

After his first tour in Vietnam, Michelle had helped Murphy pick out earth-tone blazers and sports jackets, turtlenecks in light pastel colors, and dress slacks at Jordan Marsh in Boston. That was during his assignment at Fort Devens. His CID clothing allowance didn't cover the cost of everything, so she paid for the rest. She was like that.

One time, when he did wear one of the preppie-looking blazers and a turtleneck to the office, another investigator cracked: "What'dya got? A stakeout at BC?" From then on, most of the clothes Michelle had picked out remained hanging in his wall locker. But his mother's blue-green suit always found a way into his suitcase, even if he seldom wore it.

That morning, while dashing out the front door to meet Major Hilton at the golf course, Murphy had left Waldo a pile of dirty clothes for his wife to wash. The shirt and pants he wore during his dusty motorcycle trip lay on the floor at the end of the bed.

A lot of the homes in Asmara had a system designed to catch and store rainwater on their flat roofs for use during droughts. The damaged water works made it difficult to bathe and do laundry, so a lot of thirsty Asmarinos were now tapping into their reserves. "The rains come soon, Mister John," Waldo told Murphy. "Then, no problem."

Murphy didn't shower. Instead, he took what V.D. called a "whore's bath." He filled the sink up several times with water from a five-gallon can Waldo kept filled in the bathroom for the hotel's guests and washed himself with a hand towel. As he washed, Murphy recalled the cold-water showers he'd taken in Vietnam, where hot water was often a luxury. The grunts who did the fighting, Murphy knew, sometimes went weeks without getting a shower, cold or hot.

As Murphy lay in the bed, he wondered who had shot at him. On his note pad, he wrote the names of Smyth, Hilton and Logan. These were the only three men at Kagnew Station who knew what he was doing in Ethiopia. Later, he added Romana's name, the only other person who knew about his assignment.

Recalling Smyth's reaction at the accident scene that morning, Murphy doubted the man from the American consulate would have the stomach to kill someone. And he couldn't find a reason for Hilton or Logan to want him dead. That left Romana. But, as a suspect, she also seemed a dead end.

Murphy recalled the acronym Van Dyck often used to help narrow down his list of murder suspects. "Remember MOM," V.D. would remind him. "The killer has to have a motive, the opportunity and the means." Not one of the four people Murphy had put on the list seemed to meet all that criteria. He crossed off their names, swirling a large question mark in their place.

Murphy had decided not to tell anyone about the shooting. If he filed a complaint with the CID, which had nominal jurisdiction in felonies like attempted murder, it would alert its Ethiopian brethren of his presence in Eritrea. That could cause problems.

If he could find the slugs fired at him, a ballistics test could confirm they'd come from the same rifle used to kill Wallace. But Murphy knew there would be no such test. He was off the case. "You have done enough," Hilton had told him, in so many words. "Now, go home."

Anyway, Murphy was sure the major would not want to know that someone had to tried to kill him. According to Smyth, Hilton had already found a neat solution to Wallace's murder: The Shifta did it. Another loose end, such as the attempt on Murphy's life, would only complicate matters.

Murphy doubted the Shifta, or more accurately, the Eritrean

liberation movement, had tried to kill him. He couldn't understand why the rebels would want him out of the way. What could he possibly know for them to try killing him in broad daylight less than a klick away from Tract C, one of the U.S. Army's most sensitive installations?

But someone had gone hunting for Murphy. Just before the bullet struck the rock, he'd seen a glint of light coming from the direction of the antenna field. It could have come from the sun reflecting off the windshield of a car, which meant someone had driven into the antenna field, and sought out Murphy for the purpose of putting a bullet in him.

Murphy's anger had subsided. It had been replaced with another feeling, a strange isolation.

In the past, he'd always had a back up, someone in the shadows watching his back. For nearly two years, that someone had been Van Dyck. In South Vietnam, even when he went undercover to investigate the theft of the comm wire in Da Nang, Murphy never felt alone. "He was always there," he almost said aloud. But Van Dyck had been dead for more than a year now. Since then, Murphy had been unable to place that kind of trust in anyone else.

His thoughts were interrupted by a knock on the door. After getting up from the bed, picking up his Browning and moving to a position next to the door, he asked, "Who is it?"

"Mr. John, it is Waldo," came the heavily-accented voice from the other side of the door. "I have your clothes."

Palming the Browning in his right hand, Murphy reached over with his left hand to flick open the lock. "The door's open." He quickly moved back toward the bed. "Come on in."

The door opened and Waldo stepped into the room, carrying a small pile of neatly-folded clothes in his arms. He closed the door behind him.

If Waldo noticed the gun in Murphy's hand, he didn't let on. He seemed unperturbed as he placed the small bundle of clean laundry on the bed.

Kneeling down with his back to Waldo, Murphy dropped the Browning into the pile of dirty clothes when he went fishing for his wallet. When he stood up, he handed him a red-tinged $10 Ethiopian note. In return, Waldo gave him a small envelope. "Mr. John, a lady brought this for you while you were in the bath."

The envelope contained a card, written in Italian. Murphy handed it back to Waldo. "Can you read this?"

The little brown man took the card from Murphy and studied it for a few moments. "Mr. John, it's an invitation for dinner. From a Mrs. Alley."

The name meant nothing to Murphy. However, When Waldo gave him directions to the address on the card, Murphy understood. He'd been invited to dinner that evening at Romana's house.

Murphy's mood brightened. He guessed he'd wear his suit after all.

IT WOULD HAVE taken Murphy less than five minutes to ride the Honda from the St. George Hotel to Romana's house, but he chose a much slower form of transportation.

Tesfai's gharry cart carried Murphy on a meandering route across town. The liveryman's sullen disposition hadn't improved from the day before when he took Murphy to the train station.

Murphy had told Waldo he wanted to see a little bit more of Asmara, some of its quieter neighborhoods. Waldo had given his friend precise directions before they left, so Tesfai knew exactly where they were going. Tesfai didn't say one word during the thirty-minute ride.

What Murphy really wanted to do during his sight-seeing trip was to see whether he was followed. The slow pace of two-wheeled cart made it easier for him to pick out a tail. After crossing busy Queen Elizabeth Boulevard, Tesfai's horse grudgingly clopped up a steep hill to the old Imperial Hotel, a tall wooden structure. Then, Tesfai guided his horse down a narrow tree-shaded street past A.C. Junior, an Italian social club. Slowly, they made their way to the roundabout at the bottom of the cul de sac where the Alleys, mother and daughter, lived.

As he sat in the cart's unpadded, wooden seat, Murphy felt the Browning rub against the small of his back; he had tucked the little automatic inside his belt. His slacks were too narrow to slide the gun down inside his boot, but the cut of his jacket enabled him to carry the small automatic without creating an unsightly bulge.

Murphy had hoped to get an idea of who or what he was up against. But if he had drawn a tail, he couldn't pick him out. No cars trailed behind as the gharry cart slowly made its way through the maze of side streets leading to Romana's house. Besides, most of the cars Murphy saw during his trip were little white Fiats, virtually indistinguishable from one another. At the roundabout, Murphy got out of the cart and walked up the hill. He strolled past Romana's door to the end of the cul de sac, where he waited another five minutes to see whether anyone came up the dead-end street behind him. When he was sure he hadn't been followed, Murphy walked back down the hill to the house. He was early.

Murphy's raps on the large green door, actually a Dutch door locked at bottom and top, went unanswered. After a few moments, however, he heard the metallic creak of an iron gate opening a few meters down the hill. Murphy turned to look. A well-dressed woman — a slightly darker, older version of Romana — stepped through an opening in the wall surrounding the hillside compound. Using her hands, she beckoned Murphy to come with her. Inside the small compound, Romana's mother led him across a tiled patio to the back door of the small, flat-roofed house she shared with her daughter. They came through the kitchen and walked down a short, narrow hallway, past a lavatory and into the small living room at the center of the single-story dwelling.

Mrs. Alley spoke a few words of Italian to Murphy. When she realized he didn't understand her, she motioned to the couch on the far side of the room. As Murphy sat down, the woman left the room and headed for the kitchen.

The large doorway, which Romana had used to enter the small house the day before, took up much of the wall at the front of the room. From the size of the opening, Murphy guessed the small house had been a stable once.

Against the opposite wall stood an old pedal-powered sewing machine. Neatly-folded piles of fabric sat on the table next to it, and two large wicker baskets sat on the floor under the table. On a wooden rod protruding from the wall, several dresses hung on hangers.

A small drop-leaf table, with place settings for three people, had been pushed up against the back wall. A framed picture of a squat, peppermint-stripped lighthouse, perched on a rocky cliff, hung on the wall above the table. The picture of the familiar-looking lighthouse puzzled Murphy.

On the wall above the couch, hung a crucifix and a framed photograph of JFK. This was a common sight in the homes of people in the undeveloped countries Murphy had visited. It seemed nearly every little hovel he'd stepped into contained a little shrine dedicated to the slain American president.

Murphy had been in the Army nearly two years when Kennedy, almost a neighbor of his, had been elected President. During his inaugural address, he challenged the people of Murphy's generation with the phrase: "Ask not what your country can do for you, ask what you can do for your country." For a time, that sentiment had provided Murphy with a rationale for staying in the Army. He liked the idea of being involved with something bigger than himself, and the sense of belonging that went with it.

Mrs. Alley returned after a few moments carrying a china tea service. She set the tray down on the coffee table in front of the couch and poured tea into a cup and offered it to Murphy. He took a sip. It had a pleasant orange-tinged taste.

"*Bene*?" she asked.

"It's good," Murphy nodded. "*Bene*" was another word his aunt had taught him. He set the cup down on the coffee table.

Just then, Murphy heard the sound of a key in the lock in the front door. He turned to see Romana, dressed in her nurse's uniform, step into the room. She was surprised to see Murphy. "What are you doing here?"

Murphy held up the small card that had been sent to him at his hotel. "I'm a guest. I was invited to dinner."

Romana walked over to the hallway leading to the kitchen. She spoke to her mother in rapid-fire Italian, much too fast for Murphy to pick out any words he knew. As Romana listened to her mother's response, she looked toward him. When her mother finished speaking, Romana said a few more words in Italian. Switching to English, she said to Murphy: "I am glad to see you," Romana offered her hand to Murphy. "I told my mother about our trip to Massawa, and she wanted to thank you for helping me." Her tone had changed from the day before, when she complained about his interference.

After a few moments, Murphy let go of Romana's hand. "To tell the truth, I really didn't expect to see you again. But I was glad to get the invitation."

Romana started to leave the room. Then, almost as an afterthought, she spoke again. "My mother also says you're a very handsome man." As she delivered the compliment, Romana smiled.

"What do you think?"

The answer came reluctantly. "I guess I agree." Another smile. Yes, thought Murphy, things were looking up.

Then, Murphy noticed a trace of dried blood smeared on the skirt of Romana's uniform. "Looks like you had a rough time, today." He pointed toward the stain.

"We had an emergency, and I had to help. It was a man on a motorcycle. He was hit by a sheet of metal. It cut off his face. It was horrible."

Murphy nodded. "I know. I saw the accident. How is he?"

"He died. There was nothing we could do for him."

Murphy put a hand on her shoulder. "There was nothing anyone could have done for him."

For the next ten minutes, while Romana coaxed enough water out of the roof-top cistern to shower and her mother remained in the kitchen working on their dinner, Murphy thumbed through a year-old copy of *National Geographic* he'd found lying on top of the coffee table. Before she left, she opened the top of the Dutch door to let the late-afternoon light into the sitting room. Only when Romana returned, dressed in a pink blouse and a black skirt, did Murphy notice the words "Property of Kagnew Station Library" stamped on the cover of the magazine.

"You know, the theft of U.S. government property is a federal offense," he joked. "I may have to run you in."

Romana didn't laugh.

"I say something wrong?"

The answer came slowly. "A friend of mine left that here."

Murphy thought whoever had brought the magazine to Romana's house, probably a man, had felt comfortable enough to really make himself at home. National Geographic wasn't the type of magazine usually devoured at one sitting. But it was the perfect publication to read while waiting for someone. Maybe, it was read by someone who waited for Romana a lot. After setting the magazine back on the table in front of him, he said: "I didn't know you were seeing someone."

Romana stood near the small trestle table trying to comb out the tangles of her still damp hair. "I'm not anymore."

Murphy looked down at the magazine. "Oh, he went back home?"

"No," she said. "He went to Vietnam. He was killed."

Romana's remarks ended the conversation. She went off to her room to finish combing out her hair.

Murphy recalled what Van Dyck would say when he came out with an ill-timed, insensitive remark. "Open mouth. Insert one size nine combat boot."

Murphy knew how his old partner felt. He got up, went over to the Dutch door, where he stood and smoked a cigarette while gazing out at the empty street.

DINNER STARTED with a small salad. Then came the manicotti. While they ate, the three shared a small bottle of chianti.

Mrs. Alley, using her daughter as an interpreter, peppered Murphy with questions. The older woman spoke very little English. Through Romana, she learned such mundane things as Murphy's age, his rank, his hometown, and, most importantly, his marital status.

At one point, he told Romana: "I feel like I'm being interviewed for a job."

"You are," she chuckled. She explained how every man who came through the door eventually was subjected to the same kind of grilling by her mother. "She's looking for a husband for me."

"You shouldn't have any trouble finding a husband."

Murphy had meant it as a compliment. But Romana took offense.

"I don't need a man. Besides, all of the men I meet here are interested in only one thing." She didn't have to tell Murphy what that one thing was.

Murphy did learn more about Romana. She told him her father had come from Maine. "That explains the lighthouse." He pointed toward the photograph hanging on the wall.

"That's West Quoddy Head Light," she said. "It's not far from where my father grew up."

Romana told Murphy her father's family still kept in touch. An aunt sent her clothes. "She gave me this blouse," she said.

"My mother made the skirt." An uncle had helped finance her nurse's training in Italy. "They're really nice people. They've never forgotten their brother."

After supper, Murphy stepped outside to have a cigarette. There were no buildings across from Romana's house. Instead, a short stone wall ran up the entire length of that side of the street. While he smoked, Murphy rested his elbows on the top of the wall and looked over the treetops below toward Haile Selassie Avenue, less than half a kilometer away.

A few moments later, Romana joined him.

"Your mother is a good woman," Murphy turned to flip his cigarette down the street. "She's done well to tough it out over here. I bet it hasn't been easy."

Romana, not quite tall enough to rest her elbows on the wall, stood next to Murphy with her back leaning against it. "She does what she has to. She's quite a seamstress, you know. She made that outfit I wore yesterday."

Taking his elbows down off the wall, Murphy turned and leaned back against it.

"If you can find work, it really doesn't take much to get by in Asmara," Romana continued. Then, she glanced toward her house. "We don't have to pay much for rent. It used to be a carriage house for the big house at the top of the hill. It belongs to friends of my grandfather. They spend most of their time in Italy."

Portions of a large stone villa were visible through the trees on the hillside above Romana's house.

"Your mother could have gone to the states," Murphy said. Your father's family would have looked out for her. How come she stayed?"

Romana looked up to him. "After my father died, my mother decided she wanted to stay where he was. He's buried in the

English cemetery out on the road to Massawa."

When Murphy and Romana went back inside, Mrs. Alley served them little cups of thick, black coffee. While they sat next to each other on the couch slowly sipping the coffee, the older woman sat at the dinner table with a deck of cards in her hands. After shuffling the cards several times, she began dealing them out one by one, building five stacks of cards in the sign of the cross on the table in front of her.

"She's going to tell your fortune," Romana explained. "She likes to do this with her friends."

Her mother started to turn over some cards. After studying them for a few moments, she said something in Italian.

Romana translated. "She says you are going to have a successful trip. She says you're going to find what you are looking for."

It was Murphy's turn to chuckle. "That's great. Only wish I knew what it was."

Mrs. Alley flipped over more cards. This time, she turned only a few cards before coming to an abrupt halt. After a few seconds, she held up the ace of spades so they could see it. When the old lady did speak, she was brief.

"What did she say?"

Romana turned serious. "She said she saw death."

Murphy countered with a joke. "I bet she says that to all the guys."

Romana didn't laugh. Neither did her mother, who began picking up all of the cards.

"Tell your mother not to worry." Murphy paused for a few moments to reflect on the shots that had been fired at him earlier that day. "Tell her I don't believe in any of that stuff."

"I know," Romana said. "But she does."

BEFORE HEADING back to his hotel, Murphy accompanied Romana as she delivered a dress her mother had sewn for one of her cousins to wear to a wedding.

"Sometimes, I borrow a car to make deliveries," she explained. "But this is close by, and I like to walk."

Murphy didn't mind. Exercise was good for him, and the walk gave him an excuse to spend more time with Romana.

During their walk to Ghezzabanda, Murphy was almost sure he picked out a car tailing them.

He first noticed it when they reached the roundabout. The large black sedan was parked on one of the other streets leading into the intersection. In the gloaming, Murphy was unable to determine its make. But the car caught his eye because it nearly blocked off the narrow street. In a city filled with little white Fiats, it stood out.

For a moment, Murphy shifted into operational mode. He reached inside his jacket with his right hand to feel for his gun. Satisfied he was ready, he relaxed.

Romana began to talk about Vietnam. During the conversation at dinner, Murphy had let on he'd spent two tours there.

However, he had said nothing about his wound. Murphy didn't like to talk about it. He never wore the Purple Heart ribbon he was awarded.

"Most of the people here don't even know about Vietnam," Romana said, "and those who do, don't understand what the United States is doing there."

"They've got a lot of company," Murphy replied. "Most of the men in the Army don't understand why we're there."

"Why did you go?"

"The first time I went because I was sent. I'm a soldier, and I go where the Army tells me to go," Murphy stopped to light a cigarette, tucking the bundled dress he carried for Romana under his arm as he did so. "I went back a second time because I liked it there. I enjoyed the work."

Romana led Murphy down the hill and across Ras Alula Avenue, near the glass-fronted United States Information Service office. "I don't see how anyone could enjoy that blood and carnage," she said. "It sounds like a horrible place."

"It's a dangerous place," Murphy admitted. "But it was exciting. Never a dull moment."

He didn't tell her he wouldn't be going back. Murphy had pushed his luck by returning to Vietnam. Now, he'd have to find some other locale where the work was as exhilarating but not as dangerous.

After crossing Ras Alula Avenue, the couple continued in an easterly direction. As they passed a used car lot, Murphy glanced back in time to see a black limousine pull out on the other side of the avenue from the same street they had just walked down. He wasn't sure if it was the same car he'd noticed earlier. When it turned north, in the direction of Haile Selassie Avenue, his attention returned to their conversation.

Romana talked about her dead boyfriend. "I think I know why Jim wanted to go to Vietnam. He wanted to feel what you felt. I think that is why he went."

Murphy moved closer to Romana. "You're the first to understand why I went back. Earlier this summer, I went to a wedding, and I had this same conversation with a couple of old friends, civilians. They thought I was nuts. I told them what

I just told you, and they looked at me like I had come from another planet."

Traffic was light as the young couple crossed Abuna Basilios Avenue, a broad thoroughfare.

After they crossed the street, Romana asked Murphy why he wasn't married. "You're a good-looking man. You must have someone in your life?"

Murphy exhaled a large cloud of cigarette smoke. "I did have a girlfriend once." He told her about Michelle. "I was in Vietnam about three months, and she wrote me a letter," Murphy flicked the cigarette butt in the gutter. "She ended up marrying someone else. It happens to a lot of guys in the Army. We go away for a while and another guy moves in."

"That's too bad," Romana said.

Murphy went on, almost relieved to be talking about a subject he'd kept to himself. "She really had a hard time understanding why I wanted to stay in the Army, and she worried a lot when I went to Vietnam. I guess she figured if I wasn't in her life anymore, she wouldn't have to worry."

They approached a large fountain the Italians had built at the base of the hill below Ghezzabanda. Drought and sabotage had robbed it of water. It now served as a median strip, dividing the traffic lanes of the wide boulevard leading into the residential neighborhood.

"I know how she felt," Romana said. "It was the same for me when Jim went to Vietnam. But I didn't have to worry as long as your girlfriend did. He died in a plane crash the first week he was there."

"I'm sorry."

"Jim was a lot like you," Romana said, "He could have stayed at Kagnew Station for as long as he wanted. But he just had to go to Vietnam and see what it was all about."

As they walked up the steep hillside to Ghezzabanda, Murphy shifted the package to his left side to accommodate Romana, who had linked her left arm with his right arm. Murphy remained relaxed. But when they reached the top of the hill, he stopped a moment to look back over his shoulder. This time, he saw no black limousine.

That movement piqued Romana's curiosity.

"Everything all right?"

Murphy was unsure.

"I sure hope so."

ROMANA LED MURPHY to a large tent, which ran from sidewalk to sidewalk and blocked Tigrai Street.

"This is the first night of the wedding celebration," Romana told him as they approached the tent. "It will go on all week."

She explained the mayor would perform a civil ceremony Thursday in his office at the Municipale, and the couple would exchange marriage vows Saturday morning at a Catholic Church at Gaggiret near Tract A. "After the wedding, there will be a reception at the Caravel. But most of their relatives will do their celebrating here. They come in from the villages."

A cacophony of blaring horns and high-pitched ululations greeted the pair. As they stepped through a flap at one corner of the huge canvas tent, dozens of people turned to smile in greeting.

The lighting was poor. Lanterns hung from the center posts, but the fringes remained in shadows. Still, Murphy could see well enough to know the tent was nearly filled to capacity. Men and women of all ages, and a few children, sat on wooden benches or stood in clusters.

A few of the men wore western clothes—pants, shirt and dark tweed jackets. But most were wrapped in cloaks. Older women wore cloaks and long dresses; girls wore knee-length muslin dresses. Wearing his "mother's suit," Murphy felt over-dressed. But the cordial greeting made him feel welcome.

Romana led him toward the center of the tent, where several women sat huddled around a large pan. Four layers of flat bread were stacked on the skillet, and two of the women poured the contents of a large pot onto the top layer of the gray, sponge-like bread. "That's *zigne*," Romana said. "It's very hot and spicy." The red sauce, which contained chunks of mutton and several boiled eggs, thickly spread across the top of the bread.

Soon, the women were joined by several men, who sat down on their haunches around the pan. Each man, in turn, dug into the *zigne*, tearing off a chunk of bread and using it to sop up the thick sauce. Each man took a second or third helping before giving up his place around the rim to someone else.

An old man, sitting next to the pan in front of Murphy, said a few words in Tigrinya to Romana. She gave Murphy a gentle poke in the ribs. "He wants you to join him." She glanced down at the old man, who smiled and dragged a large piece of bread through the stew. To make room, the elder slid off to one side.

Squatting down, Murphy broke off a large chunk of the bread and worked it through the sauce as he had seen the others do. Then, he crammed the stewy mixture into his mouth and started chewing. The bread was bland, relatively tasteless, but the sauce seemed quite flavorful, if a bit tangy. After a few moments, however, Murphy's mouth felt like it was on fire. He jumped up and blew air through pursed lips trying to cool it down.

The people sitting around the pan laughed at Murphy's reaction. Unable to constrain herself, Romana also laughed. "I told you it was hot."

Murphy backed away from the pan. He found himself standing next to another old man, who held a ladle in his hand. Removing the lid from one of two large wooden casks, he dipped the ladle into the milky substance inside. He filled a tin cup and handed it to Murphy. After downing the sweet-tasting liquid in nearly one gulp, Murphy handed the empty cup back for a refill.

Romana moved to his side. "That's *meis*. Honey wine. Very sweet, but very potent." Murphy took his time drinking the second cup, and he didn't ask for a refill.

Nearby, three men sat on a bench. Each held a long, slender trumpet-like instrument. When anyone entered the tent, they'd blow their horns, exhorting the people in the tent to give the new arrivals a warm greeting.

While Murphy stood nursing his cup of mes, the trio blew their horns. As Murphy turned toward the entrance, he noticed a man staring at him. Unlike everyone else in the tent, the man, who stood in the nearby shadows, didn't look toward the entrance to see who had come into the tent. Instead, his eyes glaring, he focused intently on the American.

Murphy finished his drink. After handing the cup back to the old man, he leaned toward Romana. He had to shout above the din to make himself heard. "You're right, that stuff is strong." He glanced toward an empty seat on a bench farther back in the tent. "I feel a little dizzy. I'm going to sit down for a few minutes." As Murphy wound his way through a knot of people, he stole a look in the direction of the man who had stared at him. The man now seemed engrossed in a conversation with an old woman and was no longer looking in his direction. Murphy took a seat on a bench less than ten feet away from him. He watched as the brown-skinned man, clean-shaven and not much older than Murphy, talked to the old lady. Then, as the man turned slightly, Murphy noticed the intense look in the man's eyes. He'd seen it before. It was Mekele.

Murphy remained seated, slowly scanning the tent to see whether the rebel leader was alone. Most of the people in the tent were old men and women, and none of them appeared to be much help to Mekele if things got rough. Romana now clutched the bundle Murphy had carried during their walk and stood among a small knot of people at the far end of the tent.

Lighting up a cigarette, Murphy pondered his next move. He took a few drags before he let the cigarette drop to the pavement, stamping it out with his boot as he stood up.

Slowly, Murphy slid his right hand under his jacket, pulled the small Browning automatic from its holster, and brought it to his side. Then, he stepped away from the bench and gradually moved behind Mekele, who seemed absorbed while talking to the old woman. Murphy leaned forward and, while jamming the automatic into Mekele's side, whispered: "Just pretend you're glad to see me, and you won't get hurt. And don't play dumb. I know you speak English very well."

Mekele said a few words in Tigrinya to the old woman, who shook her head and glanced up at Murphy before moving away. The rebel leader slowly turned to face Murphy, who had dropped his right arm back down to his side.

Mekele spoke in lightly-accented English. "Ah, the American from the bus." The Eritrean glanced down at Murphy's right hand, which still held the gun. "Something tells me this is not a social call."

"No." Murphy spoke evenly. "But I do want to talk to you."

"About what?"

"About the murder of Sergeant Wallace."

"I know nothing about any murder."

Just then, the horns blared. The two men both looked toward the entrance as two mufti-clad policemen, both carrying rifles, stepped through the tent flaps.

"I'm sorry," Mekele's tone was quiet, but firm. "But I must leave."

Before the rebel leader could take one step, Murphy reached out with his left arm and gripped the Eritrean's right wrist firmly. "But I've got to talk to you." He refused to relax his grip.

Mekele glanced in the direction of the policemen, who had moved toward the large pan of *zigne*. "It was foolish of me to come here." He shook his head. "If I'm found here, it will bring trouble for all of these people."

To Murphy, the two young policemen didn't look like they were in a hurry to track down any criminals, much less a rebel leader. One of them sat on his haunches in front of the *zigne*, and helped himself to the spicy dish, while the other bantered with the group of people around the large pan.

But Mekele thought differently. "One of them may wake up and recognize me. I really must go." Still, he didn't resist Murphy's grip.

Murphy remained insistent. "But I really must talk to you."

Mekele looked down at the hand locked onto his wrist. "Okay. He rubbed his chin with his free hand. "Tomorrow."

"Where?" Murphy loosened his grip slightly.

"In Keren. In the English cemetery at Keren. At noon."

"I'll be there." Murphy released Mekele's wrist.

"Come alone."

Rubbing his right wrist with his left hand, Mekele kept to the shadows as he made his way to the exit. After lifting the tent flap, he glanced back for a final look at Murphy before stepping into the dark Ethiopian night.

AFTER MEKELE left the tent, Murphy remained in the shadows smoking a cigarette.

For a time, he watched the two policemen, who seemed too busy eating, drinking, and chatting to notice his scrutiny. Then, he went to look for Romana, who had left the tent to deliver the dress her mother had made.

The tent stood in front of the bride's home.

Inside the villa, Murphy found Romana, and the teen-aged girl she'd been seeking, in an alcove off the high-ceilinged great room in the center of the large, single-story home. The girl and several of her friends were perched in front of a television set watching an episode of *Star Trek*, broadcast over the AFRTS affiliate at Kagnew Station. No *zigne*. No *meis*. Just Mister Spock.

"So much for progress," Murphy thought, recalling how Van Dyck often referred to television as the boob tube.

Murphy tried to appear calm, but he was seething. He was mad at himself for letting Mekele slip through his fingers, and he was angry at Romana for not warning him the rebel leader might be in the tent.

"You okay?" she asked, as Murphy sidled up to her. Murphy didn't think Romana knew much about him, but she apparently knew enough to see through his calm demeanor. That made it worse.

"Fine," was all he said. The girls giggled and laughed above the sound of the television; their chatter too loud for further conversation. "Can we leave? We need to talk."

But Murphy didn't say another word until they were well into their walk.

Through his earlier meanderings, Murphy had learned enough about Asmara's streets to chart his own course back to Romana's house. Their return route was different, just in case someone was waiting for them along their original route.

They left Ghezzabanda via the steep hill where the fatal accident occurred. Not far from its base, Basilios Avenue, Ras Alula, and Emperor Johannes Avenue converged. As they walked down Ras Alula, Romana broke the silence. "What's the matter?"

Murphy could no longer hide his disappointment. He spat out his words: "Why didn't you tell me Mekele was going to be there?"

Romana seemed genuinely surprised. "Mekele? At the wedding?" Then, she understood why Murphy was upset. "I honestly didn't know he would come. I didn't see him. No one said a word to me about him. If I knew he was going to be there, I would have told you."

Murphy believed her. He doubted Mekele had informed anyone of his social plans. There was no way Romana could have known the rebel leader would be in the tent.

As they walked, Romana moved closer to Murphy. She linked an arm with his, giving him a reassuring squeeze. With that, his anger melted away. "I'm sorry I was angry with you," he apologized. "Of course, you would tell me about Mekele if you knew."

Murphy hoped the change of direction would throw off anyone watching him. From experience, he knew it was easier to keep tabs on someone when you knew where they were going and how they were going to get there. The few streetlights along Ras Alula threw a dim light, so it was easy for him and

Romana to keep to the shadows, making it harder to track them. Except for a few men pedaling up the street from the city's center on bicycles, there was no traffic on the broad avenue at this time of night.

Murphy didn't think they were being followed. But he was prepared for any contingency. After they had left the wedding celebration, he'd reached under his jacket to reassure himself the small Browning was still tucked inside his waist band.

Romana went on, blissfully unaware of Murphy's concerns. She told him Mekele was a distant relative of the groom. "I'm surprised he came. He could have made a lot of trouble for his people, and he would never want to do that."

Murphy picked up the conversational thread. "Family is very important here, isn't it?"

"Family is everything here. It defines us."

"How so?"

"Every Eritrean knows who he is," she said and gestured toward three boys, who were emerging from the shadows ahead. "Ask any of those boys who he is, and he will tell you he is the son of so-and-so, who is the son of so-and-so, and on and on he will go for generation after generation."

Murphy looked at the boys, guessing they were eleven or twelve years old. "Few American kids can do that," he marveled.

Romana continued. "No, Mekele wouldn't do anything to hurt his family. That is why he acts as if he were dead."

ROMANA AND MURPHY said their goodbyes in the dark on the small patio near her back door.

"Do you want to come in for a while?" she asked. The invitation was tempting.

Much of the time Murphy and Romana had spent together had been intense. They'd gotten to know each other in a hurry. Murphy liked her, but he didn't like one-night stands, and he didn't think Romana did either. Ever since his relationship with Michelle, Murphy had yearned for something deeper than the mere physical. His fling with the airline stewardess in Taiwan had been an aberration. This was serious business.

Murphy imagined Van Dyck rolling over in his grave. One-night stands had been a staple of his sex life. "Any port in the storm," he told Murphy. To his old partner, it was always raining.

Murphy didn't know what he wanted exactly, but he did know he didn't want another meaningless relationship. Scheduled to leave Asmara in less than three days, he saw no point in getting involved.

Before he left, Romana reached up, pulled his face down toward hers and kissed him on the cheek. When he hugged her, he found the feel of her small body brushing up against his appealing. Moments later, as he walked down her street, heading toward Haile Selassie Avenue in search of a gharry cart for a ride back to the King George, Murphy wondered whether he had made the right decision. Then, he recalled something else Van Dyck use to tell him: "If you go through life kicking yourself every time you make a wrong decision, your ass is going to hurt."

Murphy crossed the roundabout at the bottom of Romana's street and headed toward the little park at the base of the hill. It was the same route Petros had driven the Opel up the previous day. While making his way down the narrow, wall-lined street, Murphy heard the roar of an automobile engine reverberate off the walls behind him. As the sound grew louder, he swore he could feel the heat from its headlights as the car bore down on him. He realized this was no reckless driver — no Ethiopian with one too many Melottis under his belt. This was someone bent on running him over.

Murphy reacted immediately. Instead of turning to look for the car, he took three long strides toward the wall on the left side of the street, the one closest to him. Then, after glancing up the hill and seeing the automobile was only a few feet away, he jumped up and grabbed the top of the wall. He felt a sharp stab of pain as a shard of glass embedded into the top of the wall cut into the side of his right hand. But he still was able to pull himself up. Looking down, Murphy saw the dark form of a large sedan flash by, less than a foot from where he had drawn his legs up under him. Farther along, the car sent sparks flying as it scrapped and careened off the wall down the narrow street.

After the car sped past, Murphy dropped to the ground. His hand hurt. Gingerly drawing his gun from its holster, he chased the receding tail lights down the street. The two red lights disappeared when the car fish-tailed through a wide left turn at the end of the street. Still, Murphy continued to chase it.

When he got to the bottom of the hill, Murphy turned the corner at full speed, too fast to avoid colliding with an old man who stood on the curb a few feet from the street corner holding a bicycle. The violent collision knocked both men to the ground. As he went down, Murphy lost hold of the pistol, and the small automatic clattered across the pavement. While he lay in the street, the tail lights disappeared into the darkness as the car, its tires screeching, headed toward Queen Elizabeth Avenue.

Remembering his gun, Murphy rolled into a kneeling position and, in the darkness, groped the pavement around him. He finally found his gun lying against the curbstone. Still on his knees, Murphy slid the pistol back into its holster.

Before Murphy could stand, however, the old man jumped on his back and screamed in Tigrinya. When Murphy did get up, the man, whose feet dangled nearly a foot above the ground, raised the volume of his screams a few decibels. He tightened his grip around Murphy's shoulders as the much bigger man took a step forward.

Murphy gently tried to shake the old man off his back. "Let go, will ya. I don't want to hurt you." But his attempts to escape the little man's hold only made him scream louder. In a few moments, the sound of running feet hitting the pavement filled the small square. Soon, Murphy and the old man were enveloped by Ethiopians. The old man remained on Murphy's back, speaking excitedly to the onlookers. He didn't relax his grip until two national policemen showed up.

Murphy was relieved. "Boy, I'm glad to see you guys." But the policemen looked at him dumbfounded. Neither apparently spoke English. They listened intently as the old man spoke rapidly to them. After listening for a minute or so, one of the policemen moved behind Murphy. Placing the barrel of his old Enfield rifle into the small of his back, the young policeman, who stood nearly as tall as the American, prodded him to move forward. The other policeman, who had taken up a position next to Murphy, also pointed his weapon at the American, and the three men began moving through the small park toward Haile Selassie Avenue. The old man, after retrieving his bicycle, followed at a distance, along with several of the people who'd come running.

Bewilderment suddenly replaced the fear and rage Murphy had felt when the car had whizzed by inches below him while he dangled from the stone wall. He had no idea why he was being marched at gunpoint through downtown Asmara. He had no clue what the old man with the bicycle had told the two policemen escorting him.

Murphy wasn't going to argue about it. As far as he could tell, neither the two policemen, nor the old man, nor the any of the people who had flocked to the commotion understood English. He wasn't going to tangle with armed men who apparently didn't understand a word he said.

Deciding to wait until someone could explain to him what was going on, Murphy calmly went along with his armed escort on a stroll through Asmara's closed and shuttered commercial district.

MURPHY DIDN'T say a word during the ten-minute walk to Carceri Centrale, police headquarters located on the north side of Haile Selassie Avenue on the edge of the Bosh.

The old man with the bicycle did most of the talking. But his babbling ceased, and the number of people in his entourage dwindled as they neared the police station, which rose out of the darkness. When they arrived, the crowd disappeared and only Murphy, the two policemen and the old man went inside. No one in Asmara went into Centrale voluntarily.

With its high, vaulted ceiling, the large, well-lit lobby had the air of a train station. However, there was no place to sit. The only furnishing was a wooden counter, running wall to wall for perhaps twenty meters across the back of the room. The two young policemen marched Murphy up to the counter, where a gray-haired sergeant eyed him warily as one of them gave his report. The old man, who had wheeled his bicycle into the police station, stood silently in the background. After listening to the briefing, the old sergeant said a few words. Then, one of the young policemen walked down the length of the counter and through a door leading off the lobby. While he was gone, no one spoke. Less than a minute later, the young policeman returned. He was followed by an older man, impeccably groomed and dressed in a dark, well-cut business suit.

"I'm inspector Tekle," said the tall Ethiopian, in slightly-accented English, "and you're an American?"

Murphy nodded. Then, he spoke. "What seems to be the problem here?"

The police inspector walked over to the old man, who stood clinging to his bicycle. "This man says you assaulted him and tried to steal his bicycle."

Murphy stood speechless.

The police inspector continued.

"Are you stationed at Kagnew Station?"

Murphy shook his head. "No. I'm visiting someone here."

Murphy had left his passport in his travel bag back at the King George. He carried his CID identification in the inside pocket of his jacket. But he didn't want Tekle to know about the shield, nor about the small gun tucked inside the waistband of his slacks.

Tekle walked to the counter and stood with his back to it so he could watch Murphy.

"Who are you visiting?"

"Smyth," Murphy answered. "I'm visiting Mr. Smyth from the American consulate."

With that, Tekle turned to the sergeant behind the counter and said a few words in Amharic. To Murphy's ear, the language sounded a little more guttural than the lilting Tigrinya he'd heard the past few days.

The sergeant picked up a telephone set from beneath the wooden counter. "We'll see if we can locate your friend," Tekle said, as the sergeant dialed. Whoever answered at the other end apparently spoke Amharic for Murphy noticed the sergeant never reverted to English during the brief conversation. After the call, he gave a brief report in Amharic to the inspector. "They're looking for your friend now," Tekle said. Then, no one spoke.

Murphy appreciated Tekle's skill as an interrogator. Murphy's reticence had made the police inspector work a little bit for information. Timing, Murphy knew, was everything in interrogations. The Ethiopian had asked a few questions. Now, he was giving Murphy time to think about his answers and about other questions he might be asked. Sometimes, during such pauses, answers to questions that haven't been asked or even contemplated came out. Murphy knew the drill. He remained silent.

During the lull, several other detectives drifted out of the squad room to see what had drawn Inspector Tekle, their supervisor, into the lobby. One of them was the detective Murphy had seen dancing at the Mocambo the night before. Another detective bore a strong resemblance to one of the men in the Mercedes Murphy had seen that morning at the accident in Ghezzabanda.

Five minutes later, the ringing of the telephone pierced the silence. The conversation was brief, the sergeant's report short. "Mr. Smyth is on his way," Tekle translated.

Then, Tekle pointed to the dried blood on Murphy's right hand. "How did that happen?"

Murphy looked down at his hand. "I must have cut it when I ran into the old man. We hit the ground pretty hard. It's nothing. Just a scratch."

Tekle pulled a clean handkerchief from the inside pocket of his coat. "Take this."

Murphy demurred. "I'm all right. It's not that bad."

A few minutes later, Smyth strode through the front door.

He wasn't wearing his dark glasses, and Murphy could tell, from the redness around his dark blue eyes, he'd apparently been aroused from a deep slumber. Still, Smyth looked quite presentable. He wore a powder-blue woolen pullover over khaki pants and had managed to pass a comb through his blonde hair before coming downtown.

Smyth had also retained his sense of humor. After greeting

Tekle like a long-lost friend, he tried, in his own way, to make light of Murphy's predicament. "So, John. In trouble with the local constabulary?"

But Murphy didn't laugh. He gestured toward the old man. "They say I assaulted this man and tried to steal his bicycle."

Smyth looked at the old man. Then, he turned toward Tekle. "How much will it cost to make this go away?"

Tekle spoke to the old man in Tigrinya. Then, he translated. "He said one hundred dollars."

"Ethiopian?" Smyth asked.

"Yes, Ethiopian."

Smyth reached into his pocket and pulled out a wad of colorful Ethiopian money. He peeled off ten notes and handed them to Tekle, who called the old man to him and gave him all the money. "Let's go," Smyth grabbed Murphy by the arm.

But Tekle wasn't done. Before the two Americans could take one step, he said, "I have one more question to ask." They turned to face the Ethiopian, who stood a little taller than either one of them. "On Sunday afternoon, the Shifta attacked the bus from Massawa." The inspector directed his gaze at Murphy. "There was an American on the bus. He was tall like you and had dark hair." Then, he pointed toward Murphy's boots. "He wore boots like those."

Murphy looked down. "A lot of Americans wear boots. We all think we're cowboys. Besides, I've never been to Massawa."

It was a minor point. But Murphy didn't want the Ethiopian police to know of his movements. Actually, he was more concerned about Romana. Murphy doubted the police inspector would be as polite if he questioned her. Tekle might force her to tell them about Mekele, and Murphy didn't want anything to jeopardize his meeting with the rebel leader in Keren the next day. So he lied.

Smyth intervened. "John spent Sunday with me. We drove the triangle route to Decamare, to Nefasit, and back up the mountain to Asmara. Not much to see, though."

With that, the two Americans left the police station.

During the walk back to his Rover sedan, which he'd left parked in the shadow of the Cathedrale in the care of a couple of street boys, Smyth asked how Murphy had happened to meet the old man with the bike.

"I was doing some roadwork," he answered, "and we literally ran into each other."

Smyth, of course, didn't believe him. "You were out running this time of night dressed like that?"

"I forgot to pack my sweats and my running shoes," came the answer.

Smyth probed no farther. Instead, he changed the subject. "You know, you violated the colonel's first commandment." Then, in a more solemn voice, he intoned: "Thou shalt not get in trouble downtown."

Smyth told Murphy the U.S. government had been trying to renegotiate its Status of Forces agreement with the Ethiopian government for several years. At the moment, he said, it was unclear who had jurisdiction, Americans or Ethiopians, when Kagnew Station personnel ran afoul of the local laws.

"The colonel wants his boys to keep their hands clean when they go downtown." The CID detachment at Kagnew Station tried to keep American soldiers out of trouble by turning potential criminal charges into civil matters, he explained. "Last month, a couple of Spec 5's from Tract C got into a disagreement with a street walker down on Queen Elizabeth near the Blue Nile. After the national policemen marched them through town at gunpoint, the two men were charged with assault, attempted rape, and destruction of private property.

Pretty serious charges. The next day, the woman agreed to drop all of the charges in return for ten dollars Ethiopian from each soldier."

The two soldiers had gotten off cheap, thought Murphy. It had cost them four dollars a piece to avoid the felony charges. Then he laughed. "So that old guy shook us down, huh?"

"It's become a cottage industry," Smyth said. "The people here are known for their honesty. But things have gotten so bad they'll do just about anything to hustle a buck. It's a bad time."

Smyth didn't notice the cut on Murphy's right hand until they'd reached his hotel. "That looks nasty. How did you do it?"

"Cut myself shaving."

Smyth didn't ask any more questions.

That afternoon, Murphy had decided not to tell anyone about the shots fired at him out near Tract C. Now, that someone had tried to run him over with a car, Murphy began to wonder about the wisdom of such a policy. But he remained silent.

After telling Waldo to fetch his first-aid kit and some warm water, Smyth led Murphy into the empty lounge where they'd met with Hilton two days before. While they waited for the little Ethiopian's return, Smyth moved behind the bar, and came up with a bottle of Johnny Walker Red. "Do you mind if I pour us a drink?"

"Be my guest."

Smyth found two shot glasses beneath the bar. After holding them up to the light to see if they were clean, he filled them to the brim. "You seem somewhat reticent," he said, carrying their drinks to the small table at the far end of the bar. Then, with a slight chuckle, "To quote the lyrics of a popular song: 'You've lost that lovin' feeling.' "

Murphy took a sip from his drink. "I'm quiet by nature."

He wanted to take the plunge. He wanted to tell Smyth about everything that had happened. But he still didn't know who his real friends were here. Until he was sure, he would have a difficult time trusting anyone.

The two men were joined by Waldo, who carried a small pan of steaming hot water and a small first-aid kit slung from his shoulder. It took a few moments to clean Murphy's wound, a narrow gash running down from the base of his little finger on the side of his hand. Waldo was gentle, but the cut stung when he applied the methylolate. After encasing the wound inside a piece of gauze, he wound three strips of white tape around Murphy's hand to keep the dressing in place. "That should do for a while, Mr. John. I'll change the dressing tomorrow if you want."

The pain had eased. But the dressing made it difficult for Murphy to open and close his hand.

When they worked together, Van Dyck had often reminded Murphy to keep him informed of his movements. "I need to know where to look for the body."

The warrant officer would laugh at his own joke. But it was sound advice.

Before Murphy went up to his room, he told Smyth: "I'm going to take a little ride to Keren tomorrow."

If he wound up missing, at least Smyth would know where to look for him.

EXCEPT FOR A BRIEF FORAY into the bathroom, Murphy spent the next morning in his hotel room.

He'd managed to coax enough water out of the stubborn shower head to thoroughly wash himself for the first time since his arrival. The waterworks were back in operation, but the water pressure remained low. Murphy imagined everyone in Asmara was washing up at the same time he was.

For breakfast, Waldo brought Murphy two hard rolls and a small pot of thick, bitter-tasting Ethiopian coffee. After the shower, he changed Murphy's dressing, replacing the long strips of surgical tape he had wound around Murphy's right hand the night before with much shorter band aids, It made it easier for Murphy to open and close his right hand.

Before leaving for Keren, Murphy cleaned his pistol. He inspected the little automatic, making sure the firing mechanism hadn't been damaged when he dropped it on the pavement.

Murphy also got some exercise. He ran in place for 20 minutes and went through his repertoire of calisthenics and isometrics. Because of the cut in his hand, he had difficulty doing pushups. Still, he managed to knock off fifty of them.

Several times that morning, Murphy cracked the shutters on the room's lone window to check the street outside the hotel. One time, he noticed two national policemen walking down the sidewalk across the street. Another, a little white Fiat buzzed down the quiet street. There was no sight of the big black limousine of the night before.

As he reassembled the Browning, Murphy wished he carried a bit more firepower, like the sawed-off carbine he had in Vietnam, or the forty-five automatic in the shoulder holster he'd left hanging in his wall locker at Fort Dix. He knew the little automatic wouldn't be much good against a squad of Eritrean rebels, but Murphy didn't want to go to his meeting with Mekele unarmed. "Good intentions can take you a long way," Van Dyck use say, "But there's nothing like a gun to get your point across." V.D. had carried a Walther PPK, a slim, seven-shot automatic noted for its stopping power.

Murphy had considered going to Kagnew Station and asking for help. Smyth already knew where he was going. But if Hilton learned of the reason, Murphy probably would never get a chance to talk to Mekele, if, in fact, he showed up for the meeting. Hilton would tell the Ethiopians about Mekele and their scheduled meeting in Keren. The rebel leader would be scared off, or worse, killed, and Murphy would lose the only possible link he had between Wallace, the dead MP, and the Shifta.

For the moment, Murphy had no problems about keeping Hilton in the dark. The major had made it abundantly clear he really didn't want Murphy to look into the case any further. Hilton had already settled on a prime suspect, the Shifta. The fact Murphy had seen an M-1 carbine, the same kind of weapon used to kill Wallace, in the hands of one of the rebels when the bus was ambushed three days before seem to buttress the major's belief the Eritrean rebels were responsible for Wallace's death. Hilton didn't seem interested in learning how the Shifta had gotten their hands on the weapon, or more specifically, the ammo apparently used to kill Wallace.

Murphy wondered why the rebels hadn't killed him when they ambushed the bus on the Massawa road. He also wondered what vital piece of information he'd picked up during the twenty-four hours following the ambush to make him worth killing now.

The shell casings Murphy had found in the antenna field out near Tract C were the only links between Wallace's death and the attempts on his life. A comparison test could tell whether those bullets were fired from the same rifle used to kill Wallace.

But Murphy knew there would be no ballistics tests. No analysis. And no help from Kagnew Station. No backup. The cavalry wasn't going to ride out of the compound on the top of the hill to save him. He was on his own. He didn't like it, but it was a situation he'd become accustomed to. That's why he made sure the Browning, the only weapon he had, was ready for use.

By the time Murphy left for Keren, the sun had burned off the gray morning overcast, and an endless procession of clouds marched across the deep-blue East African sky.

Murphy didn't try to conceal his movements when he rode out of Asmara. From Waldo, he had learned enough about the road to Keren to know it would be easy to pick out a tail in the open country. Besides, Murphy figured the real danger lie ahead. If the Shifta were out to kill him, they'd set up an ambush. It was more their style.

From what Waldo told him about the road, Murphy had deduced there were two good places to spring a trap during the hundred-kilometer ride to Keren. Those locations were in the narrow mountain passes before and after the large agricultural operation in the valley at Elaboret, more than halfway to Keren.

Outside Asmara, the paved road snaked across the rolling countryside on top of the plateau. The terrain was rock-strewn pastureland, and the Italians had built the slightly-banked road bed ten to twelve feet high to carry rainwater away from the pavement. Murphy had the road to himself. He opened up the throttle of the Honda and, while hugging the outer edge of the tarmac, weaved his way through the gentle turns at nearly sixty miles per hour.

About ten minutes into the trip, Murphy passed a small stone cross erected on the gravel shoulder as a memorial to a victim of a fatal accident. There were no dangerous dropoffs here, like on the road to Massawa. Still, the marker was a reminder. Even on this stretch of relatively benign highway he must be careful.

Murphy held the bike on a tangent on the outer edge of the tarmac, near the narrow gravel shoulder, leaning into the turns on the road, which ran for more than twenty kilometers across the plateau before beginning its descent into the series of valleys leading to Keren.

Going into one of the high-banked turns, a glint of metal in the mirror on the Honda's left handlebar caught Murphy's eye. He leaned to the left as he started to come out of the turn. When he did, he noticed the front of a black car had nearly pulled even with him, and its driver seemed to be edging it closer, trying to push the bike off the road. As the two vehicles were about to touch, Murphy leaned to the right, removing the Honda from the arc of the turn. The motorcycle's trajectory changed. The bike shot across the shoulder and went sailing into the air and off the edge of the raised highway.

It all seemed to happen in slow motion. While he flew through air, Murphy kept the Honda under him. Easing up on the throttle, he killed the engine. He managed to keep the motorcycle between his legs during the twenty-five foot flight. As he sailed through the air nearly parallel to the road, he also caught a glimpse of the distinctive logo, a propeller inside a circle, imprinted on the lid of the trunk of the black car that had run him off the road.

Murphy's flight ended abruptly. Luckily, he avoided a large boulder in the deep ditch. The Honda landed on both of its wheels among the small rocks in the bottom of the ditch and came to a full stop.

It was a rough landing, and it took Murphy a few seconds to recover. Except for a soreness in his groin, which had been mashed against the gas tank when the motorcycle made its two-point landing, he was unhurt. Slowly, he climbed off the bike. With his gun drawn, Murphy climbed up the embankment to the road. But he was too late. The car hadn't stopped. It had rounded the corner on the banked highway and was out of sight.

"SONABITCH," MURPHY MUTTERED, massaging his sore groin as he looked at the empty road, an emptiness enhanced by the barrenness of the rocky pasture around him.

Murphy carefully picked his way back down the embankment to retrieve the Honda, which lay on its side in the bottom of the ditch.

Pushing the motorcycle up the steep incline wasn't easy, especially with his injuries.

Murphy didn't inspect the machine until it was sitting on its stand on the side of the road. Even then, his inspection was cursory. But he didn't see any broken parts during his brief look, and the bike fired up almost immediately when he cranked the kick starter. Less than five minutes after flying into the ditch, he was back on the Honda traveling down the road to Keren.

Murphy still had plenty of time to get to his meeting with Mekele. Now, he wondered whether the rebel leader would keep the appointment. Murphy was sure Mekele, or one of his men, sat behind the steering wheel of the black Mercedes.

Or was he?

As he rolled along, Murphy realized someone else could have been driving the Benz.

Mekele wasn't the only one who knew Murphy was going to Keren. There was also Smyth. But Murphy doubted he had the stomach for such dirty work. Maybe, Smyth had gotten one of his spook friends to do the job for him.

Something about the car bothered Murphy. It was a

Mercedes Benz, for sure. He doubted the Eritrean rebels, the Shifta, drove such expensive automobiles, and he didn't think the CIA did either, at least not in Ethiopia. No. But the Ethiopian police did. But why would they want to kill him? Why would anyone want him dead?

If he hurried, Murphy was sure he could catch up with the car and learn the answers to those questions. However, while rolling through one of the bends in the road, the motorcycle seemed to slide out from under him. When the bike came upright, after coming out of the turn, Murphy detected a small wobble. Something was wrong with the Honda, and Murphy would have to slow down until he found out what it was. He cut his speed.

After a few kilometers, the road descended into a valley, a mere dip in the rolling fields of the highlands when compared to the deep gorges Murphy had seen on the road to Massawa. The descent was brief, and as he began to climb out of the little valley, he noticed the sky had begun to cloud up. By the time he reached the end of the short ascent, it had turned into a dismal, gray overcast. A short time later, a few large rain drops pelted him. Looking toward the horizon, Murphy saw a break in the overcast. Trying to outrun the impending deluge, he took a chance and picked up his speed along a straight stretch of road.

A few minutes later, Murphy approached a bus stopped to pick up passengers bound for Asmara. A few, small stucco buildings lined both sides of the road, and a small sign gave the name of the place as Teclesan. Off to his left, Murphy noticed the white-washed sides and thatched roofs of tukels in a small village on a slight rise no more than two hundred meters from the road. Between the village and the road, flocks of sheep and several tethered goats, unperturbed by the steady rain, grazed on the green grass which grew in tufts between the large rocks in the pasture.

As he drew closer to the bus, Murphy down-shifted to slow the Honda. When he touched the brakes to lower his speed, the rear wheel of the little motorcycle slid sideways along the wet tarmac. Easing off the throttle, Murphy threw out a leg to keep his balance and leaned the bike slightly in the direction of the skid. As he rolled past the bus, the bike came out of its slide. From then on, Murphy drove slowly through the steady rain, keeping his hands off the brakes, down-shifting to slow the bike through the few turns in the road.

While riding through the downpour, Murphy grew angrier, mostly at himself. He should have grabbed Mekele when he had the chance the night before at the wedding celebration. But Murphy had believed Mekele when the rebel leader said he didn't want to bring trouble on the heads of his friends and relations. "That's his problem," Van Dyck would have pointed out. "You should've grabbed his ass."

Murphy became more cautious when the road began to wind down a steep grade into another valley. Here, the road curled through a narrow pass, a perfect place for an ambush. He slowly tooled along as the road plunged blindly around a sharp bend. After coming out of the turn, Murphy nearly lost control of the bike as he pulled hard on both brakes to bring the Honda to a quick stop.

A flock of sheep, their bleats inaudible because of the burps of the motorcycle, blocked the road. Their unshorn wool was dirty and discolored, but the shepherd, using a gnarled wooden crook to gently prod the animals along, seemed proud of them. Dressed in rags, the man smiled at the American while slowly walking back and forth behind his flock, coaxing it across the road.

By now, the rain had subsided into a steady drizzle. Murphy wanted to stop and inspect the Honda's rear wheel. But he decided to wait until he could find a dry spot to pull over. Minutes later, it was still raining when the road climbed the far side of the valley.

A few kilometers on, the road dipped into another valley, passing through the middle of a large farm. For more than five kilometers, Murphy rolled past ten-foot high stalks of sorghum, which ran nearly up to the tarmac on both sides. Halfway across the valley, the planter's imposing stone villa sat on a small hill on the opposite side of the road. But Murphy came upon the large house too fast to chance stopping the Honda on the wet pavement. He drove on.

At the far side of the narrow valley, the road began its climb up a steep grade. As the little Honda strained up the hill, the skies lightened. Up ahead, small patches of blue broke through the gray. By the time Murphy reached the brow of the hill, the sun was shining. No rain had fallen here. The pavement was dry. Murphy looked for a spot off the tarmac to bring the motorcycle to a stop. He cut his speed as the road began to descend. A deep gorge fell three hundred meters or more from the road's up-hill lane. After slowly guiding the bike through an s-curve, Murphy noticed a narrow turnout in the opposite lane overlooking the canyon. He glided the Honda to a stop, less than two feet away from the little stone markers placed to keep motorists from driving off into the gorge.

Murphy was drenched. He got off the bike, removing his windbreaker and draping it over the handlebars to dry. After he lifted the motorcycle onto its stand, he began his inspection. As he walked around the Honda, he noticed the pain had eased. He could move without discomfort. However, the tightness returned when he crouched to inspect the rear assembly.

One of the large nuts on the rear axle had come loose, causing a noticeable wobble when the wheel turned. It was a good thing Murphy had stopped. The nut was less than a quarter-inch away from backing off the axle completely. Murphy had been very lucky. Another mile or two down the road and someone would be putting up a little monument for him.

In the storage compartment underneath the motorcycle seat, Murphy found a crescent wrench that fit the nut. He got back into a crouch behind the bike. As he tightened the nut, while holding the crescent wrench in his sore right hand, Murphy heard the sound of a footfall on the gravel nearby. His pulse quickened. Dropping the wrench, Murphy slid his right hand down into his boot to reach for his gun. Before pulling it out of its holster, he looked up.

Two tall black men walked up the shoulder of the road toward him. As they approached, the two men, clad in dirty muslin tunics, seemed to greet him in their own language. Aside from the ancient long rifles they carried, neither of the men, who both stood several inches taller than the broad-built American, looked menacing. Broad smiles played on their faces. Murphy kept his gun in its holster. He guessed the men were out for a morning hunt.

Murphy stood up behind the motorcycle. "Where did you fellas come from?" The two men seemed to understand the gist of the question. One of them responded in a language different from the lilting Tigrinya Murphy had become accustomed to hearing, while the other man used his gun, no more than a fowling piece, to point to the far side of the gorge. Turning for a moment, Murphy saw the small white tukels in a village on a ridge perhaps a kilometer away.

Just then, Murphy heard the sound of an automobile coming

down the road from Asmara. He turned in time to see a small green Simca careen around the corner. A white man sat in the driver's seat and a white woman sat next to him. When the woman saw Murphy standing with his back to the gorge, with the two armed villagers in front of him, her mouth formed a large oh, and she screamed as the car went by. The driver accelerated past the three men. Within seconds, the little green car disappeared around another corner, speeding down the mountain road toward Keren.

The two hunters seemed perplexed. But Murphy understood. The woman believed these two men, with their big rifles, were robbing him.

"She thought you were Shifta." Murphy pointed at the men and then down the empty road. "You know, Shifta."

Following a brief exchange with each other in their own language, the men laughed. "No Shifta," one of them said, shaking his head. Then, they waved their goodbyes and walked off, still chuckling. A few meters up the hill, the two men, loping along in long strides, left the road and took a path down into the gorge. Seconds later, Murphy lost sight of them as they were swallowed up in the scrub and tall cacti that grew in abundance in the arid landscape.

These two men were not Shifta. But the real Shifta, foot soldiers from the Eritrean Liberation Front, were around. They could be waiting for Murphy farther down the road. They would be in no laughing mood.

IT TOOK MURPHY a little more than thirty minutes to drive to Keren.

No ambush. No Shifta. No Mekele.

When he first arrived in Keren, site of a pivotal World War II battle, Murphy made the mistake of stopping at the Italian cemetery. It was crowded. Thin metal stakes, some of them planted only inches apart, marked each grave.

The much larger English cemetery on the other side of town, held the remains of far fewer soldiers. There was plenty of space between the earthen plots, and each burial mound was marked by a stone cross.

It was clear to Murphy which side won the battle.

Walking along the stone path toward a small grotto in the middle of the cemetery, Murphy read the headstones.

On the left were the graves of soldiers belonging to an Indian regiment. On the right were the graves of black African soldiers, members of the Kenya Rifles who had died in Eritrea. The graves at the rear of the burial ground belonged to British soldiers and, judging from their English or Dutch surnames, white South African troops who had fallen in Eritrea.

Even in death, race, or perhaps class, had kept the soldiers apart.

In the grotto, a vine-covered alcove providing the only shade in the cemetery, Murphy leafed through the pages of a large visitors' book, chained to a small wooden stand. Most of the signatures seemed to belong to American soldiers from Kagnew Station. They wrote their names and hometowns.

Some included a poignant comment like "a peaceful resting place" or "a quiet place to lie."

One wise guy, however, got carried away. He listed his name as "Elmer Fudd" from "Gwand Wapids." He wrote the cemetery was "A gweat place to hunt wabbits."

On another day, Murphy might have found the entry amusing. Not today.

Aside from two native workmen raking smooth the small white stones in the footpaths that crisscrossed it, no one else was in the cemetery.

After he sat down, Murphy reached into his boot and removed the Browning from its holster. Placing the small automatic on the stone bench under his right thigh, he lit a cigarette and waited for Mekele, sure the rebel leader wouldn't show up.

While Murphy smoked, the scraping sound of rakes grew louder as the two laborers worked their way toward him. Abruptly, the noise stopped.

"You're late." The voice sounded familiar.

Murphy looked up to see Mekele, dressed in the same garb as the two hunters he'd seen in the hills. He stood, leaning against a rake, a few feet in front of Murphy. The other man stood nearby, also holding a rake.

Murphy reached for the Browning. But when his hand closed to grip the automatic, a sharp pain coursed through the cut. He was unable to hold the gun firmly, and it fell to the ground.

"Don't bother to pick it up," Mekele intoned.

The rebel leader's face was uncovered. He looked younger than Murphy expected. The Eritrean rebel's brown face was clean-shaven, unlined.

But his eyes had the same intensity Murphy had noticed during their first meeting on the Massawa road three days before. Now, Murphy followed those eyes as Mekele glanced toward the steep bluff rising several hundred feet from the valley floor across the road from the cemetery.

"I have men up in those rocks with their rifles trained on you." Then, Mekele leaned over, picked up the gun and handed it back. "Put it away."

"Aren't you going to kill me?" Murphy slid the gun back into its holster. "You've tried hard enough."

Mekele took a seat on the bench opposite Murphy. As he did so, he said a few words in Tigrinya to the other man. Presently, the man resumed raking the path.

"If I wanted you dead, you'd be dead," Mekele shifted in his seat slightly so he could keep an eye on the road leading from town. "Now, let's start over."

Murphy relaxed. Slowly, he reached into his breast pocket and pulled out a pack of Marlboros. He offered a cigarette to Mekele before reaching into his jeans with his left hand to pull out his Zippo. After lighting Mekele's cigarette, Murphy handed him his CID identification. The rebel leader perused his ID and handed the little black badge case back. "What do you want of me?" he asked.

Murphy remained silent. He looked at Mekele for a few moments, then glanced back over his shoulder at the high bluffs.

Convinced he had nothing to lose, he decided to tell the rebel leader everything he knew about the case he was working on.

For the next few minutes, as Mekele listened in rapt silence, Murphy recounted what he knew about the shooting of Sergeant David Wallace, the dead man's contact with the liberation front in the desert outside Massawa, and the three attempts made on his own life during the previous twenty-four hours. "The Ethiopian government and a lot of the people at Kagnew Station believe your people killed Wallace," he concluded.

"Who do you think killed him?" Mekele asked.

Murphy shook his head. "I really don't know. But I do know he was killed by an M-1 carbine, and I do know I saw one of your men carrying such a weapon when you ambushed the bus on the Massawa road."

"These days, many of our men carry carbines." Mekele sat across from Murphy cradling his rake in his arms. "We recently came into possession of a lot of them."

Murphy almost was afraid to ask. After a slight pause, out came the question: "Where did you get them?"

"Kagnew Station."

Murphy took a long drag from his cigarette.

"How did you get them?"

"We bought them."

"You mean someone sold you some weapons?"

Mekele got up from his seat.

"I mean someone sold us a lot of weapons. We bought one thousand carbines."

The revelation stunned Murphy. Still, he kept his poise.

"And then you killed Wallace, the man who sold them to you?" The question came out matter of factly.

"I didn't know Wallace, and I don't know who sold the weapons to us," Mekele replied. "My assignment was to deliver the carbines to the men who needed them, and that I have done."

Murphy thought about the camel caravan and the shooting at the bus. "So it wasn't an ambush?"

Mekele caught his drift. "No, the bus was late. It wasn't supposed to be there."

Murphy remembered how he and Romana had delayed the vehicle's departure from Massawa.

"We had to kill the soldiers," Mekele explained. "No one could know we were carrying the rifles. No one could know we were there."

Then, Murphy recalled Smyth's reaction upon learning the Shifta hadn't destroyed the bus. "That's the reason you didn't blow up the bus, isn't it?"

"The soldiers in Massawa would have seen the smoke from a burning bus," Mekele explained. "They would have come to investigate. We needed more time to get away, to hide from the jet planes they would send after us."

Mekele's story seemed plausible. His commanders had given him an assignment and gave him only the information he needed to carry it out. The U.S. Army operated under the same principle. American soldiers were told only what they needed to know to perform their missions. No more, no less.

As Mekele stood up to leave, Murphy thought about his conversation on the golf course with Major Hilton. He wondered what Hilton would say if he knew what Mekele just told him. It was a piece of information the major would prefer not to hear. It didn't square with his theory about the Shifta and Wallace, a complication Murphy was sure Hilton could do without.

"Look, I'm not planning on telling anybody, at least not yet, about how you got the rifles," Murphy said. "The Ethiopian government really doesn't need to know an American sold a lot of weapons to a bunch of Eritrean rebels. They would close down Kagnew Station, and that's something my government doesn't want to happen."

Mekele smiled. "The secret is safe with me." After a slight pause, he added, "None of my men know we have purchased the guns. They think we stole them."

Mekele turned to leave. Before he took two steps, Murphy stopped him with another question. "Why have you told me all of this?"

Mekele smiled. "I spent a lot of time in your country, and I like Americans. Besides, you're a friend of Romana's, and that makes you special."

"Romana? She's in this, too?"

Mekele laughed. "Oh, no. Like many of my countrymen, she is apolitical. But that will change. The Ethiopians are stupid rulers. They will drive the Eritrean people to us."

Murphy turned and watched the two rebels walk away. The two men dropped their rakes on the ground near the entrance. Adopting the relaxed lope of the two hunters Murphy had met in the hills, they headed down the road and disappeared into a canyon away from Keren.

TO MURPHY, Mekele's revelation eliminated the Eritrean Liberation Front as his would-be killers.

He believed the Shifta had nothing to do with the attempts on his life. Who ever had tried to kill him had botched the job three times. From what he'd seen, Mekele's men wouldn't have needed more than one attempt to complete that task.

If the rebels hadn't tried to kill Murphy, they probably weren't responsible for Wallace's death either.

Murphy had no idea who tried to kill him, but he did know they had twice used a black Mercedes Benz sedan to do it. Find the car, and he would find his failed murderer and possibly the man who killed Wallace.

Murphy's search for the car began at the U.S. Army's R and R Center, located on a dusty side street no more than five minutes away from the English cemetery.

A large villa leased from its Italian owner, it was an American oasis with room for perhaps fifty overnight guests. Amenities included a three-hole, pitch-and-putt golf course with real grass greens, a small swimming pool, and a volleyball court. Like the facilities at Kagnew Station, the restaurant and bar were first-rate. It had no television, but the staff did set up a film projector in the evenings and showed old black-and-white movies.

Parked in the gravel parking lot inside the gates of the high-walled compound were several motorcycles and six cars: two late-model Fiats, a little green Corvair, a powder-blue 1954 Chrysler sedan, a lavender-colored 1958 Oldsmobile, and the little green Simca, but no Mercedes Benz.

In the small bar off the main dining room, where the staff was clearing away the dishes from lunch, Murphy encountered Billy Bodwell, the driver of the Simca he'd seen in the mountains.

A slightly-balding man perhaps five or six years older than Murphy, Bodwell seemed surprised to see him walk into the bar. "I'm sorry for leaving you in the lurch up the in the hills, brother." he apologized. "I wanted to stop. But my wife thought those men were Shifta robbing you. I had to get her out of there. She was very upset. It took her quite a while to calm down. Right now, she's down in our room trying to take a nap."

Bodwell was assigned to the StratCom facility at Kagnew Station. Sticking to his cover story, Murphy told him he was on temporary assignment at Tract C, a site he knew Bodwell wouldn't be allowed to enter because he lacked the proper security clearance.

"I borrowed a bike from a guy in B Company and came down to Keren for the day," Murphy explained. "Just visited the cemeteries." When working undercover, Murphy had learned it was wise to include a grain of truth in his cover story. "You never know who is checking you out," V.D. had counseled. "Give them something real to chew on."

Besides the Ethiopian bartender, who wore a red vest and small black bow tie like his peers in the clubs at Kagnew Station, there was only one other person in the bar—a tanned, fit-looking man not much older than Murphy embroiled in a heated telephone conversation at the far end of the bar.

"They must get here as soon as they can," he shouted into the telephone. "The boy is in a real bad way, so see what you can do to push the Ethiopians along." The man, dressed in slightly-soiled jeans and a short-sleeved, cotton-print shirt, listened intently before saying "Thanks" and hanging up the receiver. He then murmured his thanks to the bartender for the use of the phone and walked out of the room. In that instant, Murphy noted the same intensity in his eyes he'd seen in Mekele's less than a half-hour before. The man's body seemed to radiate energy. Like Mekele, he was on a mission he believed in passionately.

"The guy used to be stationed at Kagnew," Bodwell broke in. He nursed a Budweiser. "He runs an orphanage near here."

A boy had broken an arm, and a helicopter was needed to take him to one of the hospitals in Asmara.

"It's been raining up on the hill, and the Ethis don't want to fly," Bodwell nodded toward the telephone. "He was talking to the colonel, trying to get him to give them a little push."

The two men ordered lunch.

For Murphy, it was a hamburger, with a side order of onion rings, and a chocolate milk shake. For Bodwell, a mushroom pizza and another Bud.

They sat at a small table on the enclosed patio off the bar.

While they ate, the two men talked about cars. It was small talk with a purpose, as usual.

"You bring that Simca with you?" Murphy was curious at how the small, boxy-looking Swedish-made car had ended up in Ethiopia.

"No, I bought it off a guy from headquarters company before he shipped out," Bodwell said between bites. "He bought it from some United Nations guy who had it shipped here."

Soldiers at Kagnew Station always can get a good deal on a second-hand car, Bodwell told him. "We've had guys shipping cars over here for nearly twenty years, so there's quite a selection. Usually, you can buy a pretty good car at a reasonable price." Bodwell stopped a moment to take a bite from his pizza and another swig of beer. "Of course, occasionally, someone gets stuck with a lemon."

"What do you mean?"

Bodwell gave him an example of what kind of automobile was considered "a lemon" at Kagnew Station.

"Three years ago, a guy shipped a brand-new, red-and-white Marlin over here. He drove it around for seventeen months and then sold it to a buddy of his before shipping out. The next guy had it for about a year before he got transferred out of here, and he just managed to sell it before he left."

Bodwell paused to take another sip of beer before resuming his story.

"The guy who bought the car had a drinking problem. One Saturday night, he gets tanked up at the Oasis Club and drives the Marlin downtown to do some bar-hopping. In between stops, he runs over an Ethiopian kid. Drags him for more than a half mile down Queen Elizabeth. He doesn't even know he's hit the kid until he pulls up and parks the car in front of the Blue Nile. By then, it's too late. The kid's dead. There's quite a crowd down there, and the Ethis go wild when they see the kid wrapped around this guy's front bumper. He was lucky to get out of there alive."

Bodwell paused to finish his beer.

"Well, the colonel goes bullshit," he continued. "He busts him down to private and ships his ass out of here. The guy left the Marlin with one of his buddies to sell for him. Five, six months go by, and there ain't nobody who wants to buy that car. Then, some new guy in B Company shows up and plunks down a thousand dollars for it. The first time he takes the Marlin downtown, he parks it in front of the San Francisco Bar. He goes in and has a couple of Melottis. When he comes out, the car is destroyed. Tires, seats slashed. Every single piece of glass broken. All of the trim torn off. Deep gouges in the finish."

Bodwell paused for a moment. "Now, that's a lemon, brother!" he bellowed.

Murphy got the joke. But he didn't laugh. Instead, he wondered if the man who tried to run him over with the Benz was driving a lemon, a car with a history destined to cause its owner all sorts of problems.

After drawing in the last of his milk shake, Murphy posed a question: "Any of the guys up at Kagnew drive a Mercedes?"

Bodwell burped. "Way too expensive, even over here." He took one last swig of beer. "There's a couple of guys up on the post who drive some older Mercedes they picked up downtown. They say one of them used to belong to the emperor, but I doubt it, that old geezer never lets go of anything." Bodwell held up his empty Bud bottle to signal for another one.

Murphy wanted to ask Bodwell more. He wanted to know places where he could find the cars, the names of their owners, and their physical descriptions. But he didn't dare press. Up until now, his chat with Bodwell had been just that, idle chitchat. Bodwell didn't know he was talking to a CID investigator, and Murphy wanted to keep it that way.

At least, now he knew where to find the Mercedes. Kagnew Station.

MURPHY STARTED his search for the Mercedes Benz before he left Keren.

He left Bodwell in the bar, nursing another Budweiser. "I got to get going before they close the road," he explained. "I came down just for the day, and I've got to get back up the hill."

But Murphy took his time riding through Keren, a small town dominated by a huge stone fort on a mound at its center. As he went along, he looked down each dusty side street, hoping to catch a glimpse of a large black sedan. Few people were out at this time of day, and Murphy had the streets to himself.

While traveling up a slight incline leading from the dusty crossroads in the center of town, Murphy saw a black sedan parked in front of a small hotel. As he pulled close, he noticed saw the distinctive decal, the three-bladed prop, on its trunk lid. From the car's faded black finish and its lack of sharp tail fins, Murphy knew it was a much older model than the Benz sedans he'd seen the cops in Asmara drive. When he brought the Honda to a stop behind the car, he also noticed it bore the distinctive Kagnew Station license plate, which featured a gazelle head at its center. The Mercedes roared to life as Murphy climbed off the bike, showering him with pebbles and sand from its spinning rear wheels as it shot forward.

Moments later, Murphy was back on his bike chasing the Mercedes through the narrow paved road that snaked through the middle of Keren. He'd managed to pull abreast of the rear quarter panel on the driver's side of the car, when the car swerved in his direction. Murphy braked to avoid collision, falling several car lengths behind it.

Near the Italian cemetery, the big sedan left the pavement and careened down a dirt track through the outlying scrubland. The car, rocking side to side on the deeply-rutted track, sent up a dusty rooster tail. Murphy lost sight of the Mercedes, but the thick cloud told him it was just ahead. Less than a kilometer from the paved road, the dirt track forked in two directions. The intersection was obscured by the large cloud, and Murphy bore to the left, realizing too late the sedan had taken the right turn and was pulling away. He took the Honda off the track, nearly dropping the bike in the process, and drove cross country for a few hundred meters before putting the bike on the right track. By the time he trailed the car again, the dust had settled down. As he headed down the track, he noticed a wide oil slick on the ground ahead. It was too large and thick to be obscured by the debris thrown up by the Mercedes. As Murphy closed on the car, the oil streak seemed to grow narrower.

Less than a minute later, Murphy found the Mercedes stopped on the side of the track, its front end caressing a large stone pillar. As the dust settled, he noticed a group of small boys clustered around the automobile. Murphy stopped the Honda a few meters behind the car. Drawing his automatic, he approached the passenger side of the car slowly and peered through the window. The car was empty.

A group of boys clustered around Murphy, who noticed the stone pillar made up one side of the entrance to an enclosed area, surrounded by a low stone wall. Except for a small stone building inside the enclosure, there didn't seem to be any reason to put a wall up around this patch of land. As Murphy walked through the entrance, the boys chattered incessantly and drew closer to him, subtly guiding him to a large concrete mound that seemed to grow from the ground. Ten mounds, each covered with a piece of metal grating, lined the sides of the crushed stone walk that ran down the middle of the compound.

When the boys, with Murphy involuntarily in tow, stopped next to the mound, two of them left the group to slide the grating aside. Another boy picked up a long wooden pole from the ground and slid it into the opening. All the boys grew silent as their comrade leaned over the opening to peer into the hole. A few seconds later, the pole boy smiled and backed away from the hole, dragging the staff with him, withdrawing it from the hole. When the end of the pole came into view, a large brown snake hung limp from one of its two hooks. As Murphy leaned forward to look into the black hole, he noticed all of the boys had backed away from the snake pit, giving a wide berth to the snake, which had small flecks of black on its tannish hide. All of them looked in silent awe at the long reptile, whose body was the width of a man's wrist.

The stillness was broken by the crunching sound of boots running across the stone path toward Murphy, who turned to see a man flying at him. He had just enough time to side-step the man's charge, watching as his body shot past him and landed head-first inside the opening to the snake pit. Murphy reached out to grab a leg, but the man kicked him away before losing his balance and slowly slid into the hole.

Murphy and the boys, pushing each other aside to view the scene below, peered into the opening to see the man, about ten feet below them, laying face down in a sea of snakes in the bottom of the large stone cistern. Most of the snakes lay undisturbed in the coolness in the deep recesses of the cistern. But a few of them, sensing the body heat emanating from the intruder, had come to life. They lifted their heads, searching for their prey. The man, momentarily stunned by his fall, also stirred. Immediately, he realized his situation. "Get me the fuck outta here," he hollered, in a Southern drawl. "These sonsabitches are deadly."

Murphy picked up the pole and slid it back into the hole. "Grab on to this." The man failed in his first attempt to stand and take hold of the pole, falling on his back among the snakes. He screamed.

Murphy tried again. "You've got to grab hold of the pole," he hollered. Looking down into the hole, he saw the thin, grim face of Turgeon, the staff sergeant he'd seen at the rifle range the day before, staring up at him. Unsteady, Turgeon lurched forward, wrapped himself around the pole and slowly shinnied up hand over hand until he was close enough for Murphy to reach down, grab hold of his shoulders and pull the slightly-built NCO out of the snake pit.

When Turgeon, who was wearing cut-off jeans, came out of the hole, a snake remained coiled around his left leg, its fangs solidly attached to his calf muscle. When the snake cleared the opening, one of the boys reached out and grabbed the reptile, holding it with both hands behind its head. Within seconds, the snake released its grip. The boy removed his hands, and the snake fell harmlessly back into its dark lair.

Murphy helped Turgeon to his feet. "You all right?"

"I'm a fuckin' daid man," Turgeon barked. "That's a Black Mamba."

The snakes were raised for their skins for handbags and shoes, and the boys made money by showing them to the few tourists who happened to find the farm. Villagers ran for miles to avoid Mambas, one of the most feared snakes in Africa because of its lethal venom and its ability to travel quickly.

Turgeon remained unsteady on his feet. But Murphy was unsure whether it was from the snake bite or, judging from the smell, the liquor he'd drunk. He carried him to the shady side of the small stone building.

"Get me a drink," Turgeon ordered when Murphy put him down with his back propped up against the building. "There's a bottle in the car."

Already, the neurotoxins the snake had pumped into Turgeon were coursing through his nervous system. Within seconds after the snake pumped its venom into the blood stream, the toxins began to affect the operation of Turgeon's heart and his other vital organs. The hemotoxins in the venom had already started the digestive process, breaking down blood vessels and body tissues, and the alcohol in Turgeon's blood stream simply speeded up the process. He was a dead man.

Murphy returned with a half-empty fifth of Jim Beam he found on the floor in the Mercedes. After removing the cap, he handed the bottle to Turgeon, who managed to take one long pull before choking.

Sensing there wasn't much more time, Murphy began firing questions.

"Tell me about the rifles."

No answer.

"Why did you try to kill me?"

Turgeon remained silent.

."Why did you kill Wallace?"

Again, no answer.

In his mind, Murphy quickly retraced the steps he took before stumbling across Turgeon. He thought about Bodwell, and the man on the telephone in the bar, and the small hotel where Turgeon had parked his car. Maybe, because the telephone at tne R & R Center was tied up, Turgeon stopped at the hotel to look for a phone. Maybe, he called someone.

Murphy took another stab. "Who were you trying to call?"

Turgeon remained mum.

"Who's your partner?"

Throughout the brief interrogation, Turgeon, his thin lips locked in a grim expression, stared at Murphy, who crouched next to him. The boys, meanwhile, arrayed themselves in a semi-circle around the two white men, sitting on their haunches quietly murmuring among themselves.

Finally, Turgeon responded, "I ain't goin' to tell ya'll a fuckin' thang."

With his right hand, Turgeon held the bottle of Jim Beam against his chest. When he tried to raise it to his lips, it fell from his grasp. Paralysis had set in, and his arm remained where it lay. Turgeon's voice filled with alarm. "I cain't move!" At that, the murmuring among the boys, enthralled by the spectacle before them, rose a few octaves.

Murphy nodded toward the boys. "They're taking bets on how much longer you're going to last? You've got to talk to me."

Turgeon didn't say another word. A few moments later, his head slowly lolled to one side, and he fell into a sleep from which he would never awake. Murphy leaned forward, and, placing two fingers on the left side of Turgeon's neck, checked for a pulse. He felt nothing. Turgeon was gone.

Murphy didn't spend much more time at the snake farm. He had to move quickly before anyone else showed up.

He picked up the liquor bottle, walked over to the uncovered snake pit and dropped it through the opening. It landed unbroken among the dozens of black mambas coiled on top of one another in the bottom of the cistern.

Next, Murphy searched the body. Except for a chit book,

jammed into the front pocket of the dead man's cutoffs, he found nothing.

Then, Murphy checked the Mercedes. After noticing the long, deep gouge on the left front fender where the car had kissed the wall when Turgeon tried to run him over the night before, he looked inside the trunk. There, wrapped in large piece of burlap bound with a piece of twine, he found a carbine and an ammunition clip. Using his thumb to eject the .30 caliber rounds from the spring-loaded clip, Murphy discovered four rounds were missing. After feeding the bullets back into the clip, he wrapped the rifle and the magazine inside the burlap, and used the twine to tie the package to the handlebars of his motorcycle.

When Murphy went to put the car's keys back into the ignition switch, where he had found them, he noticed Turgeon's field jacket laying on the back seat. He found a wallet in one of the jacket's large side pockets. It contained Turgeon's ID card, his driver's license, twelve dollars in U.S. currency and thirty-five dollars Ethiopian. As he was sliding the money back into the wallet, Murphy found a little white business card also tucked inside it.

It was identical to the Luigi card he'd found in Wallace's boot during his first visit to Kagnew Station. On the back of it, someone had scribbled: "14 at 2200." After sliding the card inside his shirt pocket, Murphy put the wallet back where he found it.

Before leaving, Murphy paused to light a cigarette. Staring down at Turgeon, he wished the dead man could stand up and tell him what he knew.

A part of Murphy began to feel sorry for Turgeon, but another part of him fought off the emotion.

"You start feeling sorry in this business," Van Dyck told him once, "and you're going to be sorry."

DURING THE RIDE back up the mountains, Murphy adopted and rejected several theories about who sold the rifles to the liberation front.

None of them explained why anyone, especially Turgeon, would go to such great lengths to try to kill him. It didn't make sense. Until a couple of hours ago, Murphy had known nothing about the weapons. He still knew nothing about the men who stole the rifles and delivered them to the rebels.

At first, Murphy wondered whether any of Smyth's friends at the American consulate put the weapons in rebel hands. It was right up their alley. But he doubted the transfer of the weapons to the liberation front would have official sanction. The communications and intelligence operations at Kagnew Station were far too important to risk ruffling the feathers of the Ethiopian government just to score a few points with potential Eritrean leaders.

Even the CIA wouldn't be that stupid. Would it?

Then, there was Turgeon. He could have stolen the weapons and sold them to the rebels. Maybe Wallace had found out about it. Maybe Turgeon had killed him to keep him quiet. Maybe.

Finding the Luigi cards, one in a boot belonging to the murder victim and another in a field jacket belonging to a man who tried to kill him, was significant. It was a link between the two men.

The numbers, "14 at 2200," written on the back of Turgeon's card, could be of help if Murphy knew what the cryptic message meant. In military parlance, "2200" meant 2200 hours, ten o'clock at night. Murphy assumed the number "2200" written on the back of Turgeon's card referred to the time. But he had no idea what the number "14" meant.

The fact both Wallace and Turgeon had Luigi cards could mean both men had received them as a signal of some sort. The cards could had come from a third person, someone else who was involved with Wallace's murder and the sale of the carbines to the Eritrean Liberation Front.

Murphy was in an awkward position. At this stage during an investigation, especially with the unexpected turn of events during the last few hours, he'd report his findings to his superiors. It was almost instinctual. "We're like squirrels," Van Dyck told him once. "We scurry around, gathering our nuts, and, when our pile is large enough, we share them with the rest of the family."

But Murphy couldn't share what he knew with anybody. He couldn't walk into Hilton's office and lay Turgeon's rifle on his desk and tell the major someone had stolen one thousand carbines, obsolete but highly-effective weapons nonetheless, from Kagnew Station and sold them to a bunch of Eritrean rebels. It was one story the major didn't want to hear. So, instead of sharing his hoard of information, Murphy covered his tracks.

Before he left the snake farm, Murphy handed a twenty-dollar bill to the boy who pulled the black mamba off Turgeon's leg. He appeared to be the leader of the group. Recalling how Tomaso, the mechanic, had silenced his workers at his garage the day before, Murphy put a finger to his pursed lips and whispered, "Silencio."

After he left the snake farm, instead of following the dirt track back to Keren, Murphy took the little Honda overland.

He traveled through a large grove of widely-spaced, thick-trunked baobab trees for about five kilometers before linking up with the main road. It was a rough ride, and Murphy's injured hand ached and his sore groin throbbed by the time he reached the tarmac. But the route he took kept him out of Keren and put him on the road to Asmara.

On the ride back up the mountain, Murphy made one stop, pulling the bike off the pavement near the same spot where he inspected the Honda on the trip down. He couldn't ride into Asmara with a rifle strapped to his motorcycle, so he removed it from the front of the bike and heaved the weapon and its magazine, still wrapped in burlap, out over the gorge. After the package fell out of sight into the vegetation deep below, Murphy glanced toward the village on the far rim of the canyon. He wondered whether the two hunters he'd met earlier would make use of the weapon.

Later, as he cruised through the narrow mountain pass on the other side of the farm, another loose end occurred to Murphy. Another loose end. He remembered the poor shepherd, with his flock of sheep, he'd encountered at this bend in the road on his ride from Asmara. Then he thought about the two hunters with their ancient muzzleloaders. Finally, he recalled the man he'd seen shitting in the field during his first hour in Asmara.

For the first time, he wondered how the people of this dirt-poor country could afford to buy one thousand American carbines. From the economics lecture Murphy received at the Mocambo from Billings, his old Vietnam buddy, it was clear the Eritreans would have a difficult time coming up with the cash to pay for the weapons, no matter how small the price.

What could they possibly have of value to exchange for the guns?

THE WATER WAS at full force in Asmara when Murphy returned to the King George Hotel, and a long, hot shower helped ease the soreness in his body.

After the shower, instead of remaining holed up in his hotel room, Murphy walked to Kagnew Station. He was unsure of his next move, but he was certain someone was going to try to kill him. A retreat to American soil could make it more difficult. Maybe.

As Murphy was about to cross the street at the top of the hill around the corner from the main gate, a familiar voice called out to him: "Hey, Murphy, wait up!" He bent down to reach for the Browning in his boot. Before withdrawing his weapon, he turned to look behind him. It was Billings, his Vietnam buddy, dressed in khakis and quick-stepping up the sidewalk toward him. Murphy left the gun in his holster. He waited.

When Billings stopped in front of him, Murphy could see the beads of sweat rolling down the side of his face and the perspiration stains on his blouse. While he drew in huge gulps of air, Billings bent over, holding up one hand to signal he needed to catch his breath before speaking. Several moments later, while still wheezing, his first words came. "Geez, I musta run two miles up that hill." He took in another deep draught of air. "I think I got asthma."

Murphy wondered whether Billings was simply out of shape.

"What the hell are you doing running around?" Then, he resumed walking.

Billings, who wore his overseas cap at a rakish tilt, fell in beside Murphy. "I went down to see those people I was telling you about, you know, the Lebanese who were looking to change their Ethiopian money into greenbacks." He paused for a moment to take in more air. "The Ethiopian police were there. I don't think they saw me, but I took off. For all I know, the CID was there, too. But I wasn't going to stick around to find out."

Billings went on to explain how he had worked out an arrangement with the stranded entertainers to exchange their Ethiopian money for American dollars at a ten to one ratio. "They were desperate to get out of here," Then, Billings explained how he planned to set up his own little bank for some of the soldiers at Kagnew Station and convert their American dollars into Ethiopian money at a one to five ratio. "I would have doubled my money," said Billings. "It was a sweet deal."

"If you didn't get caught," Murphy commented. He wondered how Billings would react if he pulled his CID badge out of his pocket and flashed it.

Billings stopped talking when they approached the guard booth at the front gate. As the men walked through the little glass booth, the two unarmed Ethiopians posted there barely acknowledged them. The two MPs stationed on the traffic island also paid no attention to the two Americans. They were too busy talking to the Italian driver of a Volkswagen beetle trying to enter the post to notice them.

"I gotta grab a shower and change," Billings said. He led the way to the Headquarters Company barracks where he lived. "We'll go up to Oasis Club. Dinner's on me. It's Poor Boy's Night."

Billings had a room of his own on the top floor of the barracks, a lime-green building located behind the biegecolored headquarters. While he showered in the latrine down the hall, Murphy waited in his room.

From the window, he looked out once across a wide lawn toward the mess hall. Dinner was being served. Across of the street stood a long, low building. It housed the USO Club and the library. Just beyond was the Top 5 Club.

Murphy smoked a cigarette as he watched soldiers, most dressed in civilian clothes, come and go from the buildings. One man caught his eye. Sergeant K. Murphy watched as Knight, dressed in khakis and carrying a thin briefcase tucked under his arm, came out of the library, walked across a narrow street, and disappeared into the Top 5 Club. His was the only familiar face among the dozens of men walking around.

Murphy knew Knight was getting ready to leave Kagnew Station. The NCO didn't strike Murphy as someone who would spend a lot of time in a library. But the librarian would have to initial his punch-list before he could clear post. The Army didn't want anyone walking off with one of its books.

During the five-minute walk to the Oasis Club, Billings did most of the talking. "I swear I'm going to walk the straight and narrow from now on." Billings adjusted the collar on his powder-blue turtleneck sweater. "I was real lucky today. But I'm not going to push it any more."

Before their stroll was over, Murphy realized the CID in Vietnam had been right to suspect Billings of the theft of the comm wire from the signal battalion at Da Nang.

By the time the two men had reached the Roosevelt Theater, where the spaghetti western *The Good, The Bad and The Ugly* was playing, Billings told Murphy how he had sold an obsolete U.S. Army telephone system to a prominent Vietnamese businessman.

By the time they'd passed through the narrow alley near

the MP station on the far side of the wide plaza in front of the commissary and the post exchange, Billings explained how he bought weapons Marines had taken from dead VC and sold them to American airmen stationed in Da Nang.

By the time they reached the corner of the street leading to the Oasis Club, where a tall hedge hid the miniature golf course from view, obscuring everything but the top of a large windmill, Murphy had heard enough.

Individually, Billings' crimes didn't amount to much. Collectively, however, they added up to a stretch in the stockade, or worse, at the federal penitentiary at Fort Leavenworth. Murphy didn't want to know any more. "You know, you really shouldn't talk about that shit," he said. "The wrong guy might hear about it."

Billings adjusted his collar one more time. "Don't worry, I'm not telling anybody but you about this stuff." Murphy understood. To Billings, their shared Vietnam experience had made them brothers of a sort. Between them there were no secrets. Billings believed he could tell him anything. Murphy was much more reticent.

The two men had barely stepped through the front door of the Oasis Club, when someone mumbled the words "lifin' puke" to Billings as he walked past them. If the epithet bothered Billings, he didn't show it. But Murphy had to fight to keep his cool.

In Murphy's Army, rank commanded respect. But the relationship between the military's rank and file and their leaders had changed since the Vietnam War had heated up. As a result, the Army was changing.

While in Vietnam, Murphy investigated several fragging incidents, where infantrymen allegedly killed their own officers, mostly young lieutenants on their first combat assignments.

There was a wide divide, a chasm really, between the hard-charging young lieutenants intent on leading their men to hell and back and the draftees who had no intention of traveling in either direction.

At the same time, an ever-widening rift had developed between the Army's corps of non-commissioned officers and lower-enlisted men. The career men, or "lifers" as they were derisively called, no longer received the respect they had in the past, and the Army suffered because of it.

Of course, there had been no fragging incidents at Kagnew Station. But the same cancer infecting the Army in Vietnam had reached the remote base. Earlier that year, those soldiers with the rank of specialist fifth class were told they had to choose between membership in the Oasis Club or the Top Five Club. Before, they'd been eligible to join both clubs. Although on his second enlistment, apparently poised for a career in the Army, Billings had opted to join the Oasis Club.

"I guess I'm a lifer," he explained to Murphy. "But these guys are a helluva lot more fun to be around than the old alkies down at the Top Five Club." Every once and a while, however, someone hurled an insult in Billings' direction.

Avoiding the dining area where Murphy had eaten two days before following his trip to Massawa, the two men headed for the ballroom, where more formal table settings had been set up on its upper level.

Strains of Cream's "Sunshine of Your Life," piped in from the juke box in the dining room greeted them as they sat down. As they ordered dinner, Cream's mellow guitar riffs abruptly were replaced by the twangy guitar lead of Bobby Bare's "Detroit City," which had become an anthem for American soldiers far from home. After both men ordered Cornish Game Hen for dinner, Bare's plaintive tone was replaced by David

Ruffin's wailing opening to The Temptations' "Ain't Too Proud to Beg."

"You guys got some eclectic musical tastes," Murphy observed.

Billings laughed. "It's the battle of the bands between the brothers, the rednecks, and the rest of us. Happens every night."

Before dinner was served, one of Billings' friends from the finance department joined them. He was a short, squat spec four whose black-and-white nametag identified him as "Cummings." The several dark spots on his blouse also said he had already spilled one of the half-priced drinks on himself. If Cummings was cognizant of Murphy's presence at the table, he didn't acknowledge it. He apparently took Murphy for one of Billings' lifer friends and ignored him. There were no introductions. Instead, Cummings launched into a report about the death of an American soldier that afternoon in Keren. "I was over at headquarters when the call came in. Some guy got drunk down at the R and R Center and fell into one of the pits at the snake farm."

Apparently, the news of Turgeon's demise had beaten Murphy back to Kagnew Station.

Cummings explained how the Black Mambas were cultivated at the farm for their skins. "They're one of the deadliest snakes in the world. The guy probably didn't last more than five minutes." Murphy knew exactly how long Turgeon had lasted. But he wasn't talking.

Moments after Cummings left to spread the news, a waiter brought drinks: a Heineken for Billings, a Daiquiri for Murphy. "That's a helluva way to go, isn't it?" Billings asked. He didn't expect an answer. "There's all sorts of ways to get killed over here. You really got to be careful."

Murphy chuckled. "Like you, right?"

"I try to be careful. Sometimes, like this afternoon, I guess I play a little too close to the edge."

"Well, don't fall in."

While they nursed their drinks, Murphy took one of the Luigi cards out of his pocket and slid it across the table.

"Some kid handed this to me on the street today. Know anything about the place?"

Billings picked up the card and glanced at it. "Yeah, it's a bar down the street from the Mocambo. The story goes Luigi use to work as a house boy up here on post. Then, he got into real estate downtown and hit it big. That bar doesn't look like much. But he has a gold mine in that building. He must have twenty apartments out in back."

Murphy picked up the card from the table. Then, he thought for a moment. "Anybody from Kagnew live there?"

Billings frowned. "I wouldn't know. I haven't been around here long enough."

"What do you mean?"

Billings took a long pull from his bottle. "What I mean is, if someone has got a place downtown, he doesn't advertise the fact. Single guys aren't supposed to live off post. If a guy is shacking up with a girl or is just renting a pad downtown, he doesn't tell anyone but his closest friends, and I haven't been here long enough to make many friends. Besides, to most of the guys up here at the Oasis, I'm a lifer, a begging puke. Most of them won't give me the time of day."

Following Murphy's trip to Massawa, Smyth had told him the same thing at the soccer stadium.

Murphy nodded toward the business card. "Is this guy on the up-and-up?"

"Is anybody around here?" Billings emptied his beer. "I guess he isn't into anything too serious. Probably runs a few women. That's all."

Moments later, the waiter returned carrying a large tray. It held the two plump little birds, baked golden brown, and salads for both men.

Billings took a look at his bird, which sat in a bed of rice pilaf. "Life is good on our little island above the clouds."

AFTER SPENDING an hour at the Oasis Club with Billings, who picked up the eight-dollar tab for their dinner and drinks, Murphy walked down to the Top Five Club.

Before heading downtown, he became the fifth hand in a poker game in the stag bar. He had a run of good luck while playing high-low split, winning about ten dollars worth of five, ten and twenty-five-cent chits

Later, Murphy had to pick his way through a thick fog to get to the main gate. A cloud had settled over Asmara, and visibility was practically nil.

Murphy figured it would take no more than twenty minutes to walk to Luigi's, but the heavy mist made it difficult for him to find his bearings. As he walked past headquarters, he could feel tiny droplets of water brushing lightly against his face, neck, and hands. Inside the cloud, the arc lights illuminating the main gate looked like dull orbs, suspended high in the air. They gave off just enough light so Murphy could see water droplets.

As Murphy continued down the hill, visibility improved. When he reached Empress Menon Boulevard, the site of the only traffic light in Asmara, the cloud hovered about fifty meters above him, blotting out the normally star-filled East African sky.

While walking toward Queen Elizabeth II Boulevard, Murphy's thoughts turned to Van Dyck. He wondered whether V.D. would approve of how he was handling things. Van Dyck often told him, "Sometimes, you've got to make up the game as you go along." That approach had gotten V.D. killed. That thought ended Murphy's reveries.

Murphy didn't see another living soul until he literally bumped into a fellow American coming out of the alley at Big Rosie's house. "*S'cusa,*" came the apology, in a Texas twang.

A few moments later, while walking along the wide sidewalk in front of the Blue Nile on Queen Elizabeth, a woman stepped from the nightclub's doorway and grabbed his arm. "*Attar!* *Attar!*" she said. "You cumen buy me beerah." Murphy gently, but firmly, shook her off. He kept walking. A stream of Tigrinya followed him. It sounded like the woman wasn't happy with him.

A five-minute walk down brought Murphy up a slight rise, where the cloud cover hung a little lower. Through the decreasing visibility, he found a side street and followed it up a hill almost to the front door of the Mocambo. He went down sidewalk to Luigi's.

Before he went into the bar, Murphy retrieved the Browning from its holster. After tucking the small automatic in the waste band of his jeans, he stepped in. The little bar was empty. A countertop took up most of the right side of the small room, painted in a light blue pastel. A door at the far end of the counter led to another room. There, in the back room, Sergeante K sat alone at a table sipping from a bottle of Melotti.

Knight didn't seem surprised to see Murphy. "I wondered when you'd be along. Have a seat. You want a beer?"

Murphy declined the beer, but he did take a seat. "Keep both hands on the table, please." He settled into the straight back chair across the small table from Knight. "No sudden moves."

Knight set the little brown bottle down. "Don't worry. I won't try anything."

Murphy took out the card he found in Turgeon's field jacket and slid it across the table. Knight picked it up and studied the notation on the back. "Turge wasn't the brightest bulb on the Christmas tree." He placed the card back on the table. "Always wrote these little notes to himself. He had a shitty memory."

Murphy noted how Knight referred to Turgeon in the past tense. "You've heard about what happened to him, then?"

The joviality the burly sergeant had exhibited the first time Murphy met him had disappeared; replaced by a sad, somber demeanor. "Yeah, I heard about it. You kill him?"

"No." Murphy shook his head. "It was an accident. But he tried to kill me."

Knight nodded. "I told him to stay away from you, but he wouldn't listen. When you showed up at the firing range the other day, he was sure you were on to us."

"Is that why you killed Wallace? Was he on to you, too?"

Knight leaned forward. "Wallace was one of us. But he started to get cold feet, and Turgeon thought he was going to squeal. He killed him."

Murphy heard footsteps in the front room of the bar. At the first sound, he moved his right hand below the table and got a firm grip on the Browning. A tall black man, dressed in a finely-cut, three-piece suit, stepped into the room.

"Ah, Sergeante K," the man said, in accented English. "Is everything all right?"

Knight brightened. "Everything's fine, Louie. Just having a chat with a friend." Knight didn't bother to make introductions. The man backed out of the room wearing a quizzical look on his face. Then, Knight sat up in his chair. "Let's go up to my place. We'll be able to talk there."

Murphy kept hold of his gun. "All right, you lead. Slowly, please."

Knight led him out the back door into a courtyard. Glancing up, Murphy saw four sets of balconies stacked, one above the other. As they walked toward a stairwell, Murphy jabbed Knight in the side with his Browning. "Remember, I've got this." There was no response. Knight just kept walking. As Murphy followed him up the steep flight of stairs, Knight stopped for a moment. Looking back at the younger man, he said. "Don't put too much weight on the railing, it's weak in places." They slowly made their way to the third floor, where Knight led him through the unlocked door of Apartment 14, its number displayed on a small plaque attached to the door.

The one-room flat was located on the side of the building overlooking the street. It looked like a bachelor pad. A large reel-to-reel tape deck sat on a small stand next to the double bed. On the floor next to the unmade bed was a Coleman cooler. On the other side of it, where Knight took a seat in a large wooden captain's chair, an empty pizza box and several slightly-crushed cans of Bud littered the floor.

Murphy stood with his back against the wall next to the door, a few feet away from a four-drawer bureau on which a portable television sat. A small student desk in front of the window near Knight completed the furnishings.

A single light bulb hung from a socket at the end a piece of electrical conduit running down from the ceiling. Even in the dim light, Murphy could see Knight had the look of a defeated man. His perpetual smile had disappeared, and the bags under the big man's eyes had grown more pronounced.

Knight spoke first. "Where do you want me to start?"

Murphy moved away from the wall and took a seat on top of the desk. "How about from the beginning?"

Knight laid it all out. He said Wallace had come up with the idea to sell the carbines to the liberation front the previous fall, a short time after Knight had returned to Kagnew Station and Turgeon had arrived to help train the post's garrison on their newly-issued M-14 rifles.

"Davey ran into one of the Shifta leaders while hunting near Massawa," Knight said. "He had a soft spot for the Eritreans and wanted to help them. At first, he wanted to just give the rifles to them."

"But you didn't give the rifles to them, did you?"

Knight shook his head. "No, Turge also had to be in on it. He said we had a chance to make a few bucks by selling the guns to the liberation front."

Murphy interrupted. "How were you going to make a few bucks from these people? They don't have any money."

Knight nodded. "You're right. But they got plenty of hash. That's how they paid. Hashish. A hundred kilos for one thousand carbines. We threw in 100,000 rounds of ammo for nothing."

Knight continued. "Turge thought we could make fifty, sixty thousand a piece on the deal."

Murphy quickly did the math in his head. At five dollars per gram, which is what he knew soldiers from Fort Dix paid on the street in Philadelphia or New York for the drug, he calculated the hash had a retail value of five hundred thousand dollars.

Turgeon may not have been as dumb as Knight thought.

"How did you get the rifles to them?"

Knight smiled. "That was the easy part. It was my job to fill out the shipping manifests, so I just made the rifles disappear. We left them in a couple of conexes out in the desert near Massawa for the rebels to pick up."

Murphy knew exactly where the weapons had been cached. He'd seen the hiding place during the ride on the Littorina.

Knight pointed to the bureau. He told Murphy to look in the

top drawer for the paperwork.

"What about the hash?"

"I shipped it out of here months ago in another conex bound for Fort Polk, near Turgeon's home in Louisiana. I was supposed to pick it up in a week or two after I got back to the states."

"How did you get it past customs?"

"At Kagnew Station, I was customs." Knight wore a smug look. "I ran the warehouse. When I placed a seal on a shipment, it stayed sealed until it reached its final destination."

Then, Knight's sadness returned. "What are you going to do about all this?"

"What do you think?" Murphy answered his own question. "Like you said when we first met, I'm a cop. I've got to take you in."

But Murphy really wasn't sure what to do about Knight. The revelation of how three NCOs from Kagnew Station sold one thousand carbines to a group of Eritrean rebels would be disastrous, making it difficult for the Americans to maintain their operations at the strategically-important base. At best, the price of doing business with the Ethiopians would go up. At worst, the Americans would be ordered to close up shop and go home.

Knight ended the brief silence. "What do you think I'll get?"

"What are you going to get?" Murphy slowly ticked off the charges on his fingers: "Accessory to murder. Theft of government property. Smuggling. Then there's drug trafficking." Murphy paused, as if he was calculating Knight's sentence in his head. "Man, you're going to be looking at the Kansas prairie from behind the bars at Leavenworth for the rest of your life."

Knight slowly raised his left hand. Pointing at the small briefcase sitting among the blankets on top of his bed, he said. "I'm retiring tomorrow. What about my pension? "

Murphy was quick to answer. "In one word. Gone."

Knight slumped in his chair. "You know, I wasn't going to keep the money for myself. I wanted it for my kids." The big man started to cry. "The divorce cleaned me out. I don't begrudge my old lady. She spends all her money on the kids. But if I go away for this, they'll end up with nothing."

For the next few moments, silence filled the room.

It ended when Murphy spoke. "I think I know a way. But it's going to take a whole lot of balls on your part."

AFTER LEAVING KNIGHT, Murphy wandered around the backstreets of Asmara for more than an hour.

Already, he was second-guessing himself.

Before he left, he showed the burly NCO how to use the Browning. He'd chambered a round, removed the ammo clip and placed the gun on the bureau.

At first, Knight was reluctant. "I walked the straight and narrow for the last 25 years, and this is the only time I strayed off the path. Killing myself seems a big price to pay."

But the sergeant was tired and beat. His energy sapped. He looked like someone searching for an easy way out.

"It's your only way out," Murphy told him during their lengthy conversation. "This way, your ex-wife and your kids at least get to keep your pension. Any other way, they lose everything, and you spend the rest of your life behind bars."

Finally, Knight agreed. "I know I got no choice. Leave the gun and go."

Murphy took the shipping orders for the stolen rifles and ammo with him, tucking the thick sheaf of papers inside his shirt. He also slid the ammo clip into his pocket.

Now, as he walked in and out of the cloud hovering above Asmara, Murphy wondered if he'd done the right thing. The queasy feeling in his stomach told him he had not.

Even his mentor, Van Dyck, had been selective in his enforcement of the law, meting out military justice as he saw fit. "Justice, like beauty, is in the eye of the beholder," he explained.

But Murphy had always gone by the book. He was supposed to protect his fellow soldiers by removing criminals from their midst. But at Kagnew Station, he was protecting them in a different way. He was making sure an important intelligence base and a vital communications link remained in operation. In doing so, however, Murphy had let one of the bad guys determine his own fate. That wasn't supposed to happen. In the Army, the fate of anyone accused of a crime was supposed to be decided by a military court.

During his meanderings through Asmara's darkened streets, Murphy debated whether he should go back and stop Knight from doing what he had promised. Then, he thought about what the three Kagnew Station sergeants had done. Selling carbines to a group of Eritrean rebels wouldn't sit well with the Ethiopians. It would jeopardize the operations at the base.

Murphy had no other choice. But that didn't make the bad feeling he had go away.

Also, Murphy was sure he'd conned Knight into killing himself. His suicide probably would void Knight's pension. Because of the divorce, Murphy doubted Knight's children would be eligible to receive those benefits anyway, a concern he hadn't shared with Knight.

When Murphy visualized Knight placing the barrel of the Browning against the roof of his mouth and pulling the trigger, a chill ran through him. However, he fought the urge to return to the apartment. He kept walking, moving farther away from it.

Murphy didn't see anyone until he reached Five Corners, an intersection not far from the U.S. military housing complex at Tract A. There, he met three young Americans, dressed in civvies, walking along the sidewalk. "They're backed up at the

Green Doors, man," one of the teenagers told him as they passed by. "We're going to Mama K's to get some face."

Murphy didn't acknowledge the comment. He walked on, lost in his own thoughts, until he found himself at the bottom of the cul de sac leading to Romana's house.

IT WAS AFTER MIDNIGHT when Murphy awakened Romana's mother with his incessant rapping on her shutter.

The old lady used a number of different languages, until Murphy heard a question posed in English. "Who is there?"

Murphy whispered his reply. "It's John Murphy. I need to talk to Romana."

"Aspetta. Wait."

Following an excruciatingly long silence, the creak of the large Dutch door told Murphy he was welcomed.

"What do you want?" Romana asked.

Murphy stepped inside. "I need your help."

Romana, wrapped in a large quilt to protect her from the chill of the Eritrean night, moved to the couch, and Murphy took a seat across from her in a wooden chair.

For the first time in a long time Murphy wanted to talk, to get it all out. He needed to put his thoughts into words. Then, maybe, he could accept their finality. He didn't need feedback. He just needed someone to listen to him.

For nearly two years, in South Korea and then in South Viet Nam, Van Dyck had been Murphy's sounding board. He could tell the old man anything. They talked about everything. Life. Love. Lust. Sometimes, V.D. would give his advice, solicited or unsolicited, on a wide range of topics. Sometimes, he would simply share his experience, letting Murphy draw his own conclusions. Often, Van Dyck simply listened. Most of the time, that was all Murphy needed.

Until this night, he hadn't realized the void Van Dyck's

absence had created. For the past year, Murphy had withdrawn into himself. He may have needed to talk to someone, but he didn't want to. The trip to Asmara had changed things. Here, he had been left entirely on his own, with a problem he knew no one wanted to deal with, let alone hear about. Not Major Hilton. Not Smyth. Not the provost marshal. But someone had to listen to him, and that someone was Romana.

"What is this about?" she asked, taking a seat on the sofa, pulling her quilt even more tightly around her. "What do you want to talk to me about?"

Murphy lit up a cigarette. "I'm sorry for coming so late," he said. "I just need you to listen."

After he launched into his story, Romana's wariness seemed to lessen. She listened in rapt silence, absently tugging at her curls with her free hand and clutching the quilt tightly with her other hand.

Murphy told her about Wallace and how he was killed, and about Major Hilton and his theory about the Shifta. He told her about how he'd been ordered off the case. Murphy described how he had been shot at, nearly run over and forced off the road. Then, he talked about Mekele, about the meeting in the English cemetery in Keren, and about the rifles stolen from Kagnew Station. Finally, he told her about the three Kagnew Station NCOs and the theft of the carbines, about the hashish, about Turgeon and the snake farm, and about his talk with Knight a little more than an hour before.

"I just don't know if I've done the right thing," he concluded. "It's not the way I'm supposed to do things."

Romana stopped fiddling with her hair. "How are you supposed to do things?"

Murphy kept it simple. "I'm supposed to tell somebody, and

they're supposed to decide whether the Army should do anything about it."

"Why don't you do that?"

"I can't. Like I said, I was ordered off the investigation. Besides, I don't think anyone really wants to hear what I've got to say, especially the Ethiopians."

"Why should the Ethiopians care about the Shifta killing an American soldier. They don't care who the Shifta kill."

"If they found out about the rifles, they would care. They would probably want to close Kagnew Station, and the base is far too important to risk that."

Murphy wanted to tell Romana how important Kagnew Station was, but he couldn't. No one in Ethiopia was supposed to know what went on there. The actual mission of the ASA unit operating at Tract C, officially known as the 4th Radio Research Field Station, was a closely-guarded secret. But the official cover story, written in finely-crafted U.S. military bureaucratese and displayed in prominent locations inside the ASA facility, wasn't too far from the truth. The men at Tract C were instructed to tell anyone who should ask they were "involved with the scientific study and investigation of atmospheric phenomenon concerning the propagation of radio waves." In other words, they listened to everything, which is exactly what they did.

"I really don't know what to do," Murphy said. "I should be doing my job. But if I do it, it could be a disaster. If I don't do it, it could be a disaster."

Romana shrugged her shoulders. "*Inshallah.*"

"What?"

"*Inshallah,*" Romana repeated the Arabic phrase. "It means if God wills. The Moslems say it all the time. It's an answer to their problems, especially to the ones that have no answers.

Do nothing, and whatever will happen, will happen."

Murphy spent the rest of the night at Romana's. He slept on the couch, curled up in a tight fetal ball with his knees suspended in mid-air out over the front of the small sofa. No cuddling. No sex. Just sleep.

Close to sunrise, Murphy had the dream. He was back on the dunes near Pilgrim Springs way out on the Cape. He was a little boy again, frantically clawing his way up the steep mountain of sand as the big waves crashed in. As he climbed up the dune, his little legs churning as he bogged down in the sand, Murphy reached out to someone in front of him. This time, it wasn't his mother. This time, it was Van Dyck. As he stretched out his little arms to reach for his old CID partner, V.D. pulled away. He couldn't help. And the waves crashed in.

Murphy woke up, banging his knee against the small coffee table in front of the couch. The noise brought Romana running into the room.

Her voice was filled with concern. "What happened?"

Murphy described the dream. He told her about Van Dyck and how he thought about his dead partner all the time, and how he now realized he was truly on his own, and how no one could help him. It was impassioned monologue delivered by someone not given to revealing his emotions. Ever. The words came out in a torrent until Murphy had purged himself completely. Then, he settled down.

Murphy mouthed the phrase Romana had taught him. "*Inshallah.*" What would V.D. think of that?

Murphy didn't know. Nor did he care. That was a new feeling.

IN THE MORNING, after learning Murphy didn't want to spend his last full day in Ethiopia near Kagnew Station, Romana gave him directions to Gurgursum, a beach about ten kilometers off the main road near at Massawa.

Keeping his distance from Kagnew Station would prevent Murphy from walking into Major Hilton's office and telling him what he knew. That urge was still there. But he had to restrain himself, keep quiet for one more day, at least until he was well out of Ethiopia.

The trip to Gurgursum might help.

"This time of year it is hot," Romana explained. "and there won't be many people there."

Before he left, Murphy gave Smyth's card to Romana. "If anything happens to me, I want you to call and tell him what I told you." He didn't have to advise her not to tell anyone else. If she told anyone but Smyth how three American soldiers from Kagnew Station had sold a thousand carbines to the liberation front, a car full of Ethiopian police would pull up to her door. Romana would keep quiet to protect herself and her mother.

A part of him wanted to stay in Asmara a while longer, "This is goodbye," he had told Romana before walking across town to fetch his motorcycle, informing her he was scheduled to leave Asmara the next day. "I've got to go." Van Dyck, Murphy knew, was probably rolling over in his grave. "How about a good-bye screw?" was his usual farewell to a pretty woman before he left town. But Murphy was not interested in a quick roll in the hay. He'd had enough of those encounters. But there was no time for anything else. He had to leave Ethiopia.

That was the trouble with the Army, Murphy always had to leave. He marveled at couples he'd met who were able to make a go of a marriage in the Army; how the wife remained patiently at home, it seemed, waiting for a husband who might never return. Murphy hadn't met a woman willing to share that kind of life with him. He had grown use to the state of perpetual loneliness that characterized military service.

V.D., of course, held a different view. "I'm married to the Army," he'd say. "But that doesn't mean I can't fool around."

And he did.

But Murphy could no longer do that. A year, perhaps even six months ago, he would have jumped at the chance to spend a night with a woman like Romana. But Vietnam had changed him in ways he was only beginning to understand. Now, he wanted something else.

After walking across town to get his motorcycle, it took Murphy less than two hours to reach the beach at Gurgursom. Romana was right. It was deserted.

Surrounded by a reef, the beach at was one of the few safe places to swim along the Eritrean coast. At high tide, small dolphins and rays sometimes swam over the reef, but the natural barrier was high enough to keep the huge sharks patrolling the Red Sea out of the lagoon.

Wearing cutoffs he made from a pair of Chinos, Murphy used a mask and snorkel Romana's boyfriend had left behind. The incoming tide brought cooler water with it, but it didn't take long before the water inside the lagoon, no more than six meters at its deepest, matched the air temperature. By ten o'clock, it had already climbed close to one hundred degrees Fahrenheit. After less than a half hour in the lagoon, Murphy felt like he was swimming in a bathtub full of warm water. It was not invigorating at all.

As far as fish were concerned, the lagoon was a desert. For years, a cement factory, located little more than two hundred meters down the coast from the resort, had been coating the reef, which was completely exposed at low tide, with a layer of dust. Nothing grew inside it for the fish to the eat, so the schools of colorful tropical fish no longer came in to feed.

Until he walked through the shallows leading to the beach, Murphy was sure he was alone in the lagoon. But just as he was about to step out of the water he felt a strange sensation. The ground beneath his right foot seemed to move, and Murphy looked down in time to see a small ray skitter across the sea bed, its wings sending up small clouds of sand as it moved away. The odd-looking fish, measuring no more than eighteen inches from wingtip to wingtip, moved a few meters before turning around to see what had disturbed it. For a few moments, Murphy stared back. Within seconds, however, the ray, its coloring nearly the same as the sand it had churned up, settled in. Blending with its surroundings, it had become invisible again.

After getting out of the water, Murphy sat in the shade of the verandah of the beach's small restaurant smoking and thinking.

At about 11 o'clock, he was joined by two British sailors, and one of their wives.

The Brits told him they served as advisors to the cadets at the Ethiopian Naval Academy in Massawa.

"Small boats." one of them explained. "We show them how to operate small boats." The Eritrian coast line ran for more than twelve hundred kilometers. "The Ethis use the gunboats to patrol the coast and keep their Arab neighbors from smuggling arms to their Moslem brothers."

While one sailor and his wife frolicked in the shallow water near the shore, Murphy listened as the other sailor, a thin, balding man who appeared to be ten years older than he was, expounded on his solution to America's Vietnam problem.

"The Gurhkas would come in and clean up that whole lot," As he talked, he waved his half-smoked Rothman filtered cigarette in Murphy's face. "The little buggers would send the Viet Cong packing."

Murphy was aware of the fierce Nepalese warriors and how they'd found a home in the British Army several generations before.

"The Gurkhas would take care of your problem," the Brit droned on, explaining his rather simplistic solution to the complicated mess America had gotten into. "At the moment, the regiment's guarding the frontier in Hong Kong against Red China. Imagine. There's five thousand of them holding off a million chinks, all waving their little red books." He waved his cigarette. "The Gurkhas would come in and clean out Uncle Ho's men. They're a tough lot."

The sailors shared their lunch with Murphy.

They all sat at one end of the long picnic table on the verandah. Murphy bought a round of freshly-squeezed lemonade to drink with the roast beef sandwiches the sailors had brought with them. The woman, wife of the chief boatswain mate who commanded the small contingent of sailors, also had made a cucumber salad. As the sailors dawdled over their lunch, Murphy began to wonder how they were able to get away for a trip to the beach during the middle of the workweek.

"What is it? A national holiday or something?"

"Hey, what?" the chief responded. He was a burly, gray-haired man who looked like he was pushing fifty. "What do you mean?"

Murphy smiled. "Here it is in the middle of the week, and you guys don't look like you're in a hurry to go back to work. So I figured it must a holiday or something."

"I'll say we're on holiday," the chief guffawed. "You Americans have taken over the docks, and we can't get near our boats. So we gave everybody the day off."

"What's up?"

The old chief told Murphy an American supply ship was getting ready to weigh anchor. "Your boys are working their arses off to make sure she's ready to leave on time. They can't locate half the cargo. They've got stuff stashed all over Massawa, and they're having quite a time moving it. The port is a mad house, and it was a good day to get away."

A short time later, the Brits gave up on Gurgursum. They headed to the much cooler Red Sea Hotel, a luxurious, air-conditioned resort at the south end of Twalit Island.

After they left, Murphy thought about Stetson, the warrant officer he'd met during his first visit to Massawa.

He wondered whether Stetson's gang of stevedores would meet the deadline so the ship could sail on time. Then Murphy thought about his own deadline.

A SHORT TIME after the British sailors left, Murphy went looking for a loose end.

Because of the chaos on the Massawa docks, there was a chance the hashish the Eritrean rebels had used to pay for the rifles was still in Ethiopia. The stash could be sitting out in the desert, waiting to be loaded aboard the ship. Murphy had to look for it. Maybe he'd get lucky.

Murphy needed some luck. He had hidden Knight's paperwork for the rifles and the ammo in the storage compartment under the seat of the Honda. Before he left, he intended to dispose of the thick sheaf of papers, along with his scribblings about the case from his pocket-sized notebook. Those were two loose ends Murphy could tie up. However, he remained concerned about the hash.

What would happen when the one hundred kilos Knight shipped turned up in Louisiana?

Some day, someone would get curious about Knight's unclaimed shipment to Fort Polk. Some enterprising PFC would pry open one of the NCO's footlockers and peek inside. The hash would be discovered, no doubt raising a few eyebrows. Without the paperwork, there would be no direct link between Knight, the hash, and the missing carbines. But Murphy knew someone somewhere was probably on the lookout for the guns. He could only hope there would be no one at Fort Polk bright enough to draw a correlation between the three elements. Hope wasn't much of a guarantee. If he could, he had to find the hash before someone else came across it.

Shortly after leaving Gurgursum, Murphy rolled past a bus, followed closely by a U.S. Army deuce and a half with a load of young Americans sitting in its open bed. Both vehicles headed toward the beach. Moments later, he peeled off the road and pointed the Honda across the desert on a northwesterly line. Murphy intended to intersect the Massawa Road far beyond the Ethiopian Army checkpoint.

The going was rough. From his seat on the bus the other day, the desert looked flat. But once Murphy got into the terrain, he discovered The Flats, in most places, was uneven, rolling countryside. Still, there was no soft sand for the wheels of the Honda to become mired in. The dusty, hard-pan surface was perfect for traversing on a motorcycle. Murphy made good time.

Often, Murphy had to slow down to avoid the large rocks and thick thorn bushes dotting the badlands. About ten minutes after the trek began, he spooked a small brown-and-white gazelle in a narrow gully. As he backed off the throttle, the little animal bounded away. It climbed out of the gulley, and, after reaching a safe distance, stopped to watch as Murphy rolled out into the desert.

After twenty minutes of hard riding, Murphy reached the banks of the wide dry riverbed in sight of the steel bridge he'd crossed earlier during the week. He switched off the engine to listen for sounds of traffic approaching the bridge. It was a wise decision. Murphy didn't hear any cars or trucks, but he did hear something else, the whopping sound of rotary blades cutting through the air.

Hiding the motorcycle in the bushes, Murphy low-crawled to the edge of the steep bank in time to see a large helicopter, flying at no more than one thousand meters, crossed the riverbed about two hundred meters upstream. He was unable to make out the markings of the brown-colored aircraft as it followed the road through The Flats toward Massawa.

Murphy waited a few more minutes in the shade of the tall bushes. When he was sure the helicopter had left the area, he pushed the Honda down the embankment into the dry riverbed. Then, he heard another sound, the screech of a balky transmission. Murphy, his heart racing, stood motionless in the shadows of the banking. A few moments later, he watched as the first in a long line of fuel trucks, coming from Massawa, rolled across the steel span less than two hundred meters away. Murphy didn't move, or fire up the motorcycle, until long after the last truck had passed out of sight.

Riding up the riverbed for about five minutes, Murphy came to where the tracks of the Ethiopian Railway line ran across the dry wash, a few yards downstream from a trestle the liberation front had blown up several years before. He followed the rails toward Massawa. A few minutes later, Murphy found the spot in the desert he had noticed four days earlier during his ride on the Littorina. Here, about a dozen conexes, large metal shipping containers, sat on the ground next to a siding off the main line. After parking the Honda in a stand of tall bushes about ten meters from the nearest container, Murphy approached the siding on foot. When he was sure he was alone, he began his search.

At first sight, all of the conexes appeared firmly secured. But a closer inspection of the large metal shipping boxes revealed the openings to three of them were slightly ajar. Using both hands, he tried to pull open one of the doors. The metal, heated by the noon-day sun, was hot to touch. Although Murphy nearly burned his hands, he managed to open the door wide enough to peer inside.

Murphy couldn't make out anything in the darkness. He

then stepped inside. There was just enough light for him to see large sheets of the quarter-inch plywood used to build the crates containing the rifles stacked neatly against the back wall. On the floor, in another corner, he noticed a pile of metal strapping used to reinforce the crates. Stepping forward, Murphy felt something underfoot. Looking down, he saw a small pile of oily rags, apparently left in the crates by the American soldiers who had packed them.

After finding the remains of another rifle crate in a second container, Murphy marveled at the thoroughness of the Eritrean rebels. Outside the conex, the ELF fighters had left no sign they had visited the site. No footprints. No mess. Airborne reconnaissance would not reveal anything amiss, and only the sharpest-eyed Ethiopian soldier would have noticed the slight opening in the doors of the three conexes when passing through the area on patrol.

Murphy figured the Eritrean rebels removed a few guns at a time, probably at night under the cover of darkness. They used camels to transport them out of the area. Their convoy would fit in with the dozens of small caravans crisscrossing the province. He calculated it had probably taken the freedom fighters weeks, if not months, to remove the weapons. Except for a few rounds of ammunition Murphy had found lying on the floor of the second conex he'd inspected, the rebels had managed to take everything they wanted without anyone noticing.

The third conex was full. When Murphy opened the door wide, a solid wall of cardboard boxes confronted him. From the large block letters on the side of some of them, he deduced their contents were the personal belongings of a staff sergeant and his family who had rotated back to the United States.

Murphy felt hot and uncomfortable when he stood inside

the two empty conexes. He could taste the stale air. As he removed the first row of cardboard boxes and stacked them outside the third conex, he began to perspire profusely. Despite his excellent physical condition, he felt himself tiring, his strength sapped by the intense mid-day sun. He'd drank only two glasses of lemonade that morning, and he carried no water with him during his unplanned trek across the desert.

As fear of dehydration set in, Murphy slowed down. He wondered how anybody could do physical labor in this searing heat. He now understood why Stetson preferred to schedule his bull crew to work on the Massawa's docks in the cooler early-morning and late-night hours.

Murphy didn't find the object of his search until he removed nearly all of the first row of boxes from the conex. Then he discovered two wooden footlockers wedged in sideways at the bottom of the second wall of containers. Murphy no longer handled the boxes with care. He threw eight of them on the ground. Knight's name and serial number were stenciled on the lid of the wooden chests he pulled from the hiding place.

Murphy carried the footlockers from the conex and used the small slender pick he had in his pocket to spring the padlock on one of them. He opened the wooden box to find it filled with bricks of hashish, wrapped in brown cellophane, similar to the brick of hash the Ethiopian dealer had offered to sell him on his first night in Asmara. Picking up one of the bundles, Murphy thought it weighed at about two pounds and estimated the chest contained more than twenty packages. Moments later, he discovered more hash had been stashed in the other footlocker.

Sitting on one of the footlockers, Murphy smoked a cigarette while pondering his next move. He was sitting on a small fortune, but he had no desire to do anything but destroy it.

Still, the hashish had to be disposed in a manner that wouldn't draw attention to Knight, and Murphy knew he didn't have much time. The hash had to disappear before anyone from the docks came to look for misplaced cargo.

Finishing his cigarette, Murphy began to transfer the bricks of hash into the first conex he'd inspected. That task took about five minutes. After he had moved all of it, he opened several of the cardboard boxes he'd thrown on the ground. In one box, he found women's clothing, neatly folded and packed. He divided its contents between the two empty footlockers. He threw the contents of two other cardboard boxes, portions of a staff sergeant's military issue and an assortment of children's books, on the ground in front of the conex. Next, he carried several cardboard boxes into the conex containing the hashish and dumped the clothing onto the floor.

Murphy used some of the oil-soaked rags he'd found to start a fire under the hashish. As it started to burn, he opened the door of the conex wide to vent the acrid, gray smoke. When the hashish was enveloped in flames, he started a fire in the other empty conex. Then, he set Knight's two empty footlockers aflame, spilling the contents of two more cardboard boxes close by.

Murphy retrieved the shipping orders Knight had given him from the Honda's seat compartment. He used his cigarette lighter to burn away Knight's name and signature from the paperwork, Then he wedged the thick sheaf of papers in between two cardboard boxes. Next, Murphy took from the motorcycle's small compartment the photograph and the undeveloped roll of film he'd found in Wallace's apartment in Massawa. Those items were consigned to the hashish fire. Finally, Murphy threw his leather ankle holster into the fire.

After leaving the siding, Murphy drove the Honda down the

rail line toward Massawa. He didn't stop until he reached the outskirts of the village on the mainland near the causeway.

There, Murphy paused to look back.

In the distance, two thin columns of smoke wafted into the air above the desert floor.

AFTER HIS TRIP into the desert, Murphy returned to the beach at Gurgursum.

It had become crowded.

A platoon of young American soldiers who worked at the ASA site at Tract C had invaded the beach. D trick was spending its two-day break between eves and mids shifts in Massawa.

Using the deuce-and-half Murphy had seen earlier as a shuttle, the young soldiers, armed with several cases of beer, began trickling out to the beach from Massawa late in the afternoon. By the end of the day, they were joined by a motley group of people: a VW bus full of hippies, two men and three women slowly making their way through East Africa; a couple of prostitutes from town who opened for business after renting one of the dilapidated bungalows attached to the restaurant; several off-duty Ethiopian soldiers from the guard detachment at the emperor's villa at the north end of the beach; and a man offering rides on his camel for two dollars Ethiopian.

For dinner, the boys from D Trick munched on two large red snappers which they poached over a wood fire on the beach. As dusk started to fall, the Americans built a bonfire, not far from the emperor's villa, hunkered down around it Indian style, and played drinking games.

The beach had gotten too crowded for Murphy. He jumped on his motorcycle and left.

About 15 minutes later, Murphy was nursing a bottle of Heineken and wondering what to eat, when Stetson and his crew walked into the nearly-empty restaurant at the R&R Center.

The warrant officer was dressed in a sweat-stained set of jungle fatigues, probably the same outfit he'd worn in Vietnam, Murphy thought. His men looked as disheveled as their leader.

The waiters knew the routine. After Stetson's men commandeered a large table in the middle of the wood-paneled dining room, two waiters came out of nowhere each carrying two pitchers of beer and enough glasses tucked under their arms for all the men.

Stetson spied Murphy almost immediately. "Going to see an old friend," Murphy heard him say to his men. Carrying one of the pitchers, he made his way to Murphy's table. "Been spending too much time with you guys, anyway." Then, calling back over his shoulder, he added: "Drink up, boys. It's on me."

Stetson looked like he had added several more furrows to his weathered face. "Gee, Stets, you look like hell," Murphy observed. "What have you been up to?"

The warrant officer nodded. "Getting too old for this shit." He removed his baseball cap, revealing thinning gray hair pasted to his scalp. "Been one helluva week. But we got it done. She sails tonight. Right on schedule."

Murphy smiled. "That is cause for celebration." He lifted his beer in a mock toast.

They sat at a table near a window overlooking the narrow channel between the two islands. Across the water, the lights on Massawa Island were flickering to life and the soundless images of the first feature, a colored film, were visible on the screen at the old port's open-air movie theater nearly four hundred meters away.

For dinner, they started with shrimp cocktail. Each of the crustaceans was longer than the length of Murphy's middle finger.

"Just think, this morning, these big babies were swimming

in the Red Sea with nary a care in the world," Stetson said. "You can't get them much fresher than this."

For the main course, Stetson opted for the veal parmigiano, while Murphy stuck with seafood, poached Alaskan salmon. Both men had a garden salad.

"I can't believe the way you guys eat over here," Murphy marveled. "It's a gourmet's paradise."

Stetson grunted. "Got to have something to keep the boys happy here. They sure work hard enough to keep it coming."

Murphy told Stetson about his conversation with the two British sailors out at Gurgursum. "They said you guys were hurrying to get the ship loaded. They said you were having trouble locating all of the cargo."

Stetson took a long swig from his beer. "Things went from bad to worse." Whipping a large red handkerchief from his pants' pocket, he paused to wipe the sweat from his brow. "We lost some stuff in a fire out on the desert."

"A fire?"

"Yep. CID thinks the Shifta started it."

"The CID?"

If Stetson caught the concern in Murphy's voice, he didn't let on. "Happened to be in Massawa working on a case. Flew down on an Ethi helicopter for a quick trip. Ended up spending most of the afternoon here, investigating the fire."

Stetson told Murphy the contents of several conexes stockpiled on a rail siding about five kilometers out into the Flats had burned. "Usually store empty conexes out there," he explained, "and retrieve them as we need them." Stetson paused to drain his glass. "Some idiot dropped three or four loaded conexes out there by mistake. CID thinks the Shifta broke into them, took what they wanted, and then set them afire."

"Any idea what they took?"

"Not really," Stetson poured more beer into his empty glass. "Sent a couple of men out there to check it out. But the CID kicked them out of there." He took another long swig of beer. The CID had closed off the site, an indication of an active investigation.

But Stetson didn't seem fazed. "We'll check it out tomorrow. Looks like three or four families lost their entire shipment. They can send the bill to Uncle Sam."

LATER THAT NIGHT, while slowly walking toward the campfire on the far end of the beach at Gurgursum, Murphy wondered if the CID had found anything in Massawa.

When he set the fire at the conexes, Murphy didn't think the U.S. Army would be among the first to arrive on the scene, and he was concerned about what its highly-trained investigators would find.

In a way, Murphy was glad the CID came to Massawa. Anything they discovered during their visit would be on their own hook, and not on his. According to Stetson, the investigators had already blamed the Shifta for setting fire to the conexes. And there was no mention of missing guns or the residue of burnt hashish. Of course, the Army wouldn't advertise the fact it had discovered someone had walked off with a shipment of its carbines.

Still, Murphy wondered what the CID had found out in the desert. And whether he had cause for concern. Would the investigators discover the rifles from Kagnew Station were missing? Would they see the link between those weapons and the death of Wallace? Would they see how Turgeon and Knight fit in?

Murphy's ass was on the line, too. He had covered up. He'd destroyed evidence. Worst of all, he'd failed to make a bust. He'd let one of the bad guys go and decide his own fate.

As Murphy approached the campfire, he made out the shadowy figures of about twenty men sitting around it. As he came closer, he heard the young Americans count off.

"Sixteen," called out a high-pitched voice from the far side of the circle."

"Bizz," screamed the man next to him.

"Eighteen," yelled the next man.

"Nineteen," drawled the man seated next to him.

"Twenty," bellowed a deep voice.

"Bizz," called out the next man in the circle.

That "bizz" drew a round of laughter from the rest of the men in the group.

"Drink up," the boys chorused.

"The name of the game is bizz-buzz," one of them shouted above the din. "Drink up, Jonesy."

Murphy stopped next to a heavyset man standing perhaps twenty feet away from the group. He held a can of beer in his hand. "Funny game, huh?" the man said. "It's going to get drunk out tonight."

Murphy lit a cigarette. In the glow from his lighter, he could make out the features of a man perhaps ten years older than him.

"You're supposed to alternate saying bizz and buzz for every number that has a seven in it or is divisible by seven," the man explained. "When you screw up, you've got to chug your beer. By the end of the night, these guys will be lucky to make it into double digits. It makes for a happy time. A good party."

Murphy took a long drag from his cigarette. "What are they celebrating?"

"Nothing really," the man took a swig of beer. "It's a Trick Party. All of them work on the same shift out at Tract C. We get together about every three or four months to have a blow out either here or in Keren. It's good for morale."

Both men turned to the sound of bare feet running across the sand toward the water. Out of the darkness, two nude men streaked by, racing each other to the water. The trick chief chuckled. "These guys like to let it all hang out. Actually, this will be the last party for about six of them."

"Going home?"

The man finished his beer, adding his can on the pile of empties the group had started on the beach. "Nah, they're all going to Vietnam." With that, the man reached down into the cooler next to him. Pulling out two beers, he handed one of them to Murphy. "It's funny, you know. A lot of these guys got into the ASA to avoid going to Vietnam. They're all real bright kids. It takes a lot of smarts to do this work." He popped open his new beer. "It's a four-year hitch. But at least they don't have to spend it pushing a rifle." A pause. A swig. "Of course, not many of these guys know it, but one of the first U.S. soldiers killed in Vietnam was in the ASA. He was a diddy-bopper by the name of Davis. He was in the wrong place at the wrong time."

Murphy took a long swig. He thought about Wallace. Turgeon. Knight. The two Ethiopian soldiers on the bus. And Van Dyck. "I know what you mean. A lot of that has been going around lately."

MURPHY SPENT the night wrapped in an Army blanket on the beach, lulled to sleep by the lapping of the waves.

He didn't need an alarm clock. At daybreak, the sun leapt like a big orange ball above the horizon and woke him. A short time after sunrise, he left and made the trip back up the mountain to Asmara well under two hours.

When he got back to the King George Hotel, Murphy called Smyth. He asked him to check on his transportation back to the States. He showered and shaved, and he was dressing when heard a knock on his door.

It surprised him.

Murphy had no weapon. Quickly, he looked about the room to see if there was anything he could use to protect himself. Finding nothing, Murphy took up a position beside the door.

"Who is it?"

"CID," a deep American voice on the other side of the door replied.

"Just a minute." Murphy took a few moments to collect his thoughts. "I've got to get dressed."

Murphy got his gear - and his mind - in order. He pulled the sheet back from his bed and mussed up his pillow to give it a slept-in look. Then, he tossed a few of pieces of clothing—a shirt, a pair of pants and a pair of skivvies—haphazardly on the floor to give the room a lived-in look.

Murphy opened the door to find a tall, dark-complexioned American and a shorter, much-thinner Ethiopian standing out in the hallway. Both were dressed in tan tropical-weight suits.

"I'm Marquez," The American flashed his CID badge. "And this is Tekeste." When Murphy reached into his pocket for his shield, Marquez reached out with his right hand and stopped him. "It's all right. We know who you are."

"What do you want?"

"The boss wants to see you at the cop shop."

"About what?"

Before he answered, Marquez, who stood perhaps three inches taller than Murphy, subtlety shifted his eyes toward his Ethiopian sidekick, who stood behind him. The move was nearly imperceptible, a signal meant only for Murphy. Marquez was terse. "I really can't talk about it here." No need for further explanation. Murphy understood. Whatever Marquez' boss wanted to talk to him about was was not meant for the Ethiopian's ears.

Five minutes later, after a trip in a Ford Econoline made in total silence, the three men walked into a small red brick building on a cul-de-sac across the street from the Oasis Club.

Inside, in a one-room office crammed with wooden tables, desks and chairs, were Hilton, Logan, and another Ethiopian. The two Army officers wore khakis, and Murphy noticed the Military Intelligence insignia pinned to the left collar of their uniforms. He also noticed the Vietnam Service and Vietnam Campaign ribbons among the two rows of decorations pinned above Hilton's left-breast pocket. Aside from the National Defense ribbon every soldier was entitled to wear, the young lieutenant wore no decorations.

Marquez offered Murphy a seat at a cluttered desk in the center of the room. Then, the CID investigator turned toward the two Ethiopians, who were standing off to one side quietly chatting in their own language. Marquez pulled a chit book out of the pocket of his jacket and handed it to Tekeste. "Why don't you two fellas take a walk down to the snack bar and get yourself some breakfast." From the tone of Marquez' voice, Murphy knew it wasn't a request. Tekeste apparently felt the same way. The young Ethiopian accepted the chits with an especially sullen look on his face, unable to hide his feelings. He'd been kicked out of the meeting. "Take your time," Marquez shouted to the backs of the two Ethiopians as they walked out the door.

At this point, Hilton took over.

"Sort of been marking time all week, huh, Murphy?" The major reached down to pick up a briefcase from the floor next to his leg.

"I guess you could say that."

"Well, I know you did some poking around." Hilton removed a file folder from his briefcase. "We just wanted you to look at the draft of a report we're sending to the colonel later today to see if you might have anything to add to it."

The major laid the folder down on the desk in front of Murphy.

Then, the major joined the other two men in another part of the room as Murphy read the two-page draft.

The first page gave an account of the circumstances surrounding Wallace's murder, including the time and place of his death, the weapon used to kill him and several from the pathology report. Pretty straight-forward stuff.

On the second page, the writer of the report blamed the Eritrean Liberation Front for Wallace's death. He wrote, "There is evidence to indicate the ELF assumed SSG. Wallace had knowledge of its attempt to steal a shipment of M1 carbines while the weapons were in transit to the United States for disposal. Our investigation indicates SSG. Wallace unwittingly made contact with elements of the liberation front (Shifta) while hunting in the desert area near Massawa. As a result of that contact, the liberation front may have assumed Wallace had been sent to investigate the theft of weapons and ammunition from a storage area in the desert near Massawa."

The writer concluded: "In summary, SSG. Wallace, most likely, knew nothing about the pilfering of 1,000 carbines and 100,000 rounds of ammunition from the storage area. If he had knowledge of such a theft, SSG Wallace would have reported it to his superiors. But the ELF, which apparently had stumbled onto the site by accident and had been gradually removing the weapons for the past several months, couldn't afford to take a chance on whether or not SSG Wallace knew anything about its operation, and, as a precaution, silenced him."

After reading the report, Murphy put it back in the folder.

Handing the file back to Hilton, Murphy gave his appraisal. "Wrong man. Wrong place. Wrong time,"

Hilton nodded. "That's about the size of it."

As he leaned across the table to take the report from Murphy, the major accidentally swept a thick manila envelope from the corner of the table. It fell to the floor near Murphy with a clatter.

When he leaned over to retrieve the envelope, Murphy was shocked to see the short barrel of his Browning automatic poking out of it.

"What the hell is this?" Murphy asked, as he held the little automatic by its barrel.

Marquez moved next to Murphy at the center of the room. "That's what we'd like to know. We found it at an apartment downtown, and we've been wondering how it got there." The words were not said in an accusative manner, but more in a tone of bewilderment.

As his initial shock wore off, Murphy wondered whether the gun had been placed in the envelope on the table on purpose. Perhaps, he thought, the Browning had been put there to trap him. To avoid it, he feigned ignorance.

"What? Did somebody shoot somebody with it?"

"Oh no," Marquez answered. "Nothing like that."

The CID investigator explained he discovered the weapon the previous day while searching the apartment of a dead Army sergeant.

"The guy was named Knight. He got tanked up the night before last, the day before he was due to retire, and did a full gainer from the balcony in front of his apartment."

"Suicide?"

"We don't think so." Marquez shook his head. "Looks like an accident. Knight was a big man, bigger than me. We think he got drunk, lost his balance and went through the metal railing in fornt his apartment. It was pretty flimsy. Doc says he probably died as soon as he hit the courtyard. Probably laid there all night dead. They didn't find him until the morning."

"That's too bad," Murphy feigned a morbid interest. "Any wife? Kids?"

"Divorced, with three teenagers. The guy provided for his children though."

"How so?"

"Knight took out a life insurance policy when the divorce went through," Marquez explained. "It had a $100,000 accidental death rider on it. He set his kids up for college."

While Marquez talked, Murphy wondered if Knight's death had really been an accident. Or had the old sergeant staged it to make it look like one?

Murphy's attention returned to the Browning. "What about the piece?" He pointed to the manila envelope.

"We're just wondering how he got it into Ethiopia without anyone knowing about it," Marquez said. "All military personnel are supposed to register their firearms with the provost marshal when they report here. Normally, personal weapons are shipped separately. And there's no record of Knight shipping a Browning automatic or any other weapon to Eritrea."

"Maybe he bought it downtown," Murphy suggested.

"You can buy a lot of things down in the Bosh," Marquez looked at the envelope in his hand. "But that isn't one of them. No, except for the old muzzle loaders the villagers use to hunt, the Ethiopians don't like to have any weapons in the hands of their private citizens, especially here in Eritrea."

At this point, Hilton cleared his throat, a signal it was time to change the subject.

"What do you think about the report," he asked. "We leave anything out?"

Murphy looked at the folder in Hilton's hands. "I've got nothing to add." He was still concerned about being set up, "I don't even know why I am here."

Hilton tucked the folder under his arm. "Consider it a professional courtesy. After all, a lot of the information contained in the report is based on your investigation."

The major explained. "It was you who found evidence Wallace had met members of the liberation front. Also, you provided the basis for our theory Wallace was lured to the antenna field by someone he knew and was subsequently killed."

Hilton handed the folder to Logan, who hovered at the major's side. "Indirectly, you're also responsible for our discovering the carbines had been stolen, which was the real reason the liberation front was in the desert."

That caught Murphy by surprise. "Really?"

The major explained. "A CID team flew down to Massawa yesterday to follow up on your lead at Wallace's apartment. Really didn't find anything. His girlfriend had cleared out. But while our team was there, the liberation front set fire to the conexes out in the desert in an attempt to cover its tracks."

Hilton took a thick sheaf of papers from Logan. He placed the documents, half-burnt but still recognizable as shipping orders for the carbines, on the desk in front of Murphy. "We found these in one of the conexes the rebels set on fire. It looks like the paperwork had been misplaced. That explains why the rifles were left out in the desert."

Murphy noticed the signature block on the manifests was scorched, so there was no way of telling who had filled out the paperwork. "Looks like somebody screwed up."

"Yeah," The major nodded, "and it looks like we'll never know who."

MURPHY STOOD staring through the large plate glass window. He smoked a cigarette as he watched the thick, heavy raindrops explode onto the tarmac outside the main terminal at Asmara International Airport.

Smyth's timing had been precise. He delivered Murphy to the airport just seconds before the first rains of the wet season reached Asmara. When it started, the rain came in biblical proportions, thick sheets of water fell in a steady, intense torrent.

"Right on time." Smyth looked at his watch as they reached the dry safety of the terminal. "From here on in, we'll be able to set our watches every day by the rain. It will stop in about fifteen minutes."

That was ten minutes ago. The rain didn't appear close to stopping. And Smyth had gone off with Murphy's travel documents to work his magic with Ethiopian Customs.

During the ride to the airport, Smyth had briefed Murphy on the fallout following the discovery of the theft of the carbines and ammunition.

"The emperor's boys in Addis threw a fit," Smyth had explained. "The Ethis threatened to throw us out of the country."

In the end, cooler heads prevailed. But the U.S. was forced to make a large contribution toward Ethiopia's defense budget.

"It cost us enough equipment to outfit a regiment," Smyth told Murphy. "The ELF takes one thousand rifles away from us, and the Ethiopian government holds us up for one thousand more rifles. A good tradeoff."

"Sounds like a game to me," Murphy had offered.

"Maybe so. But it's a game we've got to play."

As the rain began to subside, Smyth returned with Murphy's travel documents.

"You got a problem." He waved Murphy's shot record in his hand. "Your smallpox shot is out of date."

"So, what's the problem?"

"The problem is, you can leave Ethiopia, but you might have difficulty getting into another country. Ethiopia is one of the few places in the world where they still have recorded cases of smallpox."

"What can I do?"

Smyth held out his hand. "You got ten birr?"

Reluctantly, Murphy reached for his wallet. "Too bad, I wanted to keep it as a souvenir." He handed the red-tinged note to Smyth.

After Smyth left, Murphy noticed Romana standing at a kiosk at the far end of the terminal, where a boy was selling postcards, At first, he was reluctant to approach her. He didn't want Smyth to see her with him. But he couldn't stay away.

"Ciao," she said, as he walked up next to her. While they talked, he pretended to look at the postcards.

"I didn't expect to see you here."

"I came to meet a friend, who is flying in from Addis for the wedding," Romana explained. Murphy guessed she'd borrowed her landlord's car to drive out from town.

"Oh. You didn't come to see me off?"

She smiled and looked up at him. "No. But I am glad to see you before you left."

Murphy looked to see if Smyth was coming. "My friend from the consulate is going to come back any moment, and I don't want him to see you. It could cause problems for you. But I am glad to see you again."

"I understand." Romana handed Murphy a stack of postcards. "I wanted you to have these to remember your trip to Asmara." Then, she walked to the other end of the terminal to wait for her friend.

Moments later, Smyth returned with Murphy's shot record and passport. An enterprising customs official had used a stamp to back-date the appropriate box on his shot record. Also, an exit stamp had been placed in his passport. Murphy was free to leave.

Smyth eyed the postcards in Murphy's hand. "I see you bought some souvenirs."

"Yeah. Just a few postcards."

As he followed Smyth down the length of the terminal to board his plane, Murphy glanced at the postcard at the top of the stack.

It was a picture of the Litterina crossing one of the stone trestles on the trip to Massawa. When he turned the card over, he discovered Romana had written her address. Murphy smiled.

SPACE HAD BEEN RESERVED for Murphy on a U.S. Air Force C-130 to fly back to the United States.

"It's a milk run." Smyth repeated the plane's itinerary before the two men shook hands for the final time just outside the terminal. "Dakar. Ascension Island. Recife. Should get into Homestead sometime Monday afternoon."

Murphy nodded. "Sounds like a delightful weekend."

As Murphy walked across the tarmac toward the large, gray military transport, the rain stopped and the sun started to beat down.

Three U.S. Army soldiers, dressed in fatigues, emerged from the cab of a deuce-and-a-half backed up to the loading ramp at the rear of the plane. Murphy heard scuffling sounds as they loaded cargo.

The young crew chief greeted Murphy as he entered the plane through a door just aft of the left wing. "Got a place rigged up for you to sit up forward, sir." The freckle-faced teenager assumed Murphy was an officer hopping a ride back home. A webbed seat had been set up into the side of the main cabin, not far from the steps leading to the flight deck. As he walked along the narrow corridor on his side of the cargo bay, Murphy passed several large metal pallets containing stacks of heavily-taped cardboard boxes. Each container bore the same address: "DIRNSA, Fort. Meade, Md.," as well as top-secret stamps. The boxes were filled with reams of radio intercept on its way to National Security Agency, the super-secret intelligence agency headquartered outside Washington, D.C.

The crew chief moved to the rear of the plane to raise the loading ramp. Even before it closed, Murphy heard a high-pitched whine as one of the transport's four turbo-prop engines started up. It was a long flight home, and the flight crew was itching to leave.

Murphy watched as the crew chief made his way forward, checking the rigging of the cargo to make sure it was secure and wouldn't come loose during the seven-thousand-mile flight back to the states.

"Looks like I'm your only passenger," Murphy commented as the airman eased into his perch in a pull-down metal seat at the bottom of the stairwell.

The crew chief stood up and pointed toward the rear of the plane. "You're not the only one making the trip, sir."

Murphy stood to see what the airman was pointing at. Three caskets sat on pallets in the rear of the plane.

The airman flipped through several sheets of paper attached to his clipboard. Without looking up, he said, "That would be sergeants Wallace, Turgeon, and Knight, sir."

As he looked back at the three caskets, a deep feeling of sadness came over Murphy. When Van Dyck was killed, he never felt grief, only outrage. During the months that followed, that anger had subsided, replaced by an emptiness. Although V.D. was gone, he remained very much with Murphy. In the rear of the cargo bay sat three grim reminders.

"I guess those guys won't be much company, sir," Murphy heard the airman say.

Slowly lowering himself back into his seat, Murphy felt the plane lurch forward as it started to taxi toward the runway.

"No, I guess they won't," he heard himself say.

But Murphy knew better.

Postscript

On May 24, 1993, Eritrea, after a thirty-year struggle, declared its independence from Ethiopia. Since 2000, United Nation peacekeepers have patroled the boundary between the two nations following a two-year border war.

Read Another Book by
PAUL BETIT
Phu Bai: A Vietnam War Story

It is June 1967, and United States military involvement in South Vietnam is nearing its zenith. As the war rachets up, John Murphy and Charles Van Dyck of the Army's Criminal Investigation Division investigate the murder of an American soldier at Phu Bai. War intrudes as the two investigators build their case against the most likely suspect. But a bizarre twist turns it into an unusual manhunt in the middle of a war zone.

To contact the author:
Send email to phubai@suscom-maine.net
Send letter to 1 Haywood Lane, Brunswick, ME 04011

To obtain book:
Visit Amazon.com or Barnes & Noble.com
(under books, search by author or title)
Order through your local bookstore.
Bookstores: Please order through Ingram.
For signed copy, send $16 to the author at:
1 Haywood Lane, Brunswick, ME 04011

Printed in the United States
38384LVS00003B/286-378

9 780976 653301